The Lies We Tell
For Love

BY MZ. ROBINSON

Published by:

G Street Chronicles
P.O. Box 490082
College Park, GA 30349

www.gstreetchronicles.com
fans@gstreetchronicles.com

Cover design:
        Hot Book Covers
        www.hotbookcovers.com

Typesetting & Ebook Conversion:
        G&S Typesetting & Ebook Conversions
        www.gstypesetting.com

ISBN: 978-0-9834311-4-5
LCCN: 2011938355

Join us on Facebook G Street Chronicles Fan Page
Follow us on Twitter @gstrtchroni

Dedications

"There are some people who show complete selfless acts of kindness that we do not understand but we must give thanks for."
Mz. R

This book is dedicated to my attorney Rebekah Graham. Rebekah, I can never say, "Thank You" enough for what you and your team did for me. I can not tell you how grateful I am for meeting you and how much you have touched my heart.

Best Wishes & Blessings,
Mz. Robinson

Reflections of April 27, 2011

ON THIS DAY RACE, DENOMINATION, NOR CLASS MATTERED; we were all vulnerable—helpless to a much greater power. We lost things, places, and sadly we lost loved ones. Today, although much has been re-constructed, we will forever carry the memories of that day and those we lost in our hearts and embedded in our souls. However, let us remember the lessons learned and the love that was shared. Let us never forget that when we come together and pray together, we can bounce back better than we ever were.

P.S. I have never been more proud of my city than I was during the days that followed the storms. I have never seen such unity, compassion, and love being shown. It was truly remarkable.

R.I.P. to all of those who were called home. You are gone but you shall never be forgotten.

Mz. R

Acknowledgements

To my Lord and Savior. You never cease to amaze me. I will never understand why you love me as you do or why you continue to shine your mercy and grace upon me. However, I am thankful and I will forever give you the highest praise. Thank you for sparing mine and my families lives on April 27th. I still marvel at the power you hold and I know and truly understand that we are not here because of our own doing but because of your grace and mercy.

To my parents, Ray and Shirley. Daddy and Mommy, the two of you listen to each and every ideal I have and you embrace them without passing judgment. I love you for that. You have learned to accept the individual that I am and you allow me to be me. I thank you for your prayers and your unconditional love. I love you!

To my bestie Banita Brooks. You are such a wonderful woman and an amazing friend. I have said it before and I will say it again—I could not have asked for a better sister. Blood means nothing when it comes down to loyalty and truth. I love you.

To my Uncle Kenneth. You are a great uncle and an awesome friend. As a child I could always depend on you and I am happy to say I still can. It doesn't matter where you are or what you're doing when we call you are there. I will never ever be able to repay you for how you were there after the storm and you worked like our home was your home. That is real love. You are a blessing and I love you!

To my uncles Michael, Harold, and JT. Thank you for bringing food, water, and just stopping by. Your love and kindness is forever appreciated. I love you all.

To my Uncle Dennis. Thank you for lending your tools, generator, and your helping hand. You said you were coming and you came. You shared and gave selflessly. I love you!

To Tammy. I still remember being a little girl and going places with you and how when I got out of line you would pinch me or pull my ear. I'm laughing now but it wasn't that funny back then. You have always shown my mother the love and concern of a sister and growing up you were more of an aunt than a cousin. To this day you are still supportive no matter what and for that I am very thankful. I love you!

To the Caudle, Massey, Warner, Walker, and Leslie Families. I love each and every one of you!

To K.J. I never know what you're going to say or do and sometimes all I can do is shake my head. However, I love you and we will forever be friends.

To Valerie Ann Williams. Thank you diva for your support and for always having a POSITIVE word to say. Love ya Val.

To the readers, fans, reviewers, and authors. If I could name each and every one of you I would. However, I will say thank you from the bottom of my heart for showing me love and supporting my work. Thank you!

S/O to the ladies of Wal-Mart, Huntsville Hospital, and my girls in Chattanooga(Ari & Ra-Ra). Thank you for the love and support!

To my editor Autumn. Thank you.

To Dashawn Taylor of Hot Book Covers. Thank you.

To the G Street Chronicles team. We are destined for greatness. Let's get it.

To Shawna A. Grundy, G Street Chronicles VP, thank you for everything. I truly appreciate your feedback and your words of encouragement.

Last but not least to G Street Chronicles CEO, George Sherman Hudson. Thank you for believing in my talent and gifts. You've taught me that it doesn't matter what the situation may be, you can do anything you put your heart and hustle into. Love and Respect Always.

Prologue

o you know how hard it is to know that the man you love, the man that you've always loved is not only locked by vows to another woman but that his heart is hers as well? Do you know how it feels seeing the man whom you gave your body to openly and without hesitation and surrendered your heart to with no limits, look at another woman like she is the source of love and life itself? I do.

I sat in Humphries, in the back of the restaurant in a small booth built for two, with the latest edition of Radar Magazine laying on the table in front of me. I had flipped to page 26 and was looking at the February feature for what had to be the tenth time. I frowned as I looked at Damon and his trophy wife Octavia. Damon looked handsome, as always. He wore a black one button Tuxedo and a classic white shirt with a platinum color tie. His Carmel colored skin was just as I had remembered it; smooth and flawless. The lighting from the camera reflected delicately off his smooth bald head and his dark brown eyes seemed to penetrate me from the page, causing a dampness in between my legs like morning dew on the petals of a rose. Octavia wore a platinum haltered evening gown that flowed to her toes. The dress hugged her body and had an elegant mermaid hem. Her jet black hair fell over her shoulders in a bundle of loose curls. I'm far from a hater. I believe in giving credit where credit is due, the broad looked good. I'll give her that. I can see why Damon was infatuated with her; skin the color of brown-sugar, eyes the color of honey and when it came to her figure, she was working with a banging physique. Damon stood behind her with his hands planted firmly on her waist. The two of them were smiling, showing two sets of perfect-white teeth. They looked liked something an artist created, pulling their images from the deep crevices of his untamed imagination—a portrait of perfection and poised elegance. The heading gracing the page in which they were featured read, *Successful Black Love: Overcoming All Obstacles.* I laughed out loud, drawing un-wanted attention to myself from the eyes of some of the other patrons in the restaurant. I flashed them a look that subtly asked, "Is there a problem?" Turning my head I stared in front of me, focused on nothing in particular, thinking about Damon and the last time I felt his touch. I still remember his strong hands caressing the curve of my back, the sound of his voice whispering in my ear and yes the way he brought me to multiple orgasms. He is still to this day the only man who has been capable of accomplishing such a task. I love everything about Damon and I fantasize about the day he becomes mine. I longed to be the one posing with him, the one to whom everyone referred to as *Mrs. Whitmore*—the one whose legs he spreads apart daily and to whom he made gratifying love. I was supposed to be that woman! I deserved to be that woman! I could feel my rage surfacing, bubbling slowly like lava waiting to push its way through the bounds of the Earth. Now that I think about it, I should have gotten rid of Octavia when I had the chance. I should have told her the truth about her husband. She would have dropped Damon like a pair of sweat-drenched thongs on top of a pile of dirty laundry. How do I know? Because Octavia is a simple woman—predictable—she doesn't have the dirt inside of her to be with a man like Damon. Damon is a man who has no problem with breaking a law or two to get what he wants. He goes against the grain…he's a bad boy in designer clothing. A man of his caliber needs a true ride or die bitch. He needs a woman who has no problem with getting her nails a little dirty or even bloody to get what she wants—a woman like me. Looking at my watch I saw that my lunch date was running late. I had specifically requested that he meet me at noon, it was now five minutes after. *What if he changed his mind?* I thought. I was preparing myself to call him, when I saw a man walking in my direction. He was tall with skin the color of chocolate. He wore a tan colored suit and gold tie. He slid in the booth, sitting so that he was facing me.

"Sorry, I'm late," he said. I stared at him, admiring his features. I was finally able to put a face with the voice I had been speaking with for the last two weeks. He was handsome…handsome enough that if I wasn't already in love with Damon I might have considered giving him a chance. However, until I have my man I'll give him a little action. After all, Damon was knocking Octavia's back out on a regular, while I was forced to trust my satisfaction to my fingers and my little friend Jack Rabbit. Hell, I needed someone to tie me over until I was sitting, standing and laying in Octavia's place.

"Not a problem," I said.

"You said you had an assignment for me?" He clasped his hand together in front of him, resting them on the table. He stared at me, attempting to remember where he knew me from I'm sure.

"I do." I looked at him without elaborating.

"What is it?" He seemed somewhat impatient.

"I want you to help me secure a deal," I advised him.

"What kind of deal?"

"Damon Whitmore."

"You want me to help you secure a deal with Damon Whitmore?" He looked puzzled.

"Damon is the deal," I smiled.

"I don't understand."

"I want Damon," I said, bluntly, "and you're the man who's going to help me get him."

"And what makes you *think* I would help you?" he asked, sarcastically.

I reached down in my leather bag that I had sitting on the seat next to me and pulled out the green folder I had tucked neatly inside. I placed the folder on the table in front of him.

"Open it," I told him. I watched as he read over the information I provided him.

"How'd you find out all of this?"

"Much like you, I have ties with Damon," I said, proudly. "When you have the right connections no information is unobtainable." He closed the folder then pushed it across the table to me.

"And why would I help you? How will any of this benefit me?"

The mere fact that he was still sitting with me and talking to me, told me he was interested. The gleam in his eye as he studied the documents

I provided him, told the story that I had opened a door for him that he himself wasn't capable of opening himself.

"I think we both know how you'll benefit," I replied. "Money."

"And you?"

"I told you," I said, staring at Damon's picture. "I want Damon."

Chapter 1

Damon

"Please explain to me why you keep allowing yourself to be treated like a hoe," I snapped, staring across the desk at Alicia. The two of us sat in my office discussing Kenny, the father of her daughter and the husband of my wife's best friend.

"Wh-what do you mean?" she asked, looking completely dazed and confused.

"You've been running behind Kenny for how long now?" I asked. "Six, seven years? And he still married someone else," I snapped, shaking my head.

"He stayed with *her* for money," she said defensively. "Kenny loves *me.*"

"What is it about your situation that makes you think he loves you?" I asked. "Because he cheated on his wife with you?" I questioned. "Or maybe it's because he knocked you up," I said, drumming my fingers on the desk.

Silence.

"His cheating with you was just sex," I said firmly, "and getting you pregnant was a result of bad judgment."

"Kenny loves Kiya!" she snapped.

"Oh, I don't doubt that," I said calmly. "She's a part of him. But the man doesn't love you, Alicia," I continued. "Think about it. He only loves the fact that you're convenient."

"Convenient?"

"Yes, convenient," I repeated slowly. "It's like one-stop shopping. He stops by late at night or whenever he has a few minutes on his hands, and he's in and out, so to speak."

Silence again.

"Picture a 7-Eleven," I continued, "only rather than gas or a little snack, he picks up pussy or some head. You're a grab and go for him," I said, staring into her eyes. "Only a hoe would make herself readily available for a man whose not even hers." I could see the tears welling up in her eyes. I knew my method of teaching was harsh, but there are some women who only understand tough love, and Alicia was one of them.

"I'm not a hoe, Damon," she whispered, tears rolling down her cheeks.

"Then stop acting like one," I said. Looking at the airtight spandex dress she was wearing, I frowned. The dress dipped extremely low in the front, only barely covering her nipples and not much else. "And stop dressing like one," I added. "Leave something to the imagination. If you want a man to love you—and I mean really *love* you—you have to learn to love yourself," I said. "And despite what you or the next woman says, any woman who feels like she has to set out to get a man or dress like a tramp doesn't know what self-love is."

I had my reasons for wanting to put Alicia up on some game. First, I have a daughter, and I know if she was playing herself, I would want someone to pull her aside and try to talk some sense into her. My other reason was the fact that Alicia and I had history. Looking at her in that moment, it was hard for me to believe she was the same headstrong take-no-shit girl I knew from way back. It was even harder to believe there was a time when the two of us were actually a couple. Granted, we were both teenagers, but when you see some people or certain things happen, they bring back a flood of memories. I still remember to this day how Alicia and I met.

It was my junior year at Lakeside High, and I was standing in the hallway, just talking shit with a few of my boys when I saw this skinny, awkward-looking girl stumbling down the hall. It was the first day of school, and Alicia was an incoming freshman. I remember she had on a denim skirt that went all the way down to her ankles, along with a matching denim jacket. She was carrying an armful of books and a schedule in her hand. When somebody bumped into her, it sent the load she was struggling with everywhere. I stepped away from the crowd I was standing with and went to offer my assistance.

"I got it," she said, stacking the books up before I could touch them.

"If you had it, you wouldn't have dropped them." I laughed.

She looked up at me and frowned. "Like I said," she said, standing slowly, "I got it."

I remember she marched off, leaving me standing in the hallway with my mouth open and my ass being cracked on by all my boys. My ego was somewhat insulted but not broken. Now that I think about it, even back then I was persistent as hell when it came to getting what I wanted.

Eventually, after I posted up outside Alicia's homeroom class for two straight weeks, she broke down and gave me the time of day. The two of us were an item from that point on, practically inseparable during school hours. I took her to her first high school dance, her first prom, and I was the one to take her virginity. We went together until the summer of my senior year, when Alicia's family mysteriously packed up and left Atlanta. I was young, and although my family had money even back then, I knew nothing about using your resources to get what you need. Truth be told, within three weeks after she left, I had another girl on my arm, and Alicia was just a distant memory. I discovered that Alicia Green was *my* Alicia, better known as "Lee-Lee" from Lakeside when I hired an associate of mine by the name of Lawrence to do some research on the woman who was wrecking Octavia's best friend's home.

I needed to know more about the woman who was causing so much drama for my wife's girl Shontay because she'd become a regular topic of discussion in my home. Why was it my concern? Because it was my wife Octavia's concern, and what bothers her pisses me off. You have to understand that my wife—like most women—is an emotional creature, beautiful but emotional. When something bothers her, it invades her senses to the point that other desires (like her desire to do that thing with her mouth that I so love) come up short. I'm a sucker for head—no pun intended—so you can understand why the situation with Alicia had to be dealt with and dealt with quickly. I had already decided how I was going to handle the situation when Lawrence brought me the 411 on Alicia's history.

The information Lawrence provided included everything from Alicia's Social Security number to the make of her first car. As far as I knew, I had never laid eyes on the Alicia my Octavia talked so much about, but then Lawrence brought me photos and I realized she was the Lee-Lee I knew from back in the day. Although Alicia and I hadn't spoken or seen each other in years and were on two completely different levels both mentally and socially, I was not about to have her out in the streets looking like some throw-away hoe.

"Okay, Damon," Alicia whispered lowly. I watched as she wiped her face with the back of her hands. "So help me."

Her words brought a smile to my face. Reaching across the desk, I took her hand in mine. "What happened to you, Lee-Lee?" I asked gently. "The girl I knew—"

"That's just it, Damon. She was a *girl*," Alicia said, cutting me off. "I know you have your thoughts, feelings and opinions about the things I've done as an adult, but you don't know what brought me here, to this point in my life."

I watched as the tears trickled down her cheeks, but I said nothing and allowed her to go on.

"You went on to live a happy life with loving parents, and you used that love to fuel your success. Some people aren't so lucky, like me, for instance."

"But this is a new day, baby," I told her, "a new chance."

"Where do I begin?" she asked.

"First things first," I said. "Get rid of the weave and get that cap out your mouth." I looked at her hair, wondering what in the world she was thinking. Alicia's skin was the color of deep, dark chocolate, yet she continued to knot those ridiculous platinum-blonde weaves in her head. As far as the gold cap was concerned, it was my belief that unless it was there for necessary dental purposes, it shouldn't be there at all. "Burn that dress and every other piece of clothing you own," I continued. "You have to step your wardrobe up." Staring at her, I tried to picture the pretty dark-skinned girl I had once adored; I knew she was still there, lurking somewhere under all that ghetto ensemble Alicia had put together, and I needed to find her.

"Damon, it takes money to buy new things—" Alicia stopped what she was saying when she saw me place the briefcase on the desk in front of her.

Her eyes looked like they might pop out of their sockets when I opened the case, revealing its contents. "What's this?" she asked.

"It's $125, 000," I said with a serious look on my face. "Like I said, it's a new day. This is for a new start for you and Kiya."

"And this?" I watched as she removed the gun from the top of the stacks of cash. Holding it loosely in her palms, she looked at me. "I mean, I know what it is," she said, "but what is it for?"

Leaning forward, I put my hands on the desk. "I think you already know."

***

Two Weeks Later

I pushed through the steel door leading to the roof of The Ambiance 2 and stepped into the night air with urgency. I scanned the scene with my eyes, darting from body to body. Kenny lay on his back with his eyes closed, surrounded by a growing puddle of crimson. His shirt was saturated with his own blood, evidence of the bullets that had ripped through his chest just moments earlier. Donna, his lover, looked like a sleeping angel in spite of the blood trickling from the gunshot wound in the side of her head. I pulled my eyes from their lifeless bodies just long enough to look at Alicia; she stared at me with eyes as wide as a child's. At first her expression was one of guilt and regret all wrapped into one, but then a small smile crept across her face. The gun that had been used for the crime lay on the ground a few inches from where she was standing.

I looked from her to the weapon. *Damn,* I thought to myself.

"What the...?" Savoy whispered, coming up from behind me.

"Go downstairs and get Jennings," I said, still staring at Alicia. Drake Jennings was on my payroll. He was also a detective with Huntsville Police Department. In life, it pays to have the right people on your team at the right time, and Detective Jennings was proving to be one of my wisest investments yet.

"What about...?"

"I'll handle it," I told him. "Jennings will handle the rest." I looked Savoy in the eyes, offering him some unspoken reassurance. He nodded his head before running away, and as soon as he was gone, I moved into action. I knew it would be only seconds before Octavia and Shontay came bursting through the door. Given enough time, I could have spared them from viewing the scene of death and mayhem altogether, but time was not on my side. Even if Savoy had warned Octavia and Shontay to stay away, they would have been defiant about it and done the exact opposite of what he said. I love Octavia with every ounce of blood coursing through my veins, and I love Shontay like my own sister, but the two of them are as stubborn as diaper rash on a baby's ass. Despite that, though, I would kill for either one of them; hell, when it comes to Octavia, I already have.

Much like the scene before me, Octavia was caught in a love triangle when the two of us first started dating. She was infatuated with a punk-ass bitch dope boy by the name of Beau. Don't get me wrong, Beau owned a lucrative strip club and had several other hustles, but the brother was a murderer and a woman-beater who shamelessly loved to treat his nose with heroine. I can't and won't knock Beau for his hustle, but I have a serious problem with so-called "men" who like to use their muscles to strong-arm the women in their lives. I was raised to practice and believe that a real man never uses his physical strength against a female. For some reason, though, Octavia just couldn't break free from Beau. I'm not an insecure man, so I couldn't have cared less about what Beau was or was not providing in the bedroom. The only thing I gave a damn about was getting what was rightfully mine, and that was Octavia's hand in marriage. See, I knew from the first time I laid eyes on her that she was the woman God had created just for me.

The first time I saw Octavia was in a feature article in *Black Business Woman's Monthly*. Her skin was the color of brown sugar, and she had honey-brown eyes and curly jet-black hair that I would later be pleased to find out was all naturally hers. Her face was beautiful, and her body was banging: perfectly round breasts, well-toned legs, and wide, ride-'em hips. I could tell she took care of herself, and that alone was a turn-on. However, it wasn't Octavia's beauty that earned her recognition in *BBWM;* that came from her professional accomplishments.

Octavia was a Spelman College graduate and the proud owner of Ambiance, one of Huntsville's only upscale restaurants at the time. I found this to be far more enticing than her nearly flawless appearance, but it wasn't because I needed a woman to take care of me; I'm the president of Nomad Investments and Savings, my father's company, and I also own

Gold Mortgage. I make more in a month than most people earn in an entire year. So for me, money is no object, but there is something about a woman who has her own. Octavia's beauty and credentials had me hooked, and I became infatuated with her instantly.

After reading the article, I began to study Octavia and familiarize myself with her habits. I traveled frequently from my home in Atlanta to Huntsville, Alabama, until I knew Huntsville like I knew my own nuts. Then, when I felt the time was right, I made my move. From the very beginning, the attraction between the two of us was undeniable, but as I said before, Octavia had a problem breaking away from Beau. In the end, the three of us ended up in a deadly confrontation. Beau attempted to kill both of us, but he lost his own life instead. Octavia became my wife, and three months later, our daughter Jasmine was born.

The two of us now share a wonderful life. I admit that I have some secrets, and there are some things from my past that Octavia will never know. However, what's important is that I am a protector and a provider who handles his business by any means necessary.

Removing the monogrammed handkerchief I kept in the inside my jacket, I carefully picked up the gun and positioned it in Donna's cold palm. It was not my desire to cover up the crime. I knew any partially trained rookie on the police force would be able to tell that the weapon had been moved. My reasoning behind moving the gun was based solely on my desire to spare Octavia and Shontay the horror of the truth. Fortunately, neither of them had studied forensics.

"What happened?" I asked, moving to Alicia's side.

"I killed her," she said calmly.

"And him?"

"No. Donna took care of Kenny first," she said, looking at me, "and then I returned the favor."

"That wasn't the plan," I whispered. I had given Alicia specific instructions to make sure Donna had the gun. I knew that once Donna found out Kenny was using her just like he was using Alicia, she would grow the balls to take him out, thus ending the trouble he was causing Shontay. I had never anticipated Alicia taking things into her own hands.

"Plans change," she said strongly.

"So I see."

"Thanks, Damon," she said softly.

"For what?"

"Because of you, I remember me."

I wrapped my arm around her shoulder as Octavia and Shontay came rushing in the door.

Chapter 2

Octavia

Have you ever met a woman too independent for her own good? The kind of woman who passes on love, no matter how good the man is? I used to be that woman. The only time or place I had for a man was under the sheets, pushing in between my thighs. However, something happened that made me come to the realization that all those years of having sex with no strings attached were a waste of my damn time. There came a point in my life when I had to finally admit that fear was my reason behind my failure to commit, and deep inside, I wanted what all mature adults want—I wanted real love.

My eyes were officially open when, after fifteen years, my parents, Charlene and Charles, renewed their love and remarried. I admit my parents' journey was not an easy one. When I was ten years old, my father packed his bags and walked out on my mother. At the time, I thought it was because he was in love with another woman. As it turned out, his mistress was more of the chemical sort. He had an addiction, and rather than subject my mother and me to all the bullshit that went along with that lifestyle, he walked away. Don't get me wrong…he made sure I was taken care of, but he knew he couldn't be a husband and father and love my mother like she deserved to be loved, at least not until he got his shit together. That's one of the many reasons I respect my father so much. A lot of men and women would rather take the one who loves them up, down, and through a continuous cycle of drama rather than having enough nuts to say, *"I'm fucked up right now, and you deserve better."*

Once Daddy had himself together, he let Mama know she still had his heart. As his luck would have it, he still had hers too. There was just one person standing in their way: my stepfather Bill.

Now that I think about it, Bill really wasn't a problem. The truth is that he *had* a problem. See, my loving stepfather was a raging sex addict. After doing a little research, Mama discovered that her new husband had a thing for porn, strippers, sex toys, and bondage. We also discovered during a spirit-filled Sunday morning worship service that Bill had a thing for the 60-plus, wigwearing, 300-pound mother of our church, Sister Emma. It was during that wonderful service that Bill confessed that he and Emma had been bumping the skins. As a result of my stepfather's candid confession, Mama got her dream divorce and remarried Daddy within three months.

Seeing the lasting strength of my parents' love through all of that gave me the courage to open my heart to my loving and wonderful husband Damon. If I could create an army of men, Damon would be the mold, and they'd all be captains; that's just the kind of man he is. Not only is he fine—and I do mean FINE—but he's also affectionate, loving, and understanding. He accepts me for who I am, and he takes very good care of me and our daughter Jasmine.

However, much like the love my parents share, our love is not perfect. My husband proved that to me tonight, when he looked me dead in the eyes and told me a lie.

***

I gently placed Damon's Blackberry back on the nightstand, then tiptoed back to my side of the bed. Damon lay on his back with a smile plastered on his face, sleeping like a freshly fed newborn. I wondered what he and Jada were up to in that dream world of his. My husband has openly communicated with me about his fantasies of Jada Pinkett-Smith, and I'm cool with it. It's my belief that it's not the sisters on the big screen we have to worry about, but the ones riding around in our neighborhood, looking like dick-thirsty hoes. I contemplated awakening him from his erotic dream to confront him with the information Alicia had provided to me during our phone call, but I ultimately decided against it.

Instead, I slipped back under the sheets and closed my eyes. I had a million thoughts running through my mind, and the source of their chase was my realization that my loving and wonderful husband had lied to me.

Earlier that night, the two of us had indulged in one of our many exhilarating lovemaking sessions. The loving had been so good that my boo had put me to sleep. When I woke up, I expected to roll over and find his warm body lying next to mine. Instead, I woke up at two in the morning, all alone in our king-sized bed. I climbed out of bed buck-naked and went in search of Damon, assuming he was on diaper duty with our beautiful daughter, only he wasn't. I found him downstairs, engaged in a phone call. When I asked him who he was talking to, he told me he was on the phone with his best friend, Savoy.

Not only is Savoy Damon's partner, but he's also the new boo of my bestie, Shontay. The two of them had just departed for a romantic rendezvous to Belize, so when Damon said Savoy was on the other end of the phone, I was relieved to know that my bestie and her new man had made it to their destination safely.

I would have continued to believe it was Savoy, but Shontay called me a few hours later. After we exchanged brief pleasantries, it was brought to my attention that Savoy hadn't spoken to my man since he and Shontay had left for their voyage. I ended my conversation with my girl without dropping a clue that Damon had lied to me, but don't think for one second I wasn't going to find out the truth.

After guessing the password on his phone—and believe me, I wanted to know why he had his phone locked in the first damn place—I called the last number back. Something inside me was telling me it was a home-wrecking bitch on the other line, and my instinct was right. To my dismay, it was a gutter-rat by the name of Alicia. I'd met her before, when Shontay and I rolled up and caught her at the Charles Motel with Shontay's then-husband Kenny. Alicia had been screwing Kenny for years and even had a baby by him. Although she and Kenny had put my girl through hell, Shontay had forgiven Kenny and accepted their child as part of the family. I must say my girl is a bigger woman than I am! If any man of mine brought a child up in our home of which I wasn't the baby-mama, it wouldn't be long before it would be *my* home and *my* home only. I'd have his things packed and the locks changed so fast he would nickname me Triple A. Forget "for better or for worse." I refuse to play the happy stepmother to any child of my man's conceived by some hoe. I'm a real woman, and I ain't about to play that game.

Anyway, Shontay maintained and played her role well, right up until Kenny was murdered by his girlfriend, Donna, the second girlfriend, whom Kenny was sharing with Alicia. Yes, you heard me right. Kenny, Donna, and Alicia were on some kind of kinky threesome trip until Donna shot Kenny and then turned the gun on herself.

I know Kenny was responsible for keeping his dick in his pants, but at the same time, both Alicia and Donna should have had enough respect to step back. No woman should play around with another woman's husband; that bitch called Karma will always bounce back.

You can understand why I was concerned to discover it was Alicia who had been speaking with my man. I have to give the girl some credit, as she did change her ways up just before Kenny's death. She went from dressing like a broke-down stripper to looking like a lady, but I still didn't trust her with my man. Hell, Kenny was ugly and broke, and he had her nose open. Imagine what a sexy, rich man like my husband would have done to her!

Chapter 3

Damon

I woke up with a smile on my face and my soldier standing at full command. Jada always has that effect on me.

There are really only two women I dream about: One is the beautiful woman who was lying next to me, my wife Octavia, and the other is Jada Pinkett-Smith. I rolled over and slowly pulled the covers back, revealing Octavia's beautiful round ass. I was in the perfect position to slip in and start beating it from the back, but that wouldn't have been fair to my baby. I was guaranteed to get mine, but I had to make sure she got hers first. Your woman's satisfaction is mandatory, and any man who thinks otherwise is less than a man. Squeezing her ass gently, I waited while she rolled over onto her back.

"Good morning," she said with a yawn.

"Good morning, baby." I climbed on top of her, slid down, and spread her legs with my shoulders. Her pretty pussy greeted me with a smile that I couldn't resist. Flicking my tongue over the hood of her clit, I felt like I might cum just from anticipation. I mentally whispered to my dick to be patient.

I was just preparing to suck and lick my pussy until she came for me when Octavia asked, "Why did you lie to me about your phone call earlier?"

Raising my head, I looked up to find her staring me down with those pretty brown eyes of hers, looking all intense and serious.

"Yeah, I checked your phone," she said, puckering her lips, "after I figured out your password. What's up with that anyway?" she asked, still staring at me. "You got something to hide, or was that just so I wouldn't find out about Alicia?" She fired one question after another. "What if I was up in here with my phone locked? Huh? Suspect, right?"

My first instinct was to ask her why she was going through my shit, but common sense advised me that it would've been a mistake. I knew that even if I wasn't guilty of doing wrong, questioning my wife on why she went through my phone would have been an unintentional admission of guilt. "I'm sorry I lied to you," I said, "and locking my phone is a habit. I normally keep it locked just in case I lose it. I wanted to tell you about Alicia, but I know how you feel about her," I said calmly. "And for the record, if your phone was locked, I wouldn't trip," I continued. "I trust you." I left out the part about me knowing all her passwords, and if I even thought another man was hitting my pussy, I would hurt his ass. I was still in position in between her legs, prepared to dive in.

"Um, you can come back up," she said. "It ain't even about to go down right now."

I looked at her pussy again, mentally shaking my head before sitting up in the bed.

"I spoke with Alicia," she said, sitting up against the headboard.

"And what did she tell you?" I asked.

"That you hooked her up with a job in L.A.," she said.

I was careful not to show my emotions, but I was smiling on the inside. Octavia can be hell to deal with when she's got her heart set on finding out some information. I was pleased to hear that Alicia hadn't cracked, even under pressure that would have made the CIA squeamish. "Yes," I said, trying to gauge her emotions.

"And why would you do that?" Octavia asked, folding her arms across her breasts.

I couldn't help staring at her cleavage, admiring how perfect and round her tits were.

"Up here," she said, snapping her fingers.

I redirected my attention to her eyes. "I did it for Shontay," I said. "I figured bumping into Alicia and Kiya around town would bring back too many memories, and although Shontay and Alicia have made their peace, they both need a fresh start." I left out the fact that Alicia and I had dated in high school. It wasn't important, and it wasn't going to help my case with Octavia. If I had disclosed my connection to Alicia, it would have opened up a floodgate of questions for which I knew I had no acceptable answers. Considering that Octavia's concern at that moment was that I had told her a lie, confessing that I went to school with Alicia and that we were more than friends would have caused nothing less than a nuclear disaster.

She rolled her eyes, then exhaled lightly. "I love you for what you did for Shontay, boo," she continued. "I even love what you did for Alicia, although I feel some kind of way about her."

"I know," I said, "but you don't have to worry about any other women. You're the only woman I want."

She smiled brightly. "I better be…and I trust you. I know why you did it," she added "but lying to me was wrong!"

"I know, baby, and again, I'm sorry."

"So is there anything else you'd like to tell me?" she asked, lowering her eyes in my direction. "Any other secrets you'd like to share? Rescued a litter of kittens and got them stashed out in the nursery?" she teased. "Huh, Mr. Good Samaritan?"

I pulled her into my arms and stroked her hair gently. "No, baby," I whispered, holding her tightly. "There are no more secrets I want to share." It wasn't exactly a lie.

Straddling my lap, Octavia looked at me seductively, causing my dick to instantly jolt upright at attention, like a soldier on the front lines, ready for action. "Good." She smiled, brushing her lips across mine softly. "But there is something I want to share with you."

"Oh yeah?" I whispered. "What's that?"

I watched as she slithered down my body and slid her mouth over and down the head of my rod. The warmth of her tongue and lips against my skin made my dick pulsate. Running my fingers through her hair, I moaned as she licked, sucked, and blew on my dick, causing my toes to curl. Stroking my sac gently with the tips of her fingers, Octavia rolled her tongue over the head of my dick softly. "Feel good?" she asked.

"Yes," I moaned.

"I bet this feels better," she whispered, just before taking all of my man in her mouth.

My heart rate increased until my heart felt like it might pound its way right through my ribs and out of my chest. I moaned, trying to resist the urge to thrust my hips upward. I knew if I gave into my urge, I would nut within seconds. The muscles in my thighs and lower stomach tightened as Octavia sucked me until I felt like I would explode. "Baby…" I said, breathing heavily.

Pulling herself up on her knees, Octavia moved her body until her pussy was positioned above my lips. She continued to give me head in a way that would have made a porn star jealous. Spreading her hairless lips open, I inhaled the aroma of her wetness. I wasted no time latching on to her protruding clit. Octavia has the biggest clit I have ever seen and the sweetest pussy I have ever tasted—literally. I sucked her clit with intense pressure while pushing my index finger in and out of her warmth. I felt her body tense up and her legs began to shake. Removing my finger, I dove inside her, tongue-first.

"Damon…" she groaned, arching her back.

I loved the way she said my name. I knew when it left her lips, I was hitting all the right spots at the right time. I pretended the inside of her pussy was a chess board and used my tongue as pieces. I moved from left to right, hitting corner after corner, until her sweet juices dripped down my throat.

"Right there, baby," she moaned, grinding against my face.

Rolling my tongue, I continued to penetrate her wetness until I felt heat oozing from the source of her pleasure. "Sit on it," I commanded.

Octavia obeyed my command, easing onto my rock-hard dick. I thrust up and down like a man on a mission as she threw it back. The muscles of her vagina clenched my erection like a python, preparing to devour its prey.

Grabbing her bouncing breast, I squeezed gently. "Shit!" I groaned, as I felt my eruption pushing through my body.

"Mmm…" she moaned as her muscles tightened. The aroma of sex filled the air as she came all over my dick.

I continued to push in and out of her expanding coochie until my cum was shooting up into her wet-wet. "Damnnn!" I groaned, grabbing her hips tightly. "Don't move. Don't move." The sensation going through my body was electrifying and magnificent. Once it subsided what seemed like an eternity later, I released my grip on her hips.

"Whew!" she sighed, laying her head on my chest.

I inhaled, then exhaled slowly, attempting to slow my heart rate.

"You're the best," she whispered, kissing my chest softly. "You're the best."

Stroking her sweat-soaked hair, I breathed heavily. "You too, baby. You too."

Chapter 4

Damon

One year later

$\mathcal{R}$iding down Interstate 255, I bobbed my head to the sounds of Trey Songz and Nicki Minaj that were flowing through the speakers of my Bose system. A small smile crept across my face as flashbacks of the early-morning workout Octavia had provided me ran through my mind. There is no better way to start off your morning than with a hot-wet vagina. No, wait: I take that back. There is no better way to start off your day than with a hot-wet vagina that belongs to you and only you. "Today is gonna be a good day," I declared as I moved with the flow of traffic.

Traffic seemed to move flawlessly. One of the many things I loved about living in a smaller city was that I rarely had to deal with bumper-to-bumper traffic or backups. I was halfway to my office at Nomad Investments when my cell rang. "Hey, baby," I answered.

"I just wanted to tell you I love you," Octavia said sweetly.

"I love you too." I hoped she could sense my smile through the phone. "I always will."

"The feeling is mutual."

"This morning was—"

"Un-freaking-believable." She sighed.

"Yes."

"Round 2 tonight?" she asked.

The thought of it made my nature slowly rise. "I'll be there with bells on."

"Umm, bells?" She moaned. "I prefer you naked, but if you're into Christmas decorations, we can try something new."

Shaking my head, I laughed. "My lil' freak," I teased.

"You know it."

I pulled into the parking lot of my office, then shifted my Benz into park. I smiled when I saw that all five of the spaces reserved for my employees were full; everyone was present and accounted for. It really was going to be a good day.

"Well, sexy, I have to get ready for my interviews," she said, exhaling.

I had forgotten that it was the day when she was going to be conducting interviews for a nanny for Jasmine. At first I was dead set against bringing a stranger into our home and around our daughter. It was my preference that Octavia stay at home full time, but I'm not selfish. How could I ask her to give up one of the things that made me love her? Her independence. We both agreed that a public daycare was out. We wanted Jasmine to receive one-on-one attention and care, so I finally broke down and agreed to Octavia hiring a nanny. "Let me know how it goes," I told her. "I love you."

"I will, baby, and I love you too."

***

Relaxing in my chair, I stared at the printout of the list of clients we'd acquired in the last six months. Although we were in a recession, the number of people investing their money with us had nearly doubled. I could only chalk it up to people needing something to believe in, something to hope for. They needed to know that better days were on the way. The funny thing about our clients was that not all of them were what most people would consider wealthy. Our clientele included a wide demographic, from engineers to strippers. I took pride in the fact that so many people were investing in their futures, and they were choosing to do it with my company.

"Damon?" Louisa's voice came through the speaker on the phone.

Louisa had been my assistant since I'd opened the Huntsville branch of Nomad Investments. She was with me clear back when there were only two of us. I loved her because she was efficient and punctual. Octavia loved her because she was old and comforting, like a well-worn quilt.

"Yes, Louisa?"

"You have a call on Line 2," she said sweetly.

"Thanks, Louisa. You can send them through." I waited for the buzz indicating that the call had been transferred, and then I answered, "This is Damon."

"Did I catch you at a bad time?"

I recognized the voice instantly. "No," I said, reclining in my chair. "How are you, Nadia?"

"Fine, Damon. How are you?" she echoed.

"I'm good."

"It's good to hear your voice," she said sweetly. "It's been forever."

"It has been a minute," I agreed.

"Yep."

There was an awkward silence on the phone. I knew there was more to her call than she was letting on, something other than a casual hello. Nadia and I had been friends for four years and lovers off and on for two of those years. The two of us had shared several private moments, and I knew Nadia well enough to know when she was holding something back. As it turned out, I was right.

"I'm calling to let you know I'm going to be in Atlanta next week," she said. "I'm doing a show with Tyler Perry, and I wanted to invite you to check it out."

"You're acting now?" I asked. The last time I had spoken with Nadia, she'd been performing with the Alvin Ailey American Dance Company. As a professional ballerina, she'd had the chance to travel and perform in several famous productions across the globe.

"Yes," she said cheerfully. "I'm actually starring in several plays within the next year."

"Plays? Really? What about your dancing?"

"I'm taking a break from that for a while," she said. "There have been some, uh…well, some major changes in my life over the last couple of years, so I decided to explore my career options."

"Hmm. I never thought I'd hear that from you, Nadia. You're a great dancer. I was sure you'd be pirouetting till your dying day," I joked. "What could have possibly happened to change that? Must've been something pretty drastic."

"I fell in love," she said sweetly.

"In love?" I repeated. "Congratulations, but knowing you the way I do, I never thought the day would come when you would give up your dream for a man." It was true. When Nadia and I had dated, her dancing came before everything and everyone. Hell, she even had me on a schedule when it came down to her practices and performances.

"This guy's worth it and then some," she said, and I could tell she was smiling a sickeningly sweet smile on the other end of the phone. "Besides, I'm not giving up my dream. I'm just putting it on hold for a while."

I could dig that. I, of all people, know that sometimes we have to sacrifice for love.

"I want you to meet him, Damon."

That threw me all the way off. Nadia and I were still cool and everything, as far as I knew, but the two of us chilling with our significant others was not something I saw as an option. It didn't seem like the double-date kind of scenario. "Uh, I don't know if that's a good idea, Nadia," I said slowly. "I'm a man, you know, and the last thing I want to do is kick it with one of my woman's exes." I have never had to worry about that with Octavia, but even if she had offered, I knew my answer would be *"No way!"* I have nothing to discuss with a man who used to fuck my lady. Hell, the only reason I befriended Beau before I murdered him was to ensure that he and Octavia's fling was over.

"Damon, he's not like that," she said, attempting to persuade me. "Just do me this favor. You can bring Octavia if you want."

Like hell I can, I thought to myself. I was 100 percent positive that Octavia had not forgotten the last time she'd seen Nadia. After Octavia and I got engaged, we had a short-term breakup because Beau's sorry ass sent me a sex tape of the two of them getting it on. Granted, I already knew they'd been together, and the episode had taken place before I'd actually proposed to her, but it still fucked me up seeing her lying on her back, spread-eagle, with Beau nestled all up in between her legs, getting his groove on.

During that temporary breakup, Nadia had come to visit me at my office. The two of us were walking hand and hand out to her car, reminiscing and laughing about some of the times we'd shared. Halfway to the parking lot, Nadia stopped and looked at me. "I had a wonderful time with you last week." She smiled. "It's hard to believe it's over."

I had taken a trip to Los Angeles a week prior, and I was there to make sure our L.A. office for Nomad Investments was functioning properly. However, while I was there, I made time for Nadia, just as I always did. I wanted to be the first to tell her that I had proposed to Octavia and that I couldn't see her on the level we had previously been seeing each other. Despite the announcement of my upcoming nuptials, Nadia and I still ended up in bed together. Yes, I'm a provider and a protector, a man who takes care of his lady, but I am a man, and I've never claimed to be perfect. "We both know we're not going to work out as a couple," I said to her, as gently as possible.

"We work just fine together…in bed," she laughed lightly, slightly embarrassed.

"True." I agreed.

Before I could say another word, Nadia placed her hands around my face and pressed her lips to mine. The kiss was short and sweet.

I had been so caught up in my conversation with Nadia that I hadn't noticed Octavia's car in the parking lot. It wasn't until Nadia and I began our stroll again that I noticed Octavia climbing out of her Mercedes. I froze in place as I watched her marching up the sidewalk with her keys in hand. "Octavia!" I said, releasing Nadia's hand.

"What's going on here?" my bride-to-be asked, attitude oozing from every pore in her skin.

Pissed as she was, she still looked sexy as fuck. My mind was telling me that the conversation wasn't going to end well, but my dick kept reminding me that our make-up sex was going to be fire, and believe me when I tell you it was.

"Nadia and I were just—" I tried to explain, but she cut me off.

"Nadia?" she asked. Her eyes darted over to Nadia, and I was sure World War III was going to break out right there on the sidewalk.

Nadia quietly stepped away from me, then extended her hand to

Octavia. "It's nice to finally meet you," she said politely.

Octavia stared at Nadia's hand like she had leeches crawling all over her skin. She then looked at me, and I will never forget the anger I saw blazing in her eyes at that moment. "You didn't waste much time, did you?" she said sarcastically. Now, this is one of the things that kills me about women. At that moment, she had completely forgotten the reason the two of us were arguing in the first place—her amateur porn tape. All of my fiancée's creepin' and lies went out the window the second she thought she'd been replaced by another woman.

"This is not what you think," I said, stepping toward Octavia.

"That's right," Nadia jumped in. "After what happened in L.A., I thought it was better for me to come here and try to work things out."

At that point, I had no idea where Nadia was going with her conversation. All I knew was that if she told Octavia what had really happened between us in L.A., I was going to lose my future wife, and Nadia's ass was going to become acquainted with the sidewalk after Octavia put the beat-down on her, which she was well capable of doing.

"What happened in L.A.?" Octavia asked, lowering her eyes at me.

"You didn't tell her?" Nadia asked, looking at me.

"No," I said flatly, but I felt like I might as well have been wearing a neon sign on my forehead blinking, *"I hit it! I tapped that ass in Cali."*

"Tell me what?" Octavia asked, more demanding this time. She looked from me to Nadia, then back to me again.

During those few seconds I didn't dare to breathe. My ass was on the line, and all I could do was hope Nadia wouldn't toss it under the proverbial bus.

"I came on to him," Nadia finally said. "When I found out he was going to be in town, I went to see him, and all those memories came flooding back. Well, before I knew it…" Nadia never finished her sentence, and Octavia didn't ask her to elaborate. Thinking about it now, I don't know if Nadia would have given Octavia the whole story or not. I'm just thankful I didn't have to find out.

Octavia was still pissed. She shoved her engagement ring back in my face, then drove off, leaving me screaming her name in the wind like something off of some sappy soap opera.

After we made up, I told her nothing had happened with Nadia.

Although she never mentioned that day or Nadia, I couldn't help feeling that my inviting her to see Nadia perform would bring back unwanted memories and lead to a discussion of what Nadia had left out of the conversation that day.

"I'll check on that," I lied. "However, I will be in Atlanta next week on business." I chose not to disclose the fact that I was going to be in L.A. for the weekend. My plate and itinerary for my L.A. visit was full, and attempting to make time for Nadia was not an option on that trip.

"I know." Nadia laughed lightly. "Your father told Odessa, and she told my grandmother."

I had forgotten all about the Senior Citizen Gossip Network, hosted by Odessa and Bernice, mine and Nadia's grandmothers. The women were so into gossip and rumors that they could have worked as informants for those rag mags at the checkout counters. The two of them had been friends for twenty-plus years, and if either of them had had any say in the matter, Nadia and I would have been married with a houseful of babies.

"How is Bernie?" I asked.

"She's good," Nadia said. "Full of drama, as always."

"I wouldn't expect anything less," I said honestly.

"Well, I look forward to seeing you," she said with a sigh. "The show is Tuesday through Friday at the Fox Theater. Let me know when you or the two of you would like to come, and I'll leave tickets at the window."

"I'll call you," I said.

"Talk to you then."

"Goodbye, Nadia."

"For now, Damon."

"Uh, sure...for now."

Chapter 5

Octavia

Since opening The Ambiance 2, my second restaurant, my plate of duties was running over, to the point where my in-box of paperwork was starting to look like the Leaning Tower of Pisa. Being a business owner, mother, wife, daughter, and best friend can be time consuming. Don't get it twisted...I love all the hats I wear and all the people I wear them for, but this chick is on overload seven days a week. This was one of the reasons why I couldn't understand that my wonderful husband wanted another child so badly.

Damon insisted on dropping little hints about wanting a son to go along with our beautiful baby girl, every chance he got. From name-dropping to pointing out cute little scenes with fathers and sons on TV, he had become the official spokesman for reproduction. I'm normally open to anything Damon suggests, but Baby 2 was a closed-ended conversation for me. I love being a mommy, of course, but I also missed being on the front lines of my business every day, and my office needed me there.

Before Damon and I got married, I never would have dared to give someone else full reign of my company, but after I had Jasmine, I had to step back and allow my employees to hold me down. Don't get me wrong: I had a wonderful, capable staff at both my locations, but at the same time,

I wanted to be right there at the heart of the action. I also liked to pop in at anytime and see who I might catch slipping on the job. I'm a kind-hearted, fair boss but my people gotta know that I don't tolerate any slacking, drama, or bullshit. If someone is blessed with an opportunity—like a job in one of my restaurants, for instance—they should show their gratitude by giving 110 percent, just like I do.

After pleading and practically performing an act of Congress, I got Damon to agree to let me hire a nanny so I could return to work full time. Out of a sea of *résumés*, some of which should have never been submitted in the first place and a few I could instantly tell were plagiarized or faked, I finally narrowed it down to a few people whom I actually wanted to interview. I decided to conduct interviews at The Ambiance. That way, I could get some work done in between appointments, and I wouldn't have to have strangers parading in and out of my home. It was my plan to select the perfect nanny and then invite her over for a tour.

My first two candidates were automatically knocked out of the running for being late. If they couldn't bother showing up on time for an interview, surely they couldn't be trusted to change my daughter's diaper on time, and the last thing I needed was for Jazz to suffer from diaper rash just because some lazy ass insisted on putting things off.

Candidate Number 3 was a sweet little old lady by the name of Rosa, the mother of three and grandmother of nine. She didn't smoke or drink, and she looked too old to make a move on my husband—all great qualities in my book. Rosa was batting 100 until she pulled out a King James Bible during our interview and started answering my questions with scripture verses. I wanted our nanny to have some religion, but Rosa was a little extreme for my taste. I love the Lord and everything, but I am far from a saint, and the last thing I needed was for the person helping with my child to go around passing fire-and-brimstone judgment on me.

Candidate Number 4 was too damn pretty for her own good—case closed. I couldn't have some big-titted, green-eyed, Size 2 heifer bouncing around my man. I trust my husband, but I'm not stupid, and the best way to keep your man from succumbing to temptation is to avoid having anything around that will tempt him.

Candidate 5 was a recent college graduate by the name of Alexandria. She had an impressive *résumé* and was fluent in eight different languages.

The Lies We Tell For Love

I felt I had a winner when I saw her stroll through my office door. "Hello, Mrs. Whitmore." She smiled and extended her hand to me for a professional shake.

"Please call me Octavia." I smiled, giving her the onceover with my eyes. She was tall and slim, with auburn hair worn in a simple boy-cut. She was dressed in an interview-suitable plain blue blazer and slacks. Her facial features were cute, but there was nothing that stood out about her. At first, I took her as the tomboy type, which meant Damon wouldn't be salivating over her like a hungry dog. "Have a seat." I smiled. "So, tell me a little bit about yourself," I prompted, crossing my legs. I noticed her eyes traveling from mine, down, then back up again, and something about that made me a bit uneasy.

"Well, I'm a native of Huntsville," she began.

I listened as Alexandria gave me a brief bio. Throughout the interview I noticed that her eyes occasionally strayed from mine down to my breasts, then back up again. *What the hell?* I thought. I crossed my arms across my chest, hoping it would deter her eyes, but it only seemed to attract more unwanted attention from her. I was starting to feel violated, so I decided it was time to wrap our interview up. "Thank you for coming in today." I smiled, stood, and walked over to the door. "It was very nice meeting you."

"The pleasure was all mine." She smiled and seemed to be staring at me from behind.

Did she just look at my ass?

"I hope you don't think I'm being too forward," she said, folding her hands together, "but I think you're just...well, beautiful."

"Uh, thanks." I smiled, holding the office door open for her. It was all I could do not to kick her out of it.

"Would you like to have dinner with me sometime?"

"Thank you, but no," I said nicely. "I'm straight...and happily married."

Smiling, she leaned against the doorframe. "I'm married too," she said seductively, "and he would be perfectly fine with us."

Did she just say "us"? There is no "us"! "Good to know," I said firmly. "Thank you, but you can leave now."

"You know where I'll be if you change your mind." She smiled and winked at me.

Yeah, in the unemployment line, I thought. I waited for her to walk out the door, then wasted no time closing the door behind her.

I had some time between interviews, so I decided to call and check on my girl, Shontay. I missed my bestie with a passion. After leaving Belize, Shontay and Savoy continued their voyage with a trip to London. From London, they planned to travel to Africa before returning to the States. I loved that Shontay was finally living her life on her own terms. She is a wonderful woman who has been through hell. Happiness and peace were long overdue for her.

"Okay, let me get this straight." She laughed. "You had a Bible-toting granny, too hot for the job, and a bilingual lesbian?" She couldn't seem to stop laughing after I told her about my interviews.

"Yes," I said, shaking my head.

"Shit, that sounds like a sitcom. What a mess!"

"A hot one at that," I added. "I'm afraid to see what's gonna walk in here next."

"Hopefully, the next one'll be perfect," Shontay said. "Who is she?"

Glancing at the résumé in front of me, I refreshed my memory on the next candidate. "Her name is Kelly Baker," I read. "Her résumé is impressive. She's CPR certified, elementary education major, Auburn University graduate, five years as assistant director of a daycare, and several volunteer activities. But I'm sure there's something wrong with her," I added. "You know what they say."

"What's that?"

"If something's too good to be true, it probably is."

"Well, we want only the best for my goddaughter," Shontay said. "Speaking of which, how is Jasmine?"

A smile crept across my face at the mere mention of my daughter's name. If anyone would have told me I could ever love anyone as much as I love my daughter, I would have called them a liar to their face. But it's true what they say, children are the ultimate joy. "Walking and getting bigger by the day." I smiled again just thinking of her. "Oh, and she's talking up a storm, though the only word I understand is 'Da Da'."

"A daddy's girl, huh?" Shontay chanted.

"You know it."

"And how is that brother-in-law of mine?" she asked.

"Damon is fine," I told her. "How is Savoy?"

"Perfect," she beamed, and I could hear the smile in her voice. "He is so good to me."

"That's great, Tay," I said sincerely. "I'm so happy for the two of you."

"Me too." She sighed a dreamy sigh, like a girl who'd been kissed for the very first time by her high school crush. "I pray this feeling never ends."

"Yeah, being in love is a beautiful thing," I said.

"It certainly is," she said.

There was a knock on my office door. Looking at my watch, I saw I still had thirty minutes until my next interview, so I assumed it was one of my employees on the other side of the door. "It's open!" I yelled.

The door opened, and in walked a tall, attractive brother wearing a button-down dress shirt, tie, and slacks. His skin was the color of milk chocolate, and he had a round, smooth baby-face. "Good afternoon," he said with a smile, revealing two rows of perfectly straight, gleaming white teeth.

"Good afternoon." I smiled. "Is there something I can help you with?"

"My name is Kelly Baker," he said politely. "I have a one o'clock interview."

I had been sure Kelly sounded too good to be true on paper, and I was right. *She* was a man, and there was no way in hell I was going to hire a male nanny to take care of my little girl! Call me sexist or narrow-minded or whatever you want to call me, but there are some roles I simply do not feel men are cut out to handle. "Tay, my one o'clock is here," I said. "Let me call you back."

"Good luck." She laughed, as she'd heard the masculine introduction. "Love ya."

"Love you too…and, uh, thanks." I hung up the phone and turned to my guest. "Please have a seat," I smiled, placing my Blackberry down on my desk.

"Thank you." The scent of his cologne floated across the desk as he sat down, masculine but not too strong. The brother smelled good. "Am I too early?" he asked. "I can come back if it's a problem," he added.

"No, early is good," I said. "Can you tell me a little about yourself."

"Let's see…" he began. "I was born in Japan."

"Really?"

"Yes." He smiled. "My father served in the military for fifteen years. He was stationed in Okinawa at the time of my birth."

"So you grew up overseas? In Asia?"

"No, not really. We moved to Memphis when I was one," he explained, staring at me. There was something hypnotizing about Kelly's gray eyes and the way they held my attention.

I shook my head, attempting to break the magnetic pull, and focused back on the reason he was in my office. "Interesting. Can you tell me a little about your work history?"

***

Ten minutes later, I was torn by the decision I needed to make. Kelly was perfect on paper and in person. I even tried to slip him up by crossing my legs or leaning slightly forward to see if he would stare at my breasts, but he didn't; his eyes stayed locked on mine for the entire interview. *Shit!* I thought to myself. At least if he would've scoped me out, I would have had a legitimate reason not to want to hire him. As it was, I had no excuses other than the fact that he was a man. "May I ask you a question?" I asked, staring across the desk at him.

"Sure."

"Why do you want to be a *nanny*, of all things?" I asked, putting emphasis on the word "nanny."

"Why do you say it like that?" he asked, frowning.

"Say what like what?"

"Nanny," he said. "You make it sound degrading," He waited for me to answer.

I could tell by the tone of his voice and the look in his eyes that he was bothered by my question. I was hoping he was not going to transform into one of those eye-rolling, overly sensitive men who make you want to bitch-slap their asses for being too emotional. "I didn't mean for it to sound degrading," I said, folding my hands in front of me. "It's just that you're... well, you're not what I expected."

"Because I'm not a woman?" he concluded.

"Well, yes, I did expect a woman," I said, "judging from your name and—"

"And what? The position I'm applying for?" he said, cutting me off.

That was the answer, of course, but I didn't have the nerve to agree with him out loud, so I said nothing.

"Let me ask you something," he said, adjusting his tie.

"Go ahead."

"Would you have called me for an interview if you had known I am a man?"

Hell naw, I thought to myself.

Smiling, he shook his head, as if he was reading my thoughts. "That's what I thought." He laughed.

"However, after meeting you, I'm glad I called you."

"But?"

"Well, I just don't think you're the right fit for this position."

"Because I'm a man," he concluded.

I was trying my best not to get dragged into a debate over his gender, and I had no time to get caught up in a possible sexual discrimination lawsuit. "I didn't say that," I said.

"You can be honest with me," he said calmly. "Trust me, I understand. Can you at least tell me why I am not a good fit?" he asked.

Exhaling, I looked him straight in the eyes. "I'm just not comfortable allowing a man to take care of my daughter," I confessed, and I felt like a weight had been lifted off my shoulders.

When Kelly gave me a warm, friendly smile I felt confident that he would take my words with a grain of salt. Unfortunately, I was wrong.

"So your husband is a woman?" he asked, raising his eyebrows at me.

I knew where he was going with his little line of questioning, but I decided to give him some satisfaction and play along. "No. I assure you he is all man." I smiled.

"But you just said you're not comfortable having your daughter taken care of by a man," he said, smirking at me as if he'd tripped me up.

"I'm not comfortable with a *strange* man."

"But you're comfortable hiring a strange woman?" he asked, lowering his eyes at me.

If she's qualified, yes I am! I screamed to myself. He paused, waiting for me to answer, but I never did.

"Let me ask you another question," he said. This time, he didn't wait for my reply. "As a woman, if you were told you weren't hirable because you're not a man, how would you handle that?"

I couldn't believe he actually had the nerve to turn the tables on me, but that was exactly what he was doing. "I see you're trying to make a point, Mr. Baker."

"I already have, Mrs. Whitmore," he said, rising from his chair and looking victorious. I watched as he strolled smoothly to the door and turned to face me one more time. "I think we both know you wouldn't take such obvious discrimination lightly."

He was right, of course. I would have been on the phone with my attorney before they told me the interview was over. The thought led me to ask, "So is that your plan, Kelly?"

He flashed his gray eyes at me and smiled. "Octavia, I'm a real man, and as a real man, I know how to handle other people's ignorance without involving a third party. To answer your question, though, no I'm not going to whine like a lil' bitch about how you didn't hire me." He managed to accomplish something few others ever could—he had me at a loss for words. "Again, it was nice meeting you," he said. "Have a nice day." He exited my office and closed the door behind him.

***

After getting over my run-in with Kelly, I felt optimistic about my next candidate, a Southern belle by the name of Angie who had worked with three other families. Angie was a white, heavyset redhead who had a heavy Southern accent and a pleasant personality. The two of us instantly built a repertoire. Her appearance was neat and conservative. The only mark I could give her at first was that she smelled like she had taken a bath in perfume—cheap drugstore perfume mixed with a strange but somewhat familiar odor.

"You have experience. That's good." I smiled, looking across the desk at her.

"Yes." Angie smiled. "And each one of the families I've worked for will give me an excellent referral."

"Great!" I smiled. "Well, I do require a background check," I said, sliding the release form across the desk.

"What will they check for?" she asked, frowning. "My credit's not that good."

The Lies We Tell For Love

Though the question set off some bells for me, I respected her honesty. "I don't care about your credit score," I said. "I understand that sometimes things happen." It was true, because in my opinion, a person's credit or lack thereof has nothing to do with the quality of their work. "The background check is merely done to check your criminal history," I explained.

"Oh that's not a problem then." Angie grinned. "I've only had minor traffic violations."

I was on the verge of doing the Dougie until I hit her with my next requirement. "There's also a pre-employment drug screen," I said, providing her my next form.

She shifted in her seat, then crossed her legs. The expression on her face told me we had finally bumped up against the inevitable flaw.

"Is that okay?" I asked, staring at her.

"Uh, yeah." She laughed lightly, like a shamed child caught peeking at their Christmas presents.

"Fabulous," I said, folding my hands together. "Do you have any questions for me?"

"When do I need to go for my test?" she asked, biting her bottom lip.

"Immediately," I answered, looking at my watch. "LabCorp doesn't take its last patient for another two hours."

"Oh," she said in a hushed voice. "Well, I have to pick my mother up in an hour, and it's something like a forty-minute drive."

I had heard every excuse there was when it came to buying time before taking a drug screen, and I was well aware they all meant one thing: *"That doesn't give me enough time to detox."* It was time to call her bluff. "Well, the lab is only two blocks over, and they're normally not busy around this time. You should be able to get right in and right out."

"Oh. Well, I do need to make a stop before I pick up my mom," she said, staring at her watch and trying to stretch her lie to fit neatly around her obvious avoidance.

I wasn't going to waste any more of my precious time with a junkie and a liar. I know how the game works; hell, I used to smoke a little reefer my damn self back in the day. There was a very slight possibility I was wrong about Angie, but her strained and uneasy reaction was reason enough for me to be suspicious. "I'll tell you what," I said, pushing her paperwork to the side, "I have a few more interviews lined up. I'll give you a call, and then we can schedule the screening."

"Okay." She smiled. "All I need is a little advance notice to make sure I'm free. I keep pretty busy taking care of my mother."

"Not a problem," I said, standing. "It was a pleasure meeting you."

"I'll look forward to your call." She smiled.

Yeah, when Hell freezes over, I thought, but I smiled and said, "Have a great day, Angie," as I held the door open for her.

***

After Angie left, I decided to take a breather. I was mentally exhausted and highly disappointed with the day's events. I strolled out of my office only to find Kelly sitting in one of the booths close to my office door, nibbling on a piece of my infamous better-than-sex cheesecake. He was the last person I expected to see at that moment, and I wondered if he was hanging out in my establishment plotting his sexual discrimination suit or if he was truly enjoying the atmosphere. I decided to try and do a little damage control. "Enjoying the cheesecake?" I asked, walking up to the table.

"It's misleading," he said, wiping his mouth.

"What do you mean?"

"The menu says it's better than sex," he said, looking up at me.

"And?"

"And I beg to differ."

"Well, I guess it depends on the person," I said, crossing my arms across my breast.

"I guess so," he mumbled, licking his lips.

I can't lie, the act caused a slight tingling in the pit of my stomach and quite possibly other regions of my body. I cleared my throat, attempting to calm the sensation. "Did you try anything else on the menu?" I asked.

"Nope—just the cake," he said.

"So you've been out here the whole time, and all you've tried was my cake?" I asked, shaking my head.

"If you must know, I've been trying to figure out my next move," he said, leaning back against the booth.

Here we go, I thought. "And what might that be?" I asked, placing my hand on my hip.

"Getting a job." He sighed lightly. "Pounding the pavement."

"Oh."

"You'd think with a BA and military training, a brother would be able to find something." He laughed, rubbing his hands together. "But I've been looking for a job for almost a year now, to no avail."

"I didn't know you were in the military," I said, pleasantly surprised. I didn't remember seeing it on his résumé, but I've always been very impressed by and appreciative of any man or woman who serves our country that way.

"Reserves," he said. "I know you're probably thinking that doesn't count."

"No I'm not," I said quickly. "We need all of you."

He looked at me with the ocean of gray in his eyes shining brightly, then smiled. "Do me a favor," he requested.

"What?"

"Sit down," he said, nodding to the empty space across from him. "You're making me nervous hovering over me like that."

"Why? Are you up to no good?" I asked, sliding into the booth.

"Not at all," he said. "It's just that I don't like people standing over me, especially women who tell me I'm not good enough to work for them. You've already stepped on my pride," he continued. "I don't need you making me feel even smaller."

"I didn't mean to step on your pride," I said sincerely, "and I never said you weren't good enough to work for me."

"Oh that's right. You don't feel *comfortable* with me," he mocked, snapping his fingers.

I could tell by the tone of his voice that he was taking my comment far too personally. "It's not just you," I said. "It would be the same with any man."

"But you're going to consider Queen Smokes-a-lot?" He laughed.

"Who?"

"That last woman you interviewed," he said, staring at me. "When she walked by, she smelled like a damn Cheech and Chong van. Didn't you notice?"

"Oh, her. Well—"

"Come on, Octavia," he said, leaning against the table. "Surely you're not that naïve, or were your senses confused by her swim in the cheap perfume?" he asked, laughing lightly.

Replaying the interview in my head, I had to chuckle. "Let's just say the position is still open."

"Not to *every* qualified applicant apparently." Reaching into his pocket, he removed a wallet.

I noticed a picture of him with a pretty little girl on the inside of it when he flipped it open. "Who's that? She's beautiful," I said, pointing at the photo. The little girl looked to be no older than five and had the same amazing features as Kelly, including his stormy sky-gray eyes.

Smiling, he stared at the picture. His eyes lit up as joy floated across his face like a balloon filled with warm air. "It's my daughter Ciara," he said, stroking the picture lovingly.

"You have a daughter?"

"I *had* a daughter," he said sadly. "She died two years ago."

For the second time, Kelly Baker had me at a loss for words as I saw tears swelling in his eyes.

His lips quivered slightly as he exhaled slowly and went on to explain in a near-whisper, "She had leukemia. She needed a bone marrow transplant, but we never found a match." A single tear rolled down his cheek as he looked at me.

I cleared my throat, but my attempt to dissolve the lump failed miserably. I hate seeing a man cry; it weakens me to my core. Knowing that his tears were for the loss of a child almost caused my heart to shatter. "I'm so sorry, Kelly," I said sympathetically while reaching out to touch his hand.

He turned his hand over, allowing my fingers to rest in his palm. The gesture was innocent, but the electricity between us surged from his palm through my fingertips like lightning on a stormy day. Pulling my hand back slowly, I folded my hands together in an attempt to defuse the energy I felt.

"No parent should ever have to outlive their child," he said. "The hole it leaves in your heart is unbearable."

I listened quietly as he continued to speak. The expression on his face showed that his mind had traveled far away. I imagined he was reliving the pain he'd felt when he'd first loss his precious daughter.

"As a father, I felt weak and like a failure," he said, shaking his head.

"Why?" I asked.

"Because I couldn't fix it," he said solemnly. "She needed me, and I couldn't do anything to help her. I couldn't make it right. In that way, I let her down."

"As parents, we want to wrap our children up in a blanket of love and make everything perfect," I said gently. "Unfortunately, we don't have that kind of power. Kelly, that doesn't mean we're weak or failures," I said softly. "It means we're only human."

There was silence between the two of us as he wiped his eyes with the back of his hands. Our silence was finally broken when his phone began to ring.

"Excuse me," he said. "Hello? Hey. Okay." Looking up at me, he frowned. "Unfortunately not," he said. "Okay. I'll be there in a few. Love you too," he said before hanging up. "I should get going," he told me.

"Oh, okay. Have a nice day."

"You too," he said, giving me a weak smile and dabbing the cake out of the corner of his mouth with a napkin.

"I'm really sorry for your loss, Kelly," I said, feeling more and more like crap with every passing second. If I hadn't been fully staffed at my establishments, I would've given him a job on the spot, but I had solid teams in place at both locations, and the last thing I wanted to do was hire too many people so that my employees had to lose pay and decent hours. "I'm sure you'll find something," I added.

"Thanks," he mumbled.

I watched as he pulled a ten-dollar bill out of his wallet and laid it in the middle of the table.

"No, this one's on me." I smiled, pushing the bill back toward him.

"I don't take charity," he said, shaking his head.

"This isn't charity," I said. "It's just my way of thanking you."

"For what?"

"For taking the time to meet with me," I said. It was a load of crap, and he knew it. I didn't go around buying cake for all of the applicants I turned away.

"You mean thank you for not ratting you out and telling the world you're a sexist?" he said, standing.

"I am not a sexist," I said defensively. "You just aren't—"

"I know, I know," he said. "You think I'm not the right fit. If I see someone who might be the right fit," he said, "I'll tell *her* to come see you."

He was clearly being cynical and sarcastic, on the verge of rude, but I decided to let it slide.

"Have a nice day, Mrs. Whitmore," he said before walking off.

***

It was pushing four o'clock when I wrapped up my paperwork at The Ambiance. I decided I'd had enough for one day. I was in the process of gathering my things to head home when there came a knock on my office door. "Enter," I said pleasantly.

"Sorry to bother you," said Tabitha, one of my hostesses, "but there is someone here who would like to speak to you."

"Who is it?" I asked.

"She says her name is Contessa," Tabitha said, standing in the doorway. "She doesn't have an appointment, but says she heard you are looking for a nanny."

The mere mention of the word "nanny" made me want to crawl under my desk and cover my head. I was beginning to think I was never going to find a suitable caretaker for my daughter, which meant I would have to consider the option of working part time and being a stay-at-home mom. My mother was happy watching Jasmine for me at the present, but I'd begun to notice that Mama was looking more and more tired, and the last thing I wanted was for her to get burned out. "How does she look?" I asked Tabitha. "Wait…before you answer that, is she a *she*?"

"Um, yes she is a she," Tabitha said, frowning in confusion, "and she reminds me of someone's granny."

Tabitha's answer really didn't tell me much. I wanted to tell her to tell the woman to come back the next day, but I decided it couldn't get any worse than what I'd already been through. *I might as well get rid of her today,* I reasoned. "Tell her to come in," I said.

A few seconds later, a pretty mocha-complexioned, petite older woman came through my office door. She was dressed simply but neatly in a plain white button-down blouse, a straight black skirt, and flats. Her salt-and-pepper hair was pulled back, secured in a small bun. "Hello," she said, smiling at me.

I stood and extended my hand to her. "Hello, Contessa," I said. "My name is Octavia."

"It's nice to meet you," she said sweetly.

"Have a seat," I said. "Did you bring your résumé?"

"That thing that tells you where I worked?"

"Yes, ma'am."

"No, sweetie, I didn't," she said, pushing her glasses up on her nose. "That's what's wrong with the world today," she said, waving her hand in the air. "My nephew made me one of those, but I figured I could just tell you face to face who, what, when, and where. We've become so impersonal."

I laughed lightly then nodded my head in agreement. "I agree," I admitted. "So, why don't you tell me a little bit about yourself and your work history?"

Fifteen minutes later, I knew Contessa was fifty-seven years old, a widow, and that she had spent the last ten years working for a family in Madison until eight months prior, when the father took a job out of state and the family relocated. I also sadly learned that her one and only son was in prison for armed robbery.

"I love the boy, of course, but sometimes you gotta love 'em from a distance," she said, "especially when they keep doing the same ol' thing."

She told me she had been living in Johnson Towers, apartments for seniors, on a fixed income. She advised she had been living at the Towers every since she lost her job and that it was hard finding employment at her age, especially with no other skills or a college education. She loved to cook and sew in her free time. She was healthy with the exception of being a diabetic, but she managed her disease by eating healthy and taking her insulin. She also told me her nephew lived with her. My conversation with Contessa flowed as if the two of us had known each other for years. *I finally found a winner,* I thought to myself.

"What else would you like to know about me?" she asked.

"Are you a religious woman?"

"I love the Lord, but I can't quote the Book chapter by chapter or verse by verse," she said, shrugging her shoulders.

"Neither can I," I smiled, "but I don't think He expects us to."

"Just as long as we do our best to do the right thing," Contessa said.

"I require a pre-employment drug screening, as well as a criminal background check," I advised. "Is that a problem?" I asked, practically holding my breath while I waited for her to answer. She seemed perfect, and I was not in the mood for any further busted bubbles.

"Not a problem at all." She smiled. "I promise they'll both come up clean as a whistle."

Yep. A winner, I thought, relieved already.

Chapter 6

Damon

I walked through the front door of my home and smiled instantly. The lights were turned down low, and the sound of Maxwell crooning "Bad Habits" wafted through the surround-sound system. Dropping my keys and Blackberry on the foyer table, I inhaled the aroma of what smelled like steak coming from the kitchen. Much to my delight, I found my wife wearing nothing but a pair of five-inch heels, sitting on top of our kitchen island. Admiring the glow of her skin and her well-defined curves under the soft lights, I felt my dick began to rise.

"Hello, Mr. Whitmore," she moaned seductively.

"Hello, Mrs. Whitmore." I smiled, staring at her appreciatively. "To what do I owe the honor?" I asked.

"The two of us have unfinished business," she whispered, spreading her legs. "I figured we could have dessert before dinner tonight."

I hurriedly removed my jacket and allowed it to drop to floor. "Dessert first?" I asked, removing my tie. "Won't that ruin our appetites?"

She hopped off the counter and stood with her feet shoulder-width apart. Then she grabbed me hastily by the shirt and pulled me closer. "Ruin? No," she said as she unbuttoned my pants. "I think it will only enhance it." Before I could move or jump, she had my pants and boxers down to my ankles.

"Damn." I laughed, running my fingers through her hair. "I see you're ready."

"Well, yes I am. Are you?" she asked.

"I've been waiting all day for—" I never received the opportunity to finish my sentence. I was caught off guard when she quickly opened her mouth and swallowed my stick.

***

Three hours later, I lay stretched out on my stomach with Octavia straddling my waist, massaging my back. I'm man enough to admit that after an hour of engaging in straight sex and then devouring a feast of perfectly cooked steak, shrimp, and potatoes, I was exhausted.

Octavia's hands were soft and smooth as she moved them across my skin, kneading and pounding the tension from my body like a trained expert. "How was your day, baby?" she asked.

"It was good."

"Anything big happen?"

My conversation with Nadia replayed in my head. I knew it was the perfect opportunity for me to tell her about it—that was, if I'd have had any intention of telling her. "Same ol', same ol'," I said. "How was yours, boo?" I asked.

"It was good." She laughed lightly. "Interesting, but good."

"How did the interviews go?"

"After weeding through the crazies, I actually think I found a rose."

"You gotta go through some good to get to the bad." I laughed.

"I know, baby," she whispered, kissing me on the back of my neck. "That's what I did with you."

"That goes both ways," I said.

"I'm going to make the final decision after the background and drug tests come back," she said, massaging the back of my biceps, "but I checked her references, and her former employer spoke highly of her."

"That's good, babe."

"I know," she said happily. "I also want to see how she interacts with Jasmine," she added. "I'll probably arrange a play date."

"Sounds good to me," I said, yawning lightly. I could feel my eyelids growing heavy, like they were made of lead. "You know I trust your judgment."

"I know you do," she smiled, "and that's just another thing I love you for."

"I love you more."

Chapter 7

Damon

After my last visit to Los Angeles, my father advised me that he had made the decision to close Nomad's West Coast office. He felt the company was strong enough that we could acquire and service our current clients in the West from our offices in the southern region. The decision was one my father had been toying with for years, and finally, after some coercing from my mother, he'd decided to go ahead with it. Although Nomad no longer had a working office in the city, I still had my own business to handle there. I owned three beachfront properties, along with four houses and six office buildings throughout the city. The properties were held under the name of my company, Gold Mortgage, and they were all occupied. Now that I had a family, I found myself spending less and less time in the state of California. In order to maintain the properties, keep my tenants happy, and make sure my money was always on time, I hired a licensed realtor by the name of Julian Franklin, a short, chubby, clean-cut, well-dressed brother who had the intellect and vocabulary of a college graduate and the hustle of a dope dealer. The two of us sat in the small beachfront office Julian used to conduct business, going over the profit and loss report for the second quarter.

"Everything looks good," I said, nodding my head. "Good job."

"It's what I do," he said, "and it's why you pay me."

"No doubt," I said. "Well, J., I've got a lot of ground to cover before Sunday," I said, looking at my watch.

We both stood and shook hands.

"Good seeing you again, boss," Julian said. "I'm going to get out this afternoon and do some prospecting on some for-sale-by-owners."

"Sounds good."

"By the way," Julian said as the two of us walked toward his office door, "I received a check for rent for a listing on Latitude Drive in Aliso Viejo. I don't have that particular property on my books."

"Don't worry. I'll take care of it," I said. "Do you still have the check?"

"Yeah. It's in the safe."

"I'll take it with me," I said, shaking my head. "I'll make a stop by there before I catch my flight out."

***

Déjà Vu Salon and Day Spa was a full-service salon that occupied one of my buildings. The spa had only been open for a year, but it was already showing great returns. I knew it wouldn't be long until the owner became one of my most profitable tenants. Instead of only being for the ladies like most spas, Déjà Vu catered to everyone: women, men, and children of all ages needing all sorts of beauty and pampering services. According to the latest reviews, the salon was considered to be one of the hottest one-stop shopping spots for hair-care and skincare needs. I pushed my way through the revolving doors, stepped into the salon waiting room, and smiled at what I saw. The waiting room was full to capacity, which meant the eight stations in the back were also full.

"How may I assist you?" greeted a tall, blonde female with ocean-blue eyes. She wore a hot pink shirt with the Déjà Vu logo embroidered on the front and a small name badge that read 'Joni'.

"I'm here to see Lena," I said.

"Do you have an appointment?" she asked, scanning over a list names on the pink clipboard in front of her.

"No, I do not," I said.

"I apologize, sir, but Ms. Jasper doesn't take walk-ins," she said, smiling at me. "However, I'd be happy to schedule an appointment."

The Lies We Tell For Love

I reached inside my suit jacket and removed one of my business cards to hand to her. "Give her this," I said, "and I'm sure she'll be able to squeeze me in."

Joni looked down at the card, then back at me. A small pink flush ran across her face as she nodded her head. Handing me my card back, she smiled. "That won't be necessary. Right this way, Mr. Whitmore, and I do apologize."

I followed Joni down a long corridor, past the shampoo bowl areas and the large room that housed the stylists and styling stations. We stopped in front of the closed door marked 'Office'.

Joni turned to face me. "I'll just let Ms. Jasper know you're here."

"*That* won't be necessary," I said, reaching down into my pants pocket. I pulled out my platinum money clip and slipped out a crisp twenty-dollar bill. I handed it to Joni then slightly nodded my head, a nonverbal message that her services were no longer required.

She smiled and walked away with her tip in hand.

Knock-knock.

"Come in," Lena spoke from the other side of the door.

I opened the door to the office and found myself doing a double-take. It had been a very long minute since I had seen her, and I must admit that time had been good to Lena.

She sat behind the glass desk, staring at the laptop screen in front of her. "What can I do for you?" she asked without bothering to look and see who she was talking to.

"You can start by telling me why this was mailed to my property manager," I said, holding up her check.

A huge smile crept across Lena's face as she recognized my voice and looked up at me. "Damon!" She smiled. The tone in her voice was full of surprise and what I could only assume was happiness. She stood and walked around her desk to the place where I was standing. Giving me a friendly hug she said, "It's so good to see you."

"You as well," I said. I took a step back and looked her over. She was wearing a nice fitted two-piece suit that accentuated her curves perfectly. Her hair, which she had once worn long, was short, with highlighted layers. I've always preferred long to medium lengths of hair on women, but Lena's cut complemented her face, and she was rocking the hell out of it. I would like to say I didn't notice that her breasts, which used to be C-cups at best, were now at least D's, high and perky, right where they should be—but I can't. "You're looking good," I said, and I sincerely meant it.

"Thank you." She smiled, walking back around the desk. "So are you, as always."

Sitting down in the leather armchair across from her, I nodded my head. "I appreciate that," I said. I dropped the check on the desk and stared at her. "I would also appreciate it if you would refrain from sending me money."

"I owe you that," she said softly, "and a whole lot more."

I had allowed Lena to move into the townhouse on Latitude and completely furnished the unit for her until she found a home of her choice. I had also provided her with a multitude of other little things, such as the money she needed to open Déjà Vu. Not once had I ever considered it a loan or felt like she owed me. Lena was loyal, and if I needed her for anything—and I do mean anything—she was always ready and willing to give it to me, no questions asked. That form of loyalty is hard to come by, so I considered everything I did for her to be nothing more than a token of my appreciation for her loyalty and friendship. "I'm not taking your check," I told her.

"I can't live there rent-free," she said, shaking her head.

"This isn't up for discussion," I said firmly.

Lena reclined in her chair while shaking her head. There was silence between us as she stared at me. She knew I was standing firm on my decision to refuse payment from her, and there was no way to change my mind. "Let me buy the place from you then," she finally said.

"Okay, if you insist. Make me an offer."

She smiled and folded her hands together. "I'll have the place appraised, and I'll pay you the value," she said.

"Do me a favor," I said, standing.

"Anything."

"You have a dollar on you?"

"Yeah." Lena frowned but immediately reached for her purse. She pulled out a crisp one-dollar bill and handed it to me. "All you need is one?" she asked.

"Just one," I said, slipping the dollar in my pocket. "I'll have an attorney draw up the paperwork for the townhouse. The deed will be transferred over to you within a week."

"Maybe we should hold off," she said. "I'm not sure how long the appraisal will take."

"It doesn't matter," I said, walking to the door. "The property is yours." I reached in my pocket, pulled out the dollar, and waved it at her. "You just bought it," I said.

Lena sat with her mouth open and a look of sheer disbelief on her face. Exhaling deeply, she shook her head. "You are amazing," she said. "Thank you, Damon."

"You're welcome."

"If you won't let me pay you properly," she said, "at least let me cook you dinner."

I paused, considering her offer. I was hesitant not because I was afraid something would take place between the two of us, as Lena and I were old friends, and the only feelings I had for her were platonic. I give credit where credit is due, and Lena had pulled her looks together since we had last seen each other, but I still only wanted her as a friend. My wife was more than enough woman for me, the only woman I wanted.

Lena must have sensed my apprehension. "Please, Damon?" she begged. "From one friend to another? It's just a little innocent dinner. Besides, I know you're curious about what I've done with the place, and Nae Nae would love to see her Uncle Damon." Lena's offer seemed harmless enough.

"Seven o'clock?" I asked.

"Seven would be perfect." Her sweet smile seemed to radiate across her face, illuminating the entire room.

***

I was impressed and pleased with what Lena had done with the townhouse. The ecru color that had once graced the walls of the living and dining rooms had been painted over. The living room was now covered in burnt orange, and the dining room walls were two-toned, with chocolate and cappuccino colored paint. Lena had tastefully decorated her home with black art, leather, and wood furnishings. I had fun being schooled by Lena's daughter on the Xbox 360 and then the three of us enjoyed the baked tilapia and seasoned vegetables Nae Nae's mother had prepared. When little Nae Nae headed upstairs for bed, Lena and I sat on the leather sofa in her living room, talking and enjoying glasses of chardonnay.

"Nae Nae is getting big," I said.

"She sure is." Lena smiled. "She is already asking for her own cell phone."

"They start early, huh?" I chuckled.

"They do. It's what you have to look forward to with Jasmine."

"If I could forever keep that child at the size and age she is now, I would." I said, shaking my head. "I am not looking forward to bustin' some young buck's head when he tries to lay a finger or anything else on my baby girl."

Laughing, Lena ran her fingers through her hair. "Sorry to tell you this, Daddy, but it's coming. It's inevitable. They grow up whether we like it or not."

"I know, I know."

"How is Octavia?" she asked, changing the subject.

I smiled, thinking about my wife sitting on our kitchen island in nothing but those sexy heels, waiting for me to get home. "She is great," I said, slightly bragging. "Unbelievable in fact."

"That's good." Lena pulled her eyes from mine, staring across the room with a look of reflection and meditation.

"You okay?"

Lena blinked several times, as if she was suddenly pulled out of a mind trip, jolted back to reality. "Yes, yes, I'm fine." She studdered, giving me a slight smile. She took a sip from her glass then looked at me with a straight face. "I was just wondering if I will ever have that."

"Have what?" I asked.

"A man to love me the way you love her," she said softly. "When you mention her, your face lights up, and your joy is undeniable. I want that, Damon," she said. Her voice quivered slightly as she spoke.

"You will have that someday," I reassured her. "Just be patient. And when the right man comes along," I said soothingly, "he will be extremely lucky."

Lena smiled shyly. "Thank you."

After I had Lena show me to the restroom, I rejoined her in the living room and slipped my jacket back on. "I better get going," I said.

"Do you have to?" Lena's voice oozed with disappointment.

The Lies We Tell For Love

"I do," I replied.

She cast a smirk in my direction as she stood. "I'm disappointed that you have to go so soon," she said gloomily, "but I have truly enjoyed your company tonight."

"I enjoyed yours as well," I said, walking toward the door, "and thank you for dinner."

"You're more than welcome. When will we see you again?" she asked as we stepped out her front door.

"I'm not sure, but I will be checking on the two of you," I advised her. "Call me if you need anything. I'll e-mail you about the deed."

"Thank you again." She smiled. "I love you, Damon."

"You're very welcome," I said, smiling. "And I love you too."

Chapter 8

Octavia

*D*amon was going to be out of town for a week. After he left L.A., he was going straight to ATL. With the high volume week I had projected at the restaurants, I desperately needed a helping hand. When the results came back for Contessa's criminal and drug tests, I felt like I was on Cloud 9. She passed both with flying colors, just like she said she would, and it was beginning to look more and more like she was going to officially be the caretaker of our daughter. I knew just because she looked good on paper, that didn't necessarily mean she would click with our daughter, so I decided the true test would be to see how she interacted with Jasmine. To my delight, Jasmine latched on to her like she had been a part of her life from birth.

Contessa had a Madea style, minus the ghetto, with a Mary Poppins swag, minus the I'm-perfect bullshit. After introducing her to Jazz, I took her over to meet my parents. My parents gave her the thumbs-up, and Mama even suggested that the two of them should do lunch sometime. Everything was falling into place with Contessa, and although I was clueless as to how she found out I was hiring, I was thankful someone had sent her my way.

We agreed that she would come over every morning at six and stay until I made it home from work. For the most part, I was fine with our arrangement. The only problem we were running into was that Contessa didn't have access to a vehicle because her nephew needed to have use of her car. It wasn't too big of a deal because Damon and I planned to make sure Jasmine made it to any appointments she might have. However, I did want Contessa to have transportation in the event of an emergency or if she just wanted to take Jasmine out for some fresh air.

Another concern I had was that I knew Contessa was struggling and stressing, trying to maintain her bills and pay her rent. This bothered me because I could not have the person who was looking after our daughter stressed out and distracted. In addition to that, in the short time I had known Contessa, I'd already grown fond of her. I came up with a plan that I felt would solve the transportation issue and Contessa's problem with her bills. In my opinion, the plan would be beneficial for both of us. After running my idea by my husband, I sat down with Contessa to discuss other arrangements. "How would you feel about living here?" I asked. The two of us sat poolside sipping ice tea while Jasmine lay next to us in her playpen sleeping. I had taken the day off to do some bonding with Contessa and to spend some mommy-daughter time with Jasmine.

"What you mean, how would I feel?" she asked. "I would love it!" Contessa laughed. "Who wouldn't? Look at this place! It's like being on a vacation," she commented. "I ought to be paying you for letting me share your home."

I smiled and looked over at her. "You're a joy to have around," I said.

"Well thank you." she said.

"I am serious about my offer," I informed her. "I know you have been trying to recover from being unemployed, and it's hard to maintain on a fixed income."

"Baby, you have no idea," she said. "Since I have to pay for my insulin, sometimes it's a toss-up between eating and sleeping in my own bed."

It hurt me to think about how many of our seniors are struggling. I was thankful my parents were set for life, thanks to my father's savings and the money I had set aside. *But what about people like Contessa whose children have made mistakes and can't provide for them? The way the government is looking, there isn't going to be shit left for the elderly in another ten years!*

"If you live here, you wouldn't have rent to pay," I said. "You wouldn't have to buy food either, so you could use your income to take care of your existing bills and medicine and still have plenty of money to enjoy yourself. And just so you know, this is not completely a selfless act," I said quickly. "It will also take some worry off me, since you won't be distracted and stressed while you're looking after Jasmine."

Smiling, Contessa nodded her head. "I know I told you I have a lot I'm dealing with," she said, "but trust me, I won't ever let anything happen to that little girl."

"I know," I said sweetly. "I'm just trying to make things better for all of us."

"I would love to accept," Contessa said, "but if I move here, my nephew will have nowhere to go."

I had forgotten about Contessa's nephew who was staying with her; he'd be booted out of the Towers if Contessa moved out. I opted not to say what I was thinking: *He's a grown-ass man. Why the hell doesn't he go out and get his own shit?* "Is he working?" I asked. "Is he able to get a job?"

"He's been trying, but he hasn't been able to find anything permanent," she said sadly. "He's either overqualified or doesn't have enough experience."

Bullshit, I thought. If her nephew could pick up trash, flip a burger, or scrub a damn toilet, he was qualified for at least three different positions. Whether or not he wanted those positions was another matter, but if you ask me, minimum wage bread is better than no bread at all! "Maybe he should consider applying for jobs outside of his field," I said gently, trying hard not to be inconsiderate, even though I really wanted to tell Contessa that there was no justifiable reason for any healthy young man to be sitting on his ass, living rent-free off his auntie or his mama in the city of Huntsville. I wanted to tell her that we could swing by Krystals, McDonald's, or even Ruby Tuesday's and pick him up a damn application. I know I might seem harsh, but I have a serious problem when it comes to healthy, able-bodied men sitting on their asses and sponging off the hard work of others.

"He has been," she said, "and I know it might not seem like it, but my baby has always been a worker."

"Um…"

"I'm serious, Tavia," Contessa said, straight-faced. "If you knew him like I know him, you would not be thinking like you're thinking."

"What am I thinking?" I asked.

"That he's just a sorry ass," she said. She'd hit the nail on the head, because that was exactly what I was thinking. She shook her head then frowned.

"I'm sorry, Ms. Contessa," I said. "I know I'm on the outside looking in, and I have no room to judge anyone."

She reached over and patted my hand lightly. "It's okay, sweetie," she said, shrugging her shoulders.

The two of us sat basking underneath the August sun in silence for a moment.

"So why don't you tell me about him?" I decided to try and keep an open mind about the brother. The more I thought about it, the truth was I didn't know the extent of his struggle.

I listened intently as Contessa went into an in-depth spill about her nephew's struggle to recover from the loss of his daughter and how trifling his baby's mother was. She shared with me his work history and how he almost lost himself when his little girl died from cancer. I knew a portion of the story Contessa shared with me because I had heard it before. "Kelly is a good person," she said, wiping her eyes. "He's just had a few setbacks."

"What? Did you say his name is Kelly? Not Kelly Baker?" I stated.

"Yes," she said. "You know him?"

"We've met." I said. Flashbacks of Kelly's face and beautiful gray eyes ran through my mind. "Was he the one who told you about this job?" I asked.

"He sure did," she said, "and I'm grateful. Did he apply at your restaurant?" she asked. The look on Contessa's face, combined with the innocence in her voice, told me she truly had no clue about my interview with her nephew.

"Something like that," I said. "He does seem like a good guy," I told her.

"He is, he is."

The wheels inside my brain started turning "He has some landscaping experience, does he not?"

"Yes."

"So if I could hook him up with a job," I suggested, "he could conceivably get his own place."

The Lies We Tell For Love

"Don't tell him I told you this…" Contessa said lowly; I chuckled on the inside because only she, Jasmine, and I were there, yet she insisted upon whispering. "His credit is a little bad right now," she said. "His score took a lot of damage because of all the medical bills that piled up when Ciara was in and out of treatment centers."

If Contessa had been a salesperson looking for a sucker, I'd have bought anything from her. I should have left well enough alone and just dealt with things the way they were, but that would have been too easy. Instead, I parted my pretty lips and said, "I have a suggestion." Once I enlightened Contessa, she was grinning from ear to ear, and I was happy that she was happy.

***

I asked Contessa to have Kelly call me so the two of us could arrange a sit-down to discuss the job offer. I figured he would be thrilled about it, and as long as his background check came back clear, we'd be in business. That night, I lay in bed with the phone pressed to my ear, talking to my husband. "You're really going to like her, Damon."

"So it seems like Contessa is going to work out?" he asked.

"Yes, I think she is." I said, stretching my legs out across the silk sheets. "She's great."

"I'm glad you're pleased," he said, "and I can't wait to meet her."

"She's anxious to meet you too," I said. I was preparing to drop the news on him that Kelly would be working for us and that I wanted to help him get his own apartment, but he advised me that his battery was about to die.

"Talk to you tomorrow?" he asked.

I hesitated for two reasons: one, I wanted to discuss Kelly immediately in the event that Damon had any issues with my offer; and two, because although there was nothing that could compare to having him next to me in bed, hearing his voice as I drifted off to sleep was at least a tiny bit comforting. "You better," I said. "I love you."

"I love you more."

Less than sixty seconds after I hung up with Damon, my phone began to ring. I took a quick peek at the caller ID and saw Contessa's name and number. I assumed it was Kelly calling to confirm a time for our meeting.

Part of me was admittedly anxious to hear the excitement and gratitude in his voice since he'd undoubtedly be happy not only to have a job, but also to have a nice place to sleep until he got on his feet. "Hello?"

"Hey," Kelly replied. He sounded less enthusiastic than I anticipated, but I chalked his tone up to being overwhelmed and speechless.

"Would you like to meet in the a.m. or tomorrow afternoon?" I asked.

"Neither," he said flatly. "My aunt told me about your little offer, but I'm gonna take a pass."

"Oh?" I said, slightly disappointed. Since I had decided to offer Kelly the position, I had been brainstorming, thinking of a few projects I wanted him to complete at our home. One was a small rose garden. I figured roses are foolproof, so in the event that Kelly turned out not to know a damn thing about landscaping and beautification, at least I'd have something to enter into evidence when Damon went ape-shit on me. "So you got another job?" I asked, trying to sound happy for him.

"Nope," he said, "but I'm good."

I don't know of any grown men who would be good broke and sleeping on their aunt's couch! I thought to myself. "You're good being unemployed?" I asked. "What, you don't want to work?"

"Oh, I *want* to work," he said quickly. "I just don't want to work for you."

"And exactly what is wrong with working for me?"

"First, you didn't hire me because I don't have a pus…er, a vagina," he said sarcastically. "Now you can't wait to get me on your payroll so you can move my aunt in as your live-in slave."

No the hell he didn't! "First of all—"

"Third," he said, loudly cutting me off, "my attorney advised me it's in my best interest to refrain from contact with you until after the hearing."

I didn't know if he was being honest or just a smartass. Either way, I was not feeling the ungrateful sarcasm in his voice. "I have gained a mutual respect for your auntie, and I would never treat her like anything less than a part of my family, as long as she continues to be the person of integrity that I feel in my heart she is." I was attempting to remain professional with him, but there may have been a small hint of sarcasm in my voice—okay, there was a lot of sarcasm in my voice, mixed with a big ol' drop of who-in-the-hell-does-he-think-he's-talking to. "Now, are your reservations because you fear that your aunt will be unappreciated, or is this really about our first encounter?" I asked.

"Who knows?" he said nonchalantly. "It could be a little bit of both."

"You know, Kelly, there is nothing more unattractive than a bitter brother," I said, sucking my teeth.

"That's a lie," he said. "There is something much more unattractive."

"Oh? Enlighten me," I said.

"A sister who thinks that because she has money, everyone else is supposed to bend down and kiss her black ass."

"Well, it's a good thing I'm not that sister." I laughed, the only thing that could keep me from cussing his ass out.

"Yeah, right," he chuckled, "and I ain't bitter."

Click.

The sound of the dial tone echoed in my ear while *I know he didn't!* ran through my head.

Chapter 9

Octavia

My mother always used to tell me, "A hard head makes for a soft ass." Well, just call my ass Charmin, because I was determined that even if Kelly didn't work for me, he was going to hear me out—so determined that the next morning, when he came to drop Contessa off, I was outside standing in the driveway, waiting patiently by the car as he held the passenger door open for his aunt.

"Good morning, sweetie." Contessa smiled at me. "You look pretty."

Normally, I came to the door with one eye open, my hair bound down with a scarf, sporting one of Damon's shirts or a robe, but not on that morning. That morning, I intentionally set my alarm for five a.m. so I would have time to shower and get dressed before Contessa arrived. I had straightened my hair and pulled it back into a nice ponytail that hung below my shoulders then slipped on an above-the-knee fitted t-shirt dress. The dress hung slightly off my shoulders and was one of my favorites for lounging around the house. "Good morning, Ms. Contessa." I smiled. "And thank you. Jasmine's still sleeping, but you're welcome to fix yourself some breakfast or anything else you'd like in the kitchen." I told her sweetly. "Make yourself at home. Our home *is* your home." Cutting my eyes in Kelly's direction, I waited, hoping he had something to say.

He shook his head and slammed the door shut. "Have a good day, Auntie," he said, walking around to the driver side.

"Thank you, baby," she said, waving at Kelly. "See you this evening."

I waited for Contessa to go inside before I marched up to the side of the car.

"I don't want to hear it," Kelly said flatly.

"You don't want to hear what?" I asked, confused.

"Your little spill on how I've got you all wrong," he stated, looking out the window at me.

I crossed my arms across my chest, listening in heated silence as he continued.

"How money means nothing to you or that you grew up poor and know how it is to struggle." He smirked at me while his grays stared me down. "You can save whatever little spill you were contemplating dropping on me."

I'd had enough of Kelly and his piss-poor attitude. "Let me just drop this," I said, raising my voice. "First of all, I didn't grow up poor. We weren't rich, but we were quite comfortable. My parents worked damn hard to provide for me. I know what it's like to want for things, but my needs were always taken care of, and for that I am very thankful." I cocked my head to the side, looking him directly in the eyes. "And money does mean a lot to me," I continued. "For one, it means I'm doing something right, that I'm handling mine instead of sitting around feeling sorry for myself, having a damn pity party. It means my family can eat, and they eat well. It means that when they lay their heads down, they lay them on the finest linens our money can buy. It means that when I see someone in need, I can reach out and help them, but that's only if they have enough balls to want to help themselves. Lastly, it means that despite all the wrong I've done, there is still a God who loves me and has enough mercy for me to look beyond those wrongs."

The stone-hard expression on Kelly's face softened slightly.

"I won't apologize for the things I have," I said, lowering my voice, "just like you shouldn't apologize for the things you don't." I gave him one last look before walking away.

***

The Lies We Tell For Love

My work day went by without a hitch. I was grateful for that, because after my morning conversation with Kelly, I was in no mood for any problems or complications. After work, the only thing I wanted to do was kiss my daughter, eat, and take a nice, long soak in the tub while I waited for my hubby to call. I had barely made it through my front door before I kicked off my heels and removed my blazer. After laying my things down on the foyer table, I went off in pursuit of my daughter and to see what smelled so good.

Jasmine sat in her high chair in the kitchen, knocked out. I smiled, thinking to myself that if I could see an angel, it would probably look just like that—absolutely beautiful.

I was surprised but not disappointed to find Contessa had dinner sitting on the table waiting for me. I normally felt some kind of way about other people cooking on my stove, but this was not the case with Contessa. I had been so busy that I had skipped lunch and was going on fumes from the banana I'd had earlier for breakfast. "It smells delicious," I complimented, staring at my plate of meatloaf, mashed potatoes, green beans, and crescent rolls. She had even made peach cobbler for dessert. I was a semi-happy woman—the only thing missing was Damon.

"I hope you like it." Contessa smiled. "I know you're a professional and I'm just a lil' ol' country cook, but I hope you don't mind if I put together a dish or two from time to time."

I dug into the food on my plate, and my taste buds were instantly satisfied. "Ms. Contessa, I do not think I will have a problem at all with that," I mumbled between bites.

Contessa smiled brightly. Sitting down at the table, she looked across at me. "So, will I be taking the bedroom opposite the nursery?" she asked.

Wiping my lips, I looked at her. "What do you mean?" I asked.

"If the offer still stands, I would like to accept," she said.

"Of course it stands," I said. "What made you change your mind?" I asked.

"I love it here," she said, "and if I can just learn how to work that fancy screen in the theater, I'll be doing it big."

I laughed and shook my head. "I'll be happy to teach you how to work the television, and you can choose any upstairs bedroom you like. We also have a fully equipped guesthouse that you are welcome to."

"If I get me a man, I may have to take you up on the guesthouse," she said, winking her eye. "Ms. Tessa may have to get her freak on!"

I swear I was blushing at the thought of Contessa getting her swerve on. I dropped my eyes and shook my head. "You and my mother are going to get along very well." I laughed.

"Good," she said, removing her glasses. "I need me a good friend."

"Well, she's one of the best." Speaking of my mother brought to mind that I hadn't spoken with her that day. She had advised me the day before that she and Daddy were going to Birmingham to do some shopping, but she normally always checked in. I made a mental note to call and check on the two of them. "What about your apartment?" I asked, tiptoeing around asking her about Kelly. As much as he had rocked my last nerve, I still wanted to make sure he would be straight.

"I called the Towers people today and told them I am going to be moving," she said. "My lease has been up for a while, and I've just been doing a month to month."

"Are you paid up for this month?"

"I am."

"So you'll lose that money?" I asked. I knew Contessa had no money to spare, and I couldn't stand the thought of her losing a dime. I decided at that moment that I would include the money she'd lost in her first paycheck.

"Yep, but they say they will give me my security deposit back, even though I didn't give a thirty-day notice," she said happily.

"Really? That's nice of them."

She had a look of guilt on her face as she gave me a small grin. "Not exactly," she said. "I sorta stretched the truth and told them I am moving out of town with my previous employer."

"You are moving." I giggled. "Just not out of town. So you only stretched the truth just a little," I said.

"Naw, sweetie, I told a bold-faced lie," she said, shaking her head, "but it worked." She raised up her hand to give me five.

As we slapped our hands together, I waited for her to mention something about Kelly and what her nephew's plans were. When she didn't say anything about him, I decided to bring him up. "What does Kelly have planned?" I asked, carrying my plate over to the sink.

"A friend of his called him with an offer," she said. "I think he may take it."

My back was to Contessa, so she couldn't see my expression, but there was a small smile on my face. "Good for him," I said sincerely. "Good for him."

"Yes it is," she said. Her voice lowered and was filled with sadness. "The position will require him to move out of town, but it will be good for him."

I turned around and saw Contessa dabbing at her eyes. "It'll work out," I said, "and you can visit him whenever you like. I'll make sure of that."

"Thank you, sweetie," she said.

"Offer him my congratulations," I said. I was happy for Kelly, even though our last conversation had ended on bad terms. I figured the day would come—hopefully sooner rather than later—when we would be on cordial terms. Little did I know that the day was coming sooner than I thought.

Chapter 10

Octavia

The day Contessa moved in, I took the day off so I could help her get settled. I presented the offer to hire a moving company to help with her things, but Contessa opted to bring nothing but her clothing, pictures, and a few personal items and mementos. The rest of her dishes and furniture she donated to Kelly to do with as he desired. Kelly was the designated mover, and although he advised Contessa that he didn't need my help, I volunteered my services anyway. I opened the door and waited for him to park.

He climbed out wearing a plain t-shirt, denim shorts, and tennis shoes. "I told Auntie to tell you I got this," he snapped, opening the trunk of the car.

"Yeah, she told me." I didn't comment any further. Instead, I stood waiting for him to hand me the first box. He stood looking at me with an eye of defiance, and I decided that if he wasn't going to make a move, I would. I bent over and reached for the first box I saw.

"That's heavy," he said, grabbing my hands.

I paused for a moment, noticing how soft his skin was, and then remembered that at the present moment, I still couldn't stand him. Stepping back, I waited as he pulled a clothing bag out of the trunk and handed it to me.

"Lead the way," he said. He pulled the box out that I originally intended to carry.

Contessa and Jasmine were in the home theater watching a movie as I led Kelly upstairs to Contessa's bedroom.

The room Contessa had chosen was close to the nursery, three doors down from Damon and my bedroom. I was happy about that because no matter who is in the house, when my baby and I feel the need or the mood hit, we will get it on. I knew some things would change with Contessa living with us, but my freedom to get my dick was not going to be one of them.

"This is nice," Kelly said, scanning the room with his eyes. Contessa had chosen what I playfully labeled the "purple room," since I had decorated it with deep purple and lilac—from the floral arrangements to the curtains, right down to the comforter set on the queen-sized bed. The full-sized bathroom was also accented with purple and lilac and just a hint of mint green.

"Thank you," I said politely. "Ms. Contessa loves it."

"She loves this house," he said, "and you and Jasmine."

I smiled. "We are very fond of her too," I said honestly.

"One day, I'll make sure she has a house like this," he said.

"Well, with your new job, I'm sure it won't be too long before you're able to fulfill that dream," I said, hanging the clothes bag inside the walk-in closet. When Kelly didn't respond to my comment, my instincts told me something was wrong.

"When do you leave?" I asked, stepping out of the closet. Kelly looked at me, then quickly diverted his eyes across the room.

"What's up?" I asked, easing down on the bed.

"The job fell through," he said, slipping his hands in his pockets.

"I'm sorry," I said empathetically. "What happened?"

"I'll just say the friend who offered it to me was not exactly on the up and up," he said.

There was no need for him to elaborate. I assumed whoever had offered him the job was not about the right thing. "I hate to hear that," I said.

"Thank you."

"So where are you going to live?" I questioned.

Turning around to face me, Kelly shrugged his shoulders. "Since Auntie turned in her keys, I'm going to get a room tonight and go from there," he said.

I could see in his face that he didn't have a clue what his next move was going to be. "Does Ms. Contessa know about this?" I asked.

Kelly didn't answer, but he didn't have to; the look in his stormy-gray eyes told me everything.

"You haven't told her?"

"I don't want her to worry," he said. "Besides, she needs to focus on her own happiness. I can handle mine."

I knew what Kelly was saying was easier said than done. I could tell my mother not to worry about me or that I was fine 1,000 times over, but she would still do the exact opposite. "She's going to worry regardless," I told him. "That's just a mother's way."

"I know," he said, sitting down on the bed next to me. "I just wish I had it together. I mean, it's bad enough she worries herself about Jay, but hell, I was supposed to be here to help her, not to add to her burden."

"Caring about the people you love is not a burden," I said, looking over at him. "It comes with loving them, and you can't have one without the other."

He looked at me then nodded his head. "I'm sorry for the way I came at you the other day. I was wrong to judge you," he added.

I looked away for a second then redirected my attention to him. "I also owe you an apology," I said. "When Ms. Contessa told me about her nephew who was struggling and living with her, I also judged you."

"You assumed I am some kind of moocher?" he said, laughing lightly.

"I did," I admitted, "and for that I was wrong."

"It's cool," he said. "I guess we both had the other one twisted."

"We did," I said, "but it's all good now."

"It is," he said, flashing his pearly-white smile at me.

I smiled at him in return. "You never did let me tell you about the position I'm hiring for," I said, nudging him in the side. I was waiting for him to pop off, but he never did.

"I'm listening," he said politely.

"Well, I know you have a bit of landscaping experience," I began, "and in case you haven't noticed, my flowers need a lil' bit of TLC."

"By *flowers* you mean those weeds you have out front?" he teased.

"Excuse me?" I said, putting my hands up. "Those are annuals. It's just not their season."

"Um, every season is a season for annuals," He laughed. "Hence the name."

I laughed with him. "Are you interested?" I asked. "In the position?"

"I am." He sighed. "Thank you."

"You know, Ms. Contessa told me about your credit problems," I said slowly.

Kelly stood and walked over to the window.

"But," I said quickly, "she also explained the reason why. I understand completely."

"Thanks," he said flatly.

"When she told me those things, I came up with the idea that Damon and I could put you in a place for a few months until you get on your feet."

Kelly turned around to look at me. "And why would you do that?" he asked.

"Because I respect anyone who has the desire to do better," I said. "You don't know this, but at one time, my daddy fell off. His situation was one he could control, but he still fell off. He bounced back," I said, "but he wasn't always in a happy place."

"I feel that," he said. "Thank you."

"So does that mean you're open to my suggestion?"

There was a pregnant pause until Kelly said, "Under one condition."

"What's that?"

"Once I get on my feet, I'll pay the two of you back, and I'm still looking for a position in my field. I love working with children, and I truly believe I'm destined to be a teacher."

"Most definitely," I said. "I love a person who chooses to follow their passion. Why settle for a job when you can have a career? And if I can help in any way, just let me know. Deal?" I said, extending my hand to him.

He walked up to me slowly, took my hand in his, and pressed his lips to my skin softly, causing me to feel a small twirl in between my thighs from his touch. I knew it was my hormones; I really needed my husband to come home. "Deal," he said, releasing my hand slowly.

***

That night I decided to make dinner for Contessa and Kelly, my way of welcoming Contessa to my family and letting Kelly know I was happy that we were on good terms.

After dinner, Contessa and I did the dishes while Kelly played with Jasmine.

"Well, if my work here is done, I'm going to take Jasmine up and get her ready for bed." Contessa smiled. "After that, I will be taking a long soak in my new tub, trying to figure out how to work that movie screen on my bedroom wall."

"Would you like me to come up and show you?" I volunteered.

"Thank you, but I will figure it out," she said. "I will not be defeated by all the snazzy gadgets in this place. It's bad enough it took me an hour to figure out where the garbage can was."

I laughed.

"In my day, the can sat next to the cabinets, but now they come built in," she said, shaking her head. "The Lord has truly been good to our people."

"That He has," I agreed. I placed a kiss on Jasmine's forehead then watched as Contessa and Kelly hugged goodbye.

"I'd better get going," Kelly said, walking toward the kitchen entrance.

"Which hotel are you staying at?" I asked.

"I haven't decided," he said, "but more than likely, somewhere off the Parkway."

"North Parkway?" I asked.

"Yes."

I instantly frowned. The only places to book a room on that side of town were rundown and probably bug infested. I was not feeling the thought of anyone staying in that type of environment. "Why not something on University Drive?" I asked.

Kelly slid his hands in his pockets. "My money is a little tight," he admitted.

I could tell he was uncomfortable discussing his finances, but I wanted to help if I could. "Let me help you out," I said. I was careful not to sound demanding or like I was taking pity on him. The last thing I wanted was for the two of us to get into another argument.

"No," he said. "Thank you, but no. I'll be all right."

"Please, Kelly." I was practically begging him.

"Look, you're already giving me a job," he reminded me, "and putting me in a place to stay. One night in a less-than-five-star hotel is not going to hurt me. I've slept in worse."

I couldn't imagine worse, but I was willing to take his word for it.

"So again, thank you," he said, "but no thank you."

I decided to leave the subject alone. Kelly had his mind made up, and there was nothing more I could do about it. "Well, at least take a plate with you," I said.

"That I will do." He smiled. "I have to give you props. You can definitely cook."

"Thank you," I said. "I'm the bomb," I teased.

"That you are," he said in a shy whisper. "That you are."

***

It was a quarter till midnight, and I was buck-naked, sprawled across my bed with the phone pressed against my ear. Damon and I had been on the phone for almost an hour, discussing our day. I had even told him about hiring Kelly and wanting to help him get his own place.

"That's fine, baby," Damon said. "You know, I'm all for helping any way we can."

I smiled. Damon was one in a million, and I was so glad he was mine. I could hear in his voice that it had been a long day, so I decided to do something to make my baby smile. "What are you wearing?" I asked seductively.

"Don't start with me, woman." He laughed.

"So you're not going to tell me?"

"You will not have me sleeping on swoll and I can't get none," he said.

"Fine," I said sweetly. "Don't tell me. Can you guess what I have on?" I asked, rolling over on my back.

"Octavia—"

"That's right, baby," I said softly, "nothing but my skin."

He cleared his throat lightly.

I was waiting for him to take the bait. I knew Damon hated phone sex. Correction—he hated having to masturbate, which was something he rarely did, except when I wanted him to do it over the phone with me. My hormones were off the Richter Scale, and even if he chose not to participate, I was going to force him to listen to me pleasuring myself.

"Spread your legs," he ordered.

Smiling triumphantly, I did as he requested, and the two of us talked and moaned until I was dripping all over the bed sheets, wishing I was dripping all over him.

***

The sound of my phone jolted me from my sleep. I stared at my alarm clock through hazy, heavy eyes and saw that it was two in the morning. "Hello?" I answered, clearing my throat.

"Is this Mrs. Whitmore?" asked a woman on the other line in a slight Spanish accent.

"Yes." I sat up slowly in bed.

"My name is Rose, and I am the night auditor at America's Best Inn." She spoke slowly, and I knew instantly that she was calling about Kelly.

"How can I help you?" I asked.

"One of our guests, Kelly Baker, asked me to call you." The woman sounded extremely nervous.

"Is he okay?"

"No. I'm afraid there has been an accident. Mr. Baker is on his way to the ER," she explained.

"What kind of incident?" I asked. I threw the covers back and climbed out of bed.

"He was attacked."

I listened as Rose gave me the details. I quickly threw on a pair of shorts and a tank-top, then slid my feet into the first pair of flip-flops I could find. According to Rose, one of the tenants at the motel found Kelly lying in the parking lot. She said he was beaten up pretty badly, but the paramedics didn't think his injuries were life threatening; I was thankful for that. The last thing I wanted was the responsibility of breaking the news to Contessa that her nephew—the one she loved like her own son—had been killed. I woke Contessa up to let her know I had an emergency at the restaurant and that I would be back shortly. I didn't want to alarm her until I was 100 percent sure Kelly was all right.

***

It took me less than twenty minutes to get to Huntsville Hospital. I broke the speed limit the entire way and had my Benz wide open on the highway. An hour and a half later, when I finally got in to see Kelly, I was shocked.

His face was swollen, and his lip was at least three times its normal size. There was a bandage just above his left eyebrow. His arm was in a cast, and his chest was bandaged.

There was an HPD officer present, and he explained to me that Kelly had been mugged. "Apparently, his attackers thought he had money."

I shook my head, sad that there are people in this world who would rather hurt others and take from them than going out and earning their own. It's even sadder when the victim is probably just as hard up as their attackers, if not worse.

"He has a few broken bones, including two of his ribs and his arm," the doctor, a pretty, dark-skinned female advised me. "There was a small gash over his eye that required stitches. We gave him something for the pain, and I wrote out a prescription. He was very lucky," she said. "It could have been a lot worse."

***

Kelly drifted in and out of sleep as we drove back to my house. He managed to give me a choppy description of what happened. He was leaving the vending machine when someone jumped him from behind.

"They took my wallet," he slurred. "Ciara," he mumbled. "They got her!"

I figured the meds had him high, but then I remembered the picture he had shown me. I looked over at him just as a single tear fell from his eye. I knew Kelly had nowhere to go, and he was in no condition to take care of himself, so my only option was for him to stay the night with us.

After I helped him get settled into one of the spare bedrooms, I awakened Contessa to let her know what was going on. When she saw Kelly, she cried for what seemed like hours. Once Contessa calmed down, the two of us sat in the kitchen drinking some soothing tea. It was during our conversation that I advised her about Kelly's job offer falling through, but I told her we'd come to an agreement that he would work for Damon and me.

The Lies We Tell For Love

"I appreciate it, sweetheart," she said. Her eyes were puffy and red from all the tears she had shed, and her face, which normally glowed, looked dark and slightly discolored. "I just don't know what he's going to do right now," she said. "He's going to be in a bad place until he heals." She shook her head. "I moved too fast," she said. "I should have waited to move."

"There was no way you could've known that Kelly would get mugged," I said. "It was just one of those things. The good thing is that he's alive and is going to be just fine. We will work something out," I said, yawning lightly, "and he can stay here for now. Once he is up on his feet, we can move him into the guesthouse."

Contessa's face lit up as tears began to fall from her eyes again. "Thank you, Octavia." She sniffled.

I gave her a small smile, then reached over and gave her a hug. I was full of solutions, but I only had one problem—Damon. I'd told Contessa that Kelly could stay with us until he got better, but I didn't have a clue whether or not my husband was going to go for it.

Chapter 11

Damon

"Damon!" Nadia squealed, throwing her arms around my neck. The two of us stood backstage in the midst of a crowd of cast members, stagehands, reporters, and other well-wishers.

"It's good to see you, Nadia," I said sincerely, squeezing her lightly.

It had been almost two years since we'd last seen each other, and Nadia had barely changed at all. Her light skin was still smooth and flawless, and her frame was still thin. Her face was a little fuller, and her sandy mane that had once hung down to her shoulders was now cut in a short, layered bob. Looking at her, I had to admit she was still beautiful.

She stepped back to have a look at me. "You look good."

"Thank you," I said. "So do you."

"Marriage agrees with you."

"Love agrees with you."

"Thank you," she said. "Speaking of that, where is Octavia?"

"At home."

"She didn't want to come?" Nadia questioned with raised eyebrows. Her expression told me she already knew the answer to her own question, but she just wanted to hear me say it. I hate it when women do that mind-games shit.

"I felt it was best that I didn't give her the option," I said. I gave Nadia a look that she was all too familiar with—a look that let her know I did not want to discuss the subject in further detail.

"Did you enjoy the show?" she asked, changing the subject.

"I did," I said honestly. "You were great."

"Thank you, Damon," Nadia smiled sweetly.

"So where is this mystery man of yours?" I asked, scanning the room with my eyes. "The man who has stolen your heart."

"Well, he couldn't make tonight's show, but he is going to meet us at the after-party."

"What after-party?"

"The one I'm hoping you'll attend," she said sweetly. She fluttered her lashes and smiled.

"Nadia, I don't think that's a good idea."

"Come on," she whined. "Please!"

My first instinct was to tell her "no," say "goodbye," and go about my damn business, but I couldn't help being curious. I let out a deep breath. "All right, but I can't stay long."

Nadia looked ecstatic that I had agreed to go.

My first instinct told me I should have declined Nadia's offer, and my mother always told me, "Your first thought is always the right one." This is one time I hoped my mother was wrong.

***

The after-party was exclusive, and members of the press were only allowed to attend without cameras. That was a relief to me because Nadia had been hanging all over me from the time I'd stepped into the banquet room of the W. The last thing I needed were snapshots of the two of us floating around. Her mystery man had yet to show, and I was quickly beginning to think he wasn't coming. To make the shit worse, Octavia called, so I had to tell her yet another a lie about my whereabouts. I slipped outside in the hall to take the call.

"What's with all the noise in the background?" she asked.

"Oh, I decided to have a couple of drinks," I said, walking a few steps down the corridor, away from the room.

"Really?" she asked. "With some of the fellas from the office?"

The Lies We Tell For Love

"Naw, baby. You know I roll solo," I said, and it was true. Since Savoy and Shontay had left for their trip, I either rolled alone or with my wife and daughter. Unless it was for business, you weren't going to see me chillin' with a bunch of other men. Hell, the more so-called friends a man has, the more problems he's got.

"Aw, do you miss your Bonnie, boo?"

"Like crazy," I said honestly. "Can't wait to get back and show her how much I've missed her." I spotted Nadia pushing through the banquet room doors. She looked down the opposite end of the hall first and then came in my direction. I held my finger up as a nonverbal way of telling her to be quiet, and then I watched as she strolled toward me.

"I miss my Clyde," Octavia said.

"I'll be home soon," I reassured her. "I promise. How is Daddy's girl?" I asked, gauging Nadia's expression.

She smiled as she listened to my conversation.

"Wet," Octavia said seductively. "Wait…were you referring to Jasmine or me?"

The tone of her voice was making my dick hard. "Be good," I said lightly.

"Sorry, baby. Jazz is fast asleep."

"Give her a kiss for me," I said.

"I will," Octavia said. "I love you."

"I love you more," I said sincerely before ending the call.

"Checking in?" Nadia asked, staring at me. The tone of her voice held a hint of what I thought might be jealousy, but the expression on her face was friendly and appeared innocent.

"Real men always take care of home first," I informed her.

"There is nothing you can tell me about real men, Damon," Nadia said, and then she sighed loudly. "I've had the realest of the real."

"If this man of yours was a real man, he wouldn't have left you waiting all night for him to be a no-show," I said sarcastically.

"Trust me, Damon. He has his reasons," Nadia said calmly. "And just to clarify," she continued, lowering her eyes as she looked at me, "when I said I've had the realest, I was referring to you."

***

Nadia's suite was the last place I'd planned on seeing when I'd agreed to see her show, but by the end of the night, that was exactly where I found myself. Holding Nadia tightly in my arms, I slowly carried her over to the king-sized bed. Easing her down on top of the comforter gently, I shook my head. "You never could hold your liquor." I laughed lightly.

Earlier, after watching Nadia finish off her third glass of chardonnay, I'd noticed that her words had begun to run together and she was leaning to one side, obvious signs that she had reached her limit and had too much to drink. I decided it was time to cut her off and insisted that she allow me to escort her up to her room. The two of us were feet away from the door of her suite when she let out a faint laugh, mumbled something about her baby, then collapsed in my arms.

To my surprise, when I opened the room door Nadia's personal assistant, María, an older woman of Latin descent, was waiting in the living room. After introducing myself, I asked María to point me in the direction of Nadia's bed. I slipped Nadia's heels off of her feet and dropped them on the carpeted floor.

"Dame," she moaned lowly.

"Yes?"

"I-I miss you," she said.

"Go back to sleep, Nadia," I said, ignoring her flirtatious slur.

Slowly sitting up in the bed, Nadia ran her fingers through her hair. Giving me a glazed stare she asked, "Don't you miss me? Don't you miss the times we shared?" she continued, leaning toward me. "The fun we had? The way we used to fuck for hours?" Stroking the side of my face with one hand, Nadia slid her other hand across my lap. She grabbed my crotch gently, causing my man to jump slightly.

"Chill, Nadia," I said, brushing her hand away. Standing, I readjusted myself. Despite being turned off by Nadia's sloppy drunkenness, my body—no, my dick—still responded to her touch by growing slightly. I decided it was time for me to make my exit. I had no intention of sleeping with Nadia, and I was not in the mood to deal with the emotional outbreak my intuition was telling me was about to take place.

"Why are you leaving, Damon?" Nadia asked. She was following so close behind me that she was practically walking on the back of my heels. "Stay here with me, just for tonight," she pleaded.

"You know I can't do that," I said. "I have a family now, Nadia."

We stood face to face in the living room of her suite. At the mere mention of my family, I saw a change in Nadia's expression. Her eyes narrowed to tiny slits.

"Fuck your little Bama Barbie," she snapped. "You act like the sun rises and sets on her ass!"

"Ms. Nadia," María said, quickly entering the room, "please keep your voice down."

Nadia spun around quickly to look at her. "Don't tell me what to do!" she snapped. "Last time I checked, you work for me, not the other way around!"

"But I—"

"But nothing!" Nadia said, cutting María off. "Go back to your room NOW!"

María bowed her head and obediently shuffled out of the room. The expression on her face reminded me of a child who had just been scorned by her mother.

"Was that really necessary?" I asked, shaking my head.

"Is it really necessary for you to remind me every opportunity you get about that bitch you chose over me?"

"You need to watch your mouth," I said firmly. I didn't appreciate, nor was I going to continue to tolerate, Nadia disrespecting my wife.

"You need to live up to your promises, Dame," she said with tears in her eyes. "What happened to you being here for me when I need you? What happened to the Damon I used to know?"

"I'm still me," I said, "but now I have a wife and a daughter to take care of."

"Fuck your wife and daughter!" Nadia screamed, glaring at me. "What about me? What about us? What about your son?!"

I erupted in laughter. "Nadia, you really need to go sleep that shit off," I said, walking toward the door. "You're trippin'." As I opened the hotel door, I glanced over my shoulder. "You went from having an imaginary man to me having a son. That's a whole new level of bullshit." I walked out the door, slamming it behind me. I was halfway down the hall when I heard Nadia shouting.

"So you're just going to walk away, Damon? From me? From your son?"

I was fed up with Nadia's ranting and raving. I turned around, deciding to check her ass once and for all. "Fuck you and your crazy…" I stopped what I was saying when I saw Nadia standing in the hallway holding the hand of a small boy who looked no older than two. The child was handsome, with Nadia's skin color, a head full of curly hair, and big brown eyes. When I first turned around, I'd wanted to tell Nadia that our friendship was officially over and that she could lose my number, but for the first time in my life, I was speechless. The little boy standing next to Nadia looked all too familiar to me, and I knew exactly why. The child held a striking resemblance to my baby girl, Jasmine.

Chapter 12

Octavia

The first couple days following his attack, Kelly spent his time doped up on painkillers and sleeping. Contessa was ecstatic when he finally broke out of his sleep coma and rejoined the rest of the world. I had just made it in from The Ambiance 2 when he came downstairs to speak with me. The swelling in his face had gone down considerably, and his lip was now only twice its normal size. I noticed he was starting to look better by the moment.

"You want me to stay here?" he asked.

"Until you heal," I said. "I think that would be best, and you'll love the guesthouse," I said enthusiastically. Our guesthouse, which was normally reserved for visitors or whenever Shontay needed a getaway, was twice the size of a king-sized hotel room. It was fully equipped with a full-sized kitchen, all the latest appliances, and everything you would find in a studio apartment.

Kelly looked like he was pondering the offer until he sighed lightly. "I don't think so," he mumbled. Kelly was as stubborn as shit on the bottom of a shoe! Even in his broken condition, he insisted on holding on to his pride. I can respect a man holding his nuts, but he was seriously in no position to turn down my hospitality at that moment. *Look what happened the last time he did,* I thought.

"Look, you're in no condition to take care of yourself right now," I said. "Once you're repaired, you can sleep anywhere you please. However, Ms. Contessa and I agree this is the best arrangement at the moment, and we are not going to argue with you about it. It's settled." I gave him a cocky grin then continued flipping through the stack of mail.

"And what about the man of this house?" he asked. "Did you and Auntie consult with him?"

The arrogance and confidence I had been feeling earlier dwindled away quickly, like a bubble in the wind. "I'm sure Damon will be fine with it," I said firmly.

Kelly shook his head. "We'll see," he said. "We will see."

***

I was anxious and excited that Damon was returning home from his business trip, so much so that I decided to invite my parents over for a little cookout and pool party, to which Contessa and Kelly were also invited. I won't lie, I knew Damon was less likely to go off about Kelly in front of my parents. You can call me a coward if you want to, but my mother did not raise a fool. To avoid a blow-up by your man, you have to put him in the right place at the wrong time.

My father and Kelly hit it off instantly. After discussing his attack and his injuries, the two of them continued to converse on everything from politics to women. Their conversation flowed freely, and it was almost as if the two of them had met before. I liked the fact that Kelly seemed to be having a good time in spite of his injuries.

Mama, on the other hand, kept her conversation with Kelly short and sweet. She was polite, but I knew there was something behind her quietness. Whenever Mama nods or just smiles, it's a guarantee that she is up to something. "That Kelly seems really nice," she said to me as we sat by the pool. Contessa had excused herself to go and put Jasmine down for a nap.

"I think he's good people," I said, looking across the patio at Kelly, who was standing with my father by the grill.

"He's not bad to look at either," Mama added. "The canvas is a little banged up right now, but you can still see the art."

Admiring the khaki shorts Kelly wore and dark blue polo, I silently admitted what I had already privately acknowledged—Kelly was fine. "I haven't noticed," I lied. Looking at Mama, I gave her a sly smile.

Turning her lips up and lowering her eyes, she stared at me. "Is there suddenly something wrong with your eyesight?" she asked sarcastically.

"No," I said lightly. "It's just that I only have eyes for my man."

Laughing lightly, she shook her head. "Your father and I have been together for thirty-five years, and never have my eyes been only for him."

"Well, Damon has my heart," I said sincerely, "and that's all that truly matters."

"True," she agreed, "but temptation will always come a-knocking. We just have to make sure we don't open the door when it does."

I meditated on my mother's words while watching Kelly. "I have no intention of opening that door, Mama."

"Are you sure you haven't already?" she asked.

The sound of the phone ringing saved me from having to respond. "Hello?" I answered quickly.

"Hey, baby." Damon sounded exhausted on the other end.

"Hey, boo. I was just thinking about you," I said, ignoring Mama's hand, which I assumed she had extended for the phone.

"Let me talk to him," she said firmly.

I turned away, trying to ignore her.

"Is that Mama?" Damon asked.

"Yes," I said sweetly. "Daddy's here too. I decided to have a cookout and invited the two of them over. Contessa's here…and Kelly too."

"Kelly?" he asked.

"Yes, babe, Ms. Contessa's nephew that I hired."

"Oh, that's right," Damon sighed. "I forgot about him. What do Mama and Charles think of him?" he asked.

"They like Kelly," I said, clearing my throat. At no point in time had I told Damon that Kelly was shacked up in our guesthouse. I had lost my courage, and it just didn't seem like the right time to tell him. I was buying myself a little extra time, trying to muster up some more courage. "What time will you be here?" I asked, changing the subject.

"That's the thing, babe," he said, sounding disappointed. "Something's popped up at the office, so I'm stuck here till Tuesday."

"Tuesday?" I said, genuinely concerned. "Is everything all right?"

"Everything is fine, baby," he said. "It's just that I have an important meeting I need to handle."

I knew if Damon wasn't returning home as he originally planned, whatever had taken place had to be major, but I was still ready to see my man and to feel his arms around me. "Well, you gotta handle your business," I said, attempting to sound cheerful instead of disappointed.

"If you want, I can come home tonight and return to Atlanta early tomorrow," Damon offered.

Hell yeah, that's what I want! I thought to myself. "Naw, it's fine, boo," I said to him. "Handle your business."

"Are you sure?"

"Positive," I said sweetly.

"Octavia…"

"Yes, baby?"

"You know I love you," Damon said, "right?" There was something in his voice that wasn't quite right, but I couldn't put my finger on it—or maybe it was my own guilt. Then again, it could have been the fact that Mama was practically sitting on my lap, hanging on my every word.

"I know you do," I said softly, "and I love you. Nothing will ever change that."

"The feeling is mutual," he said.

Mama gave me a look that said, *"You better tell him before I do."*

What ever happened to mother-daughter loyalty? I thought to myself. "About Kelly," I said, gathering my words, "Daddy checked him out and said he looks good on paper."

"And in person," Mama stated softly.

Cutting my eyes at her, I shook my head.

"I told you I trust your judgment," Damon said. "I'm sure he'll work out fine, and if not, we know how to make him go away."

"Yeah we do." I laughed lightly.

"I'll let you go for now," he said. "I love you, baby."

"I love you too." I smiled. "Talk to you later."

***

"Damon handled the news about Kelly well," Mama said, handing me an empty bowl.

After the two of us ate with Daddy and Kelly, I excused myself to the kitchen to wash dishes. Mama volunteered to tag along. Daddy and Kelly sat in our home theater watching a movie on the big screen.

"What news?" I asked, confused.

"Oh, that's right," she said, snapping her fingers. "I forgot…you didn't tell him!"

"No, not yet, but when I do," I said, "I know he will support my decision. He trusts me," I said proudly.

Covering her mouth with her hand, Mama yawned softly, her third yawn in less than ten minutes. As I stared at her beautiful brown face, I noticed something I had never seen before. Mama looked tired—drained, to be exact.

"You look exhausted, Mama."

"Don't change the subject," she said, looking at me.

"I'm not, but you need to go sit down," I ordered. "I got this."

On any normal occasion, Mama would tell me she was fine and find something else to wash, clean, or disinfect, but this time, she did exactly as I asked and walked over to the kitchen table and took a seat. "Your father has got to stop keeping me up at night," Mama said, letting out another soft yawn. "I try to remind him I'm not twenty-one anymore."

"Mommy, I do not need a visual," I said, frowning.

"That wasn't a visual, baby," she said. "Trust me, you couldn't handle the visual." She laughed lightly and coughed a little.

"Are you coming down with a cold?"

"Probably just the change in the weather," she said, shaking her head. "Don't worry about me, baby. Just make sure you keep everything under control in this beautiful home you and Damon share."

I could hear the warning in my mother's voice, and I knew that considering my past history with lovers, she had a genuine reason to be concerned. However, Damon was not just my lover. He was my man, my friend, my husband, and the father of my child. He was everything I needed and more than I ever wanted. I had my hormones under control when it came to every other man, and there was no way I was going to allow Kelly—no matter how pretty he was—to disrupt my happy home.

"You don't have to worry about that," I told her.

"Ladies, it's been a wonderful afternoon, but I think I'll call it a night," Kelly said, entering the kitchen. "Auntie and Jasmine are both getting their beauty naps, and as you can see, I need mine."

Looking up from my dishes, I gave him a small smile.

"Thank you for everything," he said.

"You're very welcome."

"But mostly for allowing me to be a part of your family and share your home." He flashed his eyes at me then said with a straight face, "I promise your generosity and hospitality will not be in vain."

There was an awkward silence in the room until Mama loudly cleared her throat.

"It was a pleasure meeting you, Mrs. Ellis," Kelly said, redirecting his attention to my mother, whom I was certain had been watching the two of us like a hawk. "I look forward to seeing you again," Kelly said.

"Have a great night, Kelly," she said sweetly. "See you soon."

The two of us watched as Kelly exited out the patio doors and walked in the direction of the guesthouse.

"Listen to me, little girl," Mama said, staring at me. "Be very careful with that one."

"I have a good feeling about him, Mama," I said reassuringly. "I think he'll be a hard worker."

"It's not his work ethic I'm worried about," Mama said, rising from the table slowly.

"Stop worrying about me," I said, walking over and taking her hand in mine. "I told you I have everything under control."

"Mm-hmm," she mumbled, leaning on my shoulder. "Right."

***

I love the fact that Damon is a business owner and a major player when it comes to making money, but I hate sleeping without his arms around me. I hate it so much that I rarely ever sleep when he's gone, and that night was no exception.

After the two of us indulged in another lengthy phone conversation that included some steamy phone sex, we said "I love you" and then "Goodnight." Afterward, I took a long, hot bath, slipped into a pair of shorts and a fitted tank-top, then popped in to check on Jasmine. After tucking my baby back in, I decided to have myself a nightcap. I was sitting in the kitchen enjoying a glass of Rose when I heard the roaring of our hot tub. I opened the French doors leading out onto the patio and saw Kelly sitting in it. The full moon in the sky cast an illuminating light down, reflecting off the water like diamonds in a mirror and bouncing off Kelly's skin, causing it to glow. It wasn't until he turned to climb out that I noticed he was only wearing his birthday suit. I suddenly felt like a horny stalker and decided to return to the kitchen and my drink.

Moments later, Kelly knocked on the patio doors.

"Come in," I said before downing the last of my drink.

When he opened the doors, I was completely caught off guard by his appearance. He was bare-chested, wearing nothing but a towel wrapped around his waist. I could tell he was naked under the terrycloth. His chiseled chest glistened with droplets of water covering his smooth brown skin. He held his fractured arm up against his body as if he were still wearing a sling. "I'm sorry," he said. "I thought everyone was asleep. I know Auntie is knocked out, and I just assumed you and Damon were. Otherwise, I would have never—"

"It's fine," I said, trying hard to push the image of Kelly buck-naked out of my head but failing terribly.

"I'll apologize to Damon in the morning," he said, nervously shifting his weight from one leg to the other. The action caused the front of the towel to slip open slightly.

"Damon's not home," I said, looking away. "Not yet anyway."

"Oh. Well, my apologies to you," he said. "The heat is good for sore muscles, and I'm trying to ease the soreness without the pills."

"I can respect that," I said honestly. I had seen far too many specials on people who had become addicted to prescription drugs. I couldn't blame him for looking for alternative healing methods.

"If it's not too much trouble," he began, "may I have something to drink?" he asked.

"It's no trouble, Kelly," I said, redirecting my attention to him. "Take whatever you want from the fridge."

Staring in my eyes, he smiled brightly. "Thank you," he said. "However, right now I'll just take the water."

I watched as he walked slowly over to the refrigerator and pulled out three bottles of water. I couldn't help noticing that his thighs were as defined as a track star's, small, but all muscle and not an ounce of fat. The towel covered his ass, but it could not hide the fact that it was also sculptured and toned. When he turned around and started walking toward me, I forced myself to stop my silent gawking and instead looked at my nails, pretending I was inspecting them.

"Thank you again," Kelly said, standing next to my chair. "There is one more thing you can help me with."

"Oh yeah?" I said, looking up into his eyes. They were lowered and staring directly into mine. "What's that?" I asked.

"I'll be right back," he said.

***

When he returned from the guesthouse with his bandages, I was thankful to see he was finally wearing pants.

Kelly flinched slightly as I pulled the wide Ace bandage around his chest as the two of us stood in the kitchen. He closed his eyes, and an expression of sheer pain flashed across his face. He leaned forward slightly, as if at any moment he might fall. I wrapped my arms around his waist, allowing him to place his weight on me, to use me for stability.

After a few seconds, Kelly opened his eyes and looked down at me. There was a hint of water, evidence of tears floating below the grayness that penetrated me through his stare. Placing his hand on my neck just below my hairline, he whispered, "Thank you." His fingers were extremely warm, almost to the point of feverish against my skin. His touch caused a small sensation to course from my neck down my back. Our eyes remained locked until Kelly dropped his hand from my neck at the same time I released the grip I had around his waist.

I continued the task of reapplying his bandage. "I'm sorry if I'm hurting you," I said. I knew the pressure the bandage would put on his ribs would help alleviate some of the pain, but the process of me getting it on him seemed to make it worse, and I hated that I was hurting him.

"It's not you," he said. "I'm okay."

I continued to wrap the bandage around his skin tightly then secured it against his body with two small metal clasps. "All done," I said.

"Thank you." He smiled slightly.

"That's something you should do more often," I said.

"What?"

"Smile," I said.

"Moment of truth?" he said.

"I'm listening."

"It's somewhat hard not to when I'm around you," he said, looking at me intently.

I remained quiet, choosing not to comment.

"Thank you again. Goodnight, Octavia," he said. "Sweet dreams."

"You too," I said pleasantly.

Exiting the kitchen, Kelly pulled the door closed behind him. He was gone, but the sensation that had flowed through my body was still present, even in his absence. I closed my eyes while exhaling lightly as Mama's words echoed through my head: *"Be very careful with that one."*

Chapter 13

Damon

I had question after question for Nadia, but the one I wanted answered more than anything was why she hadn't told me about her son. *How could she allow damn near two years to pass and not once pick up the phone and let me know that she had a child, especially if I could be the father?*

"I thought another man was his father," Nadia said while the two of us sat in the hotel lobby consuming breakfast. "However, he always had his doubts and insisted upon a paternity test." Taking a sip of her mimosa, she looked at me. "Once the test came back stating that he was not the father, I knew Donovan was your son."

"You should have told me," I said, "even if you thought there wasn't a chance that he's mine. Just in case, you should have told me."

"But we always used protection," she said, shrugging her shoulders. "I figured there was no possible way for you to be his father, but that last night we were together, we slipped up."

Nadia was right. I always wore a condom when the two of us were involved, so it didn't make sense that I could have fathered her child. If Donovan didn't resemble Jasmine so much I would have told Nadia to kiss my ass and call Maury Povich about her baby's father. However, I couldn't ignore or deny the resemblance. Granted, the last time Nadia and I slept together was a distant and cloudy memory, and I did remember there being a large amount of alcohol involved—so much that I wasn't 100 percent sure that the condom hadn't broken or torn. *Hell, did I even remember to put the damn thing on?* I wasn't sure. The only thing I was sure of was that I needed confirmation and I needed it immediately. "When did you find out that the other man was not Donovan's father?"

"Shortly after he was born," she admitted.

"So you've know for two years?" I asked, trying to maintain my composure while resisting the urge to wrap my fingers around her neck. I was angered by the fact that Nadia had taken it upon herself to keep me completely shut out and in the dark about Donovan for the first two years of his life. "Why did you wait until now?" I asked, staring at her.

"I thought I could do it on my own," she said lowly. "I can financially, but emotionally, keeping this type of secret is too much to bear. I don't want to lie to my son for the rest of my life, Damon. He deserves to have you in his life, and you deserve to have him. Plus, I knew you had a new home and family," she added. "I didn't want to disrupt that."

I was so busy trying to get answers to my questions and to come to grips with the fact that I might have a son that I actually had not taken the time to think about how and what I was going to tell Octavia. Her feelings about Shontay's deceased husband Kenny having a child with another woman was less than favorable. Although Nadia's child was conceived before I exchanged vows with Octavia, my mind was telling me that my wife would still not accept it and most likely wouldn't forgive me.

"You can't—correction, you won't—disrupt my family," I said. "In fact, no one is to know about this but you and me." I was giving Nadia a hidden warning, and the look in her eyes told me she completely understood the consequences and repercussions that would fall upon her if she brought even an ounce of havoc to my home or marriage. "Have you told anyone that I could possibly be your son's father?" I asked.

Sighing lightly, Nadia shook her head. "No, Damon," she said. "I wanted to wait until I told you, then—"

"There is no then," I said firmly. "You are not to speak a word of this to anyone until I give you the go-ahead. Do you understand?" I asked, locking my eyes with hers. I had known Nadia for years, and there was a time when I truly loved her, but if she did or said anything to harm Octavia, I would not think twice about hurting her—or worse.

"Yes," she said lowly. "Yes."

"Good," I said lightly. Looking down at my Rolex, I saw that it was almost ten a.m. "You should go upstairs and get Donovan. Our appointment is at ten thirty," I reminded her. "I don't want to be late, and as soon as the test is done, I have to go so I can try to wrap up my business before I get on the road in tomorrow."

Nadia's eyes narrowed slightly. "You haven't spent any time with Donovan," she said, sounding irritated. "I figured you would at least want to spend some quality time with him before you leave." She was right, if he was my kid, but I was still hoping Donovan was not my son. Hell, for all I knew, Nadia obsessed over me so much when she was pregnant that her child came out with my family resemblance. I knew it was a long shot and that I was thinking like a dumbass, but I was willing to take any explanation I could get with the exception of me being the father.

"I have to wrap up some deals, and then I have to get home, Nadia," I said, laying a 100-dollar bill on the table for the waitress. "I have a business to run and—"

"And a family," she said, rolling her eyes.

"You make a drunken announcement at two in the morning that I have a son," I whispered, leaning forward in my chair. "What in the hell do you expect me to do?" I asked. "Forget everything and everyone I'm responsible for?"

"Your responsibilities just increased by one," she said, standing.

"We don't know that yet," I said.

"I know," she said, smiling, "and whether you admit it to me or not, you do too."

***

It took less than a minute for the pretty blonde technician at the DNA Diagnostics Center to run the cotton swab across the inside of my cheek, but the results I expected to receive two weeks later could possibly affect my life forever. I had a million thoughts running through my head, and I needed to try and clear some of them before I returned home to Alabama. I decided to cancel my morning appointments and instead stop in at Stone Mountain to visit with my parents, Damon Sr. and Ilene. If my mother had known I had been in the city and was just now paying them a visit, she would have given me a royal ass-whipping. She believes in handling your business, but in her mind, family is and must always remain first and foremost.

My parents had been together for thirty-two years, and they appeared to be more and more in love every time I saw them. That was the kind of love and longevity I wanted to share with Octavia, and I would have moved mountains to obtain it.

My mother opened the door to their home. She looked beautiful, as always, like a runway model in her cream, knee-length silk dress that hung off her shoulders and gold open-toed Jimmy Choos. Her mocha-colored skin looked smooth and refreshed. Running her fingers through her short, tapered hair, she flashed her gray eyes at me. "DJ, darling," she purred, throwing her arms around my neck. "What a pleasant surprise!"

"You look beautiful, Mama," I said sincerely, squeezing her tightly.

"Thank you, baby," she said sweetly. "You look handsome, as always."

"Good genes," I said, returning her smile.

"Only the finest."

"Where are my daughter and granddaughter?" she asked, stepping back to look past me.

"At home," I said. "I had some business to take care of, and I decided to pop in on you and Pops before I head out tomorrow."

Mama searched my face with her eyes. Touching her hand to her neck, she rubbed the sparkling ruby hanging from the platinum chain around her neck. "Is everything all right?" she asked; like many mothers, it was as if she could see right through me, the way a fortune teller might see through a crystal ball. I could tell by her expression that she knew something was on my mind.

"Everything is fine," I lied. "Just feeling a little guilty."

"Guilty? About what?" she asked with raised eyebrows.

"That I've been here for a while but am just now stopping in to see my family." This time, it was only partially untrue.

"Um," she said, cutting her eyes at me, "I raised you better than that."

"I know," I said, kissing her cheek, "and I apologize."

"Just don't let it happen again. Always remember, family first."

"Yes, ma'am," I said with a smile. "Where is Dad?" I asked.

"Out on the golf course with some colleagues," she said, rolling her eyes, "trying to make the ninetieth hole or whatever it is they do."

I laughed and shook my head. Unless it involves shopping or spending money, Mama couldn't care less about my father's hobbies. She is a true diva, and she will undoubtedly be one until the day she died.

"Do you have time to sit for a moment?" Mama asked.

Although, she was asking me a question, I knew telling her "no" was not an option. "Of course I do."

Flashing me a huge white smile, she batted her eyelashes. "Perfect," she said. "Let's go sit in the family room."

***

Five minutes later, the two of us sat side by side on my parents' sofa drinking iced tea and discussing my mother's latest shopping adventure in Paris.

"You have to take Octavia soon," she said. "She would love it."

"Yeah, that's definitely on my to-do list," I said.

"It better be," Mama ordered. "Only the best for Whitmore women."

"Speaking of Whitmore women," I said, "when was the last time you seen Grandma?"

The mere mention of my father's mother turned my mother's pleasant expression sour. My mother and Grandmother Whitmore were like vampires and werewolves—natural-born enemies who hated the scent of the other. "She made an appearance a week ago," Mama said, "her and that wretched best friend of hers. What's that old bat's name?" she asked, tapping her nail against her lips. "Bitchnese, Bitchatrice, Bitchtilla?"

"Bernice," I said, shaking my head. "Her name is Bernice, Mama." To say Mama's dislike of my grandmother flowed over to her friend would be an understatement. My grandmother and Bernice were like two peas in a pod, and they were both on my mother's shit list. Mama's and Grandmother's hatred for each other went as far back as the day my father met my mother and fell in love. My grandmother accused my mother of being manipulative and cunning and said she wanted my father merely for his money. On the contrary, Mama said she didn't want Daddy at all at first, money or no money. She was single, beautiful, and the object of many men's affections. However, much like my desire to win over Octavia, Dad was determined to have Mama, and once he showed her how a real man can love and hold his woman down, Mama fell for him too. Her love of designer shoes, clothes, and expensive trips came much later.

"That's right. Bernice." Mama giggled slyly. "Anywho, the two of them flew in to see your former whore perform," she said, referring to Nadia.

I wasn't in the least bit surprised that my mother referred to Nadia as a whore. She had always let it be known that she didn't care for her and thought she was nothing more than a gold-digger. I had explained time and time again that Nadia had never truly asked me for anything and that she was passionate about her career and talents, but Mama's response each and every time was, "Give her a moment, and she will eventually come begging. She's a gold-digging whore, Damon, but a smart one. Trust me, one day, the truth will eventually reveal itself."

To this day, it still amazes me how people turn against each other. Believe it or not, there was a time when Mama actually liked—or at least tolerated—Nadia. When Nadia and I first met and began dating, my mother actually allowed her to stay at their home while she visited during the summer. Nadia worked for us for a short period of time out of our L.A. office for Nomad Investments. Mama and Nadia got along well back then, and I thought Nadia had earned a guaranteed spot in our family and might someday be my bride. But then Mama flipped the script and turned against her. I think when she found out that Nadia was connected to Bernice, it left a sour taste in her mouth. I've discovered that in life, it doesn't matter how good of a person you are; it's human nature to be judged and to judge others by the blood they carry and the company they keep.

"They saw her show last week?" I asked. "The production with Tyler Perry?" I was surprised to hear Mama say that my grandmother had gone to see Nadia's show the week before. I specifically remember Nadia stating that she was going to be performing in Atlanta that week and that one week only.

"DJ, you know I don't know or care who, what, or when, when it comes down to that girl," Mama said, sucking her teeth, "except when it comes down to my baby boy." Eyeing me suspiciously, she paused. "You are staying away from that trash, aren't you?" she asked.

"I haven't touched Nadia in a very long time, Mama," I said honestly, conveniently leaving out the fact that I had seen her just hours earlier.

"But you've spoken with her," Mama stated without hesitation.

"How did you know?"

"A lioness always knows when her cub is in danger," she said, shaking her head.

"Nadia is neither a threat nor a danger to me."

"Not alone," Mama said, rising from the sofa. I watched as she walked over to the window then looked out, seemingly lost in her thoughts. "However, along with the two bitches of the East egging her on, she could be a problem."

I meditated on my mother's words. "Our conversation was innocent," I said, joining my mother at the window. "You have nothing to worry about."

"Innocent?" she asked. "DJ, you and I both know that conversations with old lovers are rarely innocent, especially when said lovers have a hidden agenda."

"And what do you think is on Nadia's agenda?"

"The same thing that has always been on it," she said, looking over at me. "Money."

Chapter 14

Octavia

"Good morning," Kelly greeted me as I entered the kitchen. He stood at the kitchen island dropping pancakes onto a plate. I admired the fact that he was managing pretty well with one arm.

"Good morning, Kelly." I smiled, and walked over to Jasmine, who sat in her high chair, feeding herself Cheerios. Her curly hair was neatly pulled back into two pigtails, and she was already dressed. I was pleasantly surprised and a little relieved, due to the fact that I was already running late for work. Kissing her forehead lightly, I inhaled the scent of fresh baby lotion. She giggled lightly, then flashed her big brown eyes at me and smiled. Despite the fact that I was running on less than four hours of sleep, it was one of the busiest days of the week at my restaurants, and I was late, which was a sure sign that my day was going to be a rough one; nevertheless, all seemed right in my world the moment my daughter smiled. "Where is Ms. Contessa?" I asked.

"She's in the laundry room," Kelly advised me. "She ate then told me she had one more load to finish."

"She made breakfast," Kelly said. "Pancakes, Canadian bacon, scrambled eggs, and freshly squeezed OJ."

"That was really sweet of her," I said sincerely, "but I'm already late, and

I've got to get to my office."

"You're the boss," Kelly said. "You can never be late. Now sit."

"True, but if I don't get started early, it will take forever for me to finish my paperwork."

Placing a full plate on the table, Kelly nodded his head. "Understandable," he said, looking at me. "Now sit down."

"I thought I was the boss around here," I teased.

Pulling my chair out for me, Kelly laughed. "You are, but the boss does not always know best."

"Well, if I'm going to eat, you have to join me," I told him. "So grab a plate and pull up a chair."

"You don't have to tell me twice," he said with a hungry-looking smile.

***

Not only was breakfast delicious, but it was just what I needed to get my energy level up. After enjoying our meal, the two of us sat talking and often laughing as Kelly told me stories about his childhood.

"Am I interrupting something?"

I was so engulfed in my conversation with Kelly that I hadn't heard Damon come in. He looked stressed, but he was still fine in his green Ralph Lauren polo and creased khakis. In less than ten seconds flat, I was out of my chair and had my arms wrapped around his neck. To say I missed my man would have been an understatement. Smiling sweetly, I shook my head and answered, "No, not at all." I kissed him, then chanted, "Welcome home, baby."

Jasmine was also thrilled to see her father. She kicked her legs excitedly against her chair, singing, "Da! Da! Da!"

"Hello, princess," Damon spoke to her. "Hey, beautiful," he whispered to me softly while squeezing me tightly. Pulling away, he stared at Kelly. I watched as he walked over, lifted our daughter out of her chair long enough to give her a hug and a kiss, then sat her back down. He stood at the edge of the table, towering over Kelly with a look on his face that was as serious as that of a judge during a murder trial. "I don't think we've met," Damon said to Kelly.

"Damon, this is Kelly," I said quickly. "Kelly, this is my husband, Damon."

The Lies We Tell For Love

Easing back from the table, Kelly stood then extended his hand to Damon. "Nice to meet you, Mr. Whitmore," he said politely.

I held my breath as Damon stared at Kelly for a second or two, silent and still. For a second there, I thought he was going to leave Kelly's ass hanging, but he finally he shook his hand. "Call me Damon," he said.

Exhaling lowly, I smiled.

"In that case, would you like some breakfast, Damon?" Kelly asked.

I could tell he was a little uneasy around Damon, but I assumed it was due to the stone-cold looks my man was giving him.

"Yes, I would," Damon said, looking at me suggestively.

My kitty began to throb because we both knew what was on my husband's mind.

Pressing his lips to mine, Damon kissed me like it was the very first time.

Kelly cleared his throat lightly and stepped away from the two of us. "I'll be happy to make you a plate," he offered.

"Thanks, but what I'm about to devour doesn't require silverware." Damon laughed.

I noticed Kelly seemed uncomfortable with Damon's statement so I looked down at my wrist, checking my watch for the time. I had made time for breakfast, and now I would make time for my man. Another of my personal beliefs is that if you don't make time for your man, another woman will, and I'll be damned if I'd give another chick the opportunity when it comes to my Damon.

Chapter 15

Damon

Stroking Octavia's naked back with my fingertips, I exhaled. The two of us lay buck-naked on top of our bed after two sweaty rounds of banging sex. Although I was sexually satisfied, I couldn't seem to shake my mental frustration. I was concerned about the DNA test I had taken earlier. The testing center advised me that I would receive the paternity test results in the mail within two weeks, and I had given them my office address because I knew Octavia would never see the mail. Still, knowing I was concealing a secret from her—especially one of such magnitude—was eating away at me inside. I had lied to her before to protect her, but I had to admit to myself I was only keeping the secret from her to protect myself from losing her. To further add to the frustration, I knew if the results came back positive, I would have to break down and tell her about Donovan, and I was sure that would bring our relationship to a crashing halt.

"You're awfully quiet," she said, looking up at me.

"I'm sorry, baby," I said, squeezing her tightly. "I was just thinking."

"I know what you're thinking about," she said, "and don't worry."

"What do you mean?" I asked, confused.

"About Kelly, babe," she said, propping herself up on her elbow. "I saw the way you were looking at him."

I'll admit when I first saw him in the kitchen with my wife and daughter, I thought I was going to commit murder for a second time in our home, but from the looks of the brother, someone had already put their foot in his ass. Surely, he wasn't stupid enough to earn another one. "I was surprised," I confessed. "I just wasn't expecting see another man sitting at my breakfast table, that's all."

"I'm sorry, boo," Octavia said sweetly. "I can only imagine how it must've looked."

"And what happened to him?" I asked. "It looks like he went to war and lost."

"He got mugged a couple days ago," she said. "Two broken ribs, fractured one of the bones in his arm, plus his face was ten times worse than what you just saw."

I shook my head in silence. "Wrong place, wrong time?" I asked, running my fingers through her hair.

"Exactly," she said, "but I think he's good people, and the two of you are going to get along very well."

I was not looking for, nor did I need any new friends. My wife had hired Kelly to do a job, and that was the only thing he needed to do. I was home, and I was going to make sure he did that job and did it well. "Where is Contessa?" I asked, changing the subject.

"She was in the laundry room last I heard." Octavia laughed. "However, *someone* could not wait around for introductions."

I had been away from my wife for a week. I was anxious to meet Contessa, but our introduction was not one of my top priorities when I'd first walked through the door. "I'll apologize to her later," I said.

"Well, babe, it was good as always, but I gotta go." Octavia gave me a quick peck on the lips then jumped out of bed.

"You're just going to leave me?"

"Business is business, baby," she said, walking into our master bathroom, "but I still love you!"

"Love you too, boo." I laughed lightly. "Hey, babe?"

"Yes?"

"If you like, I can drop you off today," I suggested, "play chauffer for you for the day."

"You're not going into the office today?" she asked, peeking her head back out the bathroom door.

"Naw. I think I'm going to relax today."

"Okay, babe." She smiled. "Should I let Contessa know she has a free day?"

"Keep her on call in case something major pops up at the office," I told her, "but Jazz can roll with her daddy today."

"I'll tell her," she said. "She'll probably spend time with Kelly."

"How far does he stay from here?"

"Oh, not far at all," she said. She had that awkward look on her face that she always gets when she thinks I'm going to be upset about something.

"How far?"

"The guesthouse," she said quickly before shutting the bathroom door.

"What the hell?" I asked, jumping off the bed to march in the bathroom behind her. She had the shower on and was humming softly, so I opened the glass shower door and stared at her like she had lost her mind. "You let him move in to our guesthouse?" I asked.

"Just until his broken bones heal!"

"Oh? And how long do you think that will be?" I asked, watching as she lathered soap over her skin. I was pissed off, but I couldn't resist looking at how sexy she was, soaking wet and covered in bubbles.

"Just a few weeks," she said.

"Hell naw," I said.

"And why not, Damon?" she questioned. "He is Contessa's nephew, and he's hurt."

I don't know if I was bothered because she hadn't cleared her decision with me first or if I was afraid karma was biting me in the ass for not informing her that I might have an illegitimate son. "I know it's only temporary, but baby, we know nothing about this man," I said.

"Would you be bothered if it was Contessa's niece instead of nephew?" she asked, cutting her eyes at me and daring me to say the wrong thing.

I didn't answer.

"So you wouldn't care?"

"I didn't say that," I said.

"But you were *thinking* it," Octavia said, sucking her teeth. "What difference does it make if a person is male or a female?" she asked. "What would that mean to you?" she interrogated further, refusing to let the issue drop and downright turning the tables on me.

"Don't try and change the subject," I said calmly.

"Answer the question, Dame."

I wanted to tell her the difference was that I wouldn't have to worry about a female stepping out of line and making a move on my wife, but even if she did, *that* I could accept; shit, I'd probably find that to be a turn-on. But another man? Well, that would lead to major problems and complications, not to mention someone getting hurt, and that someone wouldn't be me. "It wouldn't make any difference," I lied.

"All right then," she said. "So either way, we would be taking a chance. Right or wrong?" she asked.

I was not in the mood to debate or argue with her, so I decided to let the subject rest for the moment. "A couple of weeks," I answered, "but then he has to go."

"Thank you, baby," she said, extending her hand to me. "Now, get in here and help me wash my back."

"If I do, you will never make it to the restaurant," I warned her.

She looked like she was considering it. "Hmm. You're right." She smiled. "Rain-check?" she teased.

"Sure. For tonight?"

"Definitely." Octavia smiled victoriously.

I gave her a short kiss then returned to our bedroom. I waited till I heard her singing a loud, off-key rendition of Jennifer Hudson's "Where You At?" before I picked up my Blackberry.

"Talk to me."

"I got an assignment for you," I said, stretching out across the bed.

"I assumed so," Lawrence said sarcastically. "That's the only time you call."

He was right. Lawrence was good to have on my team to do a little dirty work now and then, but he was not true friend material. I trusted the work he did because I was paying him. If he hadn't been on my payroll, I wouldn't have dealt with him at all. "So you already know the deal?" I said.

"Yeah. What you got for me?"

"I need you to check someone out for me."

"Wifey stepping out already?" He laughed. "After everything we went through so you could put that ring on her finger?" Lawrence had been the one who had assisted me in getting close to Octavia, and he'd committed several crimes to help me snub out the competition. When I think back, I realize how blessed we were that Lawrence's crazy-ass tactics hadn't cost Octavia her life.

"My wife is a happy and faithful woman," I advised him firmly.

"Are you sure 'bout that?" Lawrence chuckled. "Hell, I thought the same thing about my ex-bitch until I found her sucking off the neighbor."

"If I remember correctly, that was after she caught you beating out her best friend."

"Shit, her friend was fine as hell!" he yelled. "I told her about bringing those tramps in our home. The dumb bitch shoulda listened."

I shook my head. Not only was Lawrence an arrogant, heartless prick sometimes, but he was quite possibly the most psychotic person I knew. I made a mental note that after that assignment, I would release him from my team. He simply wasn't stable, and that can be a liability. "Listen, I'm in a hurry," I said, changing the subject. The shower was no longer running, and I knew Octavia would be coming out of the bathroom any minute.

"What you need?"

"I need you to check out someone for me," I began.

"A new bitch?" Lawrence laughed. "I knew the pimp in you wasn't dead."

I blew loudly into the phone. It didn't matter how many times I told Lawrence that I was committed to my wife, he always seemed to think there was a glimmer of hope that one of us was going to step out on the other. There may have been things I kept from Octavia, but faithfulness was not nor ever would be one of them. "Just listen," I said impatiently. I gave Lawrence Kelly's name and the information Octavia had shared with me and told him to let me know what he could find on him. Despite Lawrence being a colossal asshole, he was good at what he did, and a name and a brief description was all he needed. The man could find anybody, even if they were underground, hiding in an unmarked grave.

***

I spent the rest of my day with my daughter. I enjoyed our father-daughter time, which included watching her play at the park, making a major mess feeding herself, and taking a nap on my chest. I wished she could always remain small so I could hold her in my arms and protect her from anything that came her way. Out of everything I've ever made or built, she is, without a doubt, my greatest creation. That evening, I treated her and my wife to dinner at Ruth's Chris Steak House then later treated my wife to a heaping helping of dessert in our bedroom.

After we shared a nice hot bath, I lay in bed watching Octavia as she dug through the pile of clothes I had taken on my trip, separating the ones she planned to take to the dry cleaners from those that would be washed at home. "I told you I could handle that, baby," I stated.

"I got this, boo."

I smiled. My wife was far from the typical housewife, but she definitely still took care of our home, and everything she did, she did well.

"So you approve of Ms. Contessa?" Octavia asked, looking over her shoulder at me.

"I do," I said, reflecting on the conversation I'd had with the woman earlier. Contessa seemed sweet and spunky. She was also slightly feisty for an older woman. "I like her. She reminds me of my grandmother a little."

Octavia turned around to look at me. "Who?" she asked with raised eyebrows.

"My father's mother."

Octavia pouted her lips slightly then shook her head. "Odessa?" She frowned.

I laughed. "Yes, my sweetheart of a grandmother, Odessa." My grandmother had made a less-than-favorable impression on Octavia when the two of them first met. In fact, my grandmother insisted that the only reason I wanted to marry her was because I had gotten her pregnant. At the time of their meeting, though, Octavia wasn't pregnant; my grandmother just refused to accept that I was marrying someone outside of her best friend's granddaughter. To this day, Octavia and my grandmother barely have two words to say to each other. Out of respect and love for me, they have been cordial to each other on the rare occasions when they were together; however, out of my respect and love for both women, I have never, nor will I ever demand that they be friends or even spend time together.

Octavia smacked her lips loudly. "A lie, don't care who tells it," I heard her mumble.

"I heard that!"

"I know you did," she said sarcastically. "That's why I said it aloud!" She rolled her eyes and stuck her tongue out at me.

"Let's agree to disagree." I laughed. "You keep on with that shit, and I'm going to show you what to do with that tongue."

"I agree to disagree," she said, batting her eyes at me, "and if I remember correctly, I already *showed you* what I can do with this tongue." She turned her back to me and continued sorting clothes.

"That you did," I said. "I'm thinking Round 2."

"Not a problem," she said. "Let me finish this, and then I'm all yours."

I settled in against the headboard, folding my arms behind my head. I closed my eyes and exhaled. It felt good to be home, back in my own bed. I was in my own zone, reflecting on the fact that it had been a good day.

"Baby, who is Lena Jasper?" I heard Octavia ask.

I opened my eyes and saw that she had her pretty brown eyes locked directly on me; she was waiting for my response. "Who, baby?" I asked slowly. I was in no way attempting to play stupid, but I did wonder how she knew about Lena.

"Lena Jasper," she repeated, walking over to the edge of the bed. "Who is she?" she asked, "and why is she writing you checks for four grand?" She was holding the same check I had returned to Lena during my visit. It was obvious that Lena had slipped the check in my jacket when I had excused myself to use her bathroom.

"Ms. Jasper is a tenant of mine," I said, sitting up straight. "I meant to deposit that."

"Shame on you," she said, laying the check on the nightstand.

"I know," I said. "I was so anxious to get the trip over with so I could get home."

"I understand, Mr. Whitmore," she said, climbing into the bed. She straddled my waist and kissed me slowly. "However, we cannot forget to take care of our business and handle the money," she whispered.

"It won't happen again," I said, rolling her over on her back.

I took my time making love to Octavia for the second time that night. After her climax was complete, she fell asleep on my chest, and I held her tightly in my arms. I lay in the darkness staring at the ceiling. My mind wondered what Lena was thinking slipping the check in my jacket, and I came to the conclusion that she probably assumed I would find it before I returned home. I could only assume it was an innocent gesture. As I ran my fingers down the curve of Octavia's back, thoughts of Nadia and Donovan floated through my mind; I silently said a prayer asking God—no, begging Him—to please let Donovan be someone else's child.

Chapter 16

Octavia

It was after ten when I arrived at The Ambiance 2, and to my delight, we were packed to capacity. My crew was holding me down, and everything was running smoothly. After walking through my establishment and greeting the patrons, I excused myself to the comfort of my office so I could focus on my paperwork and closing payroll.

I was sitting behind my desk going over numbers when Katlyn knocked on the door and came in carrying a large green and black gift basket. Katlyn was a pretty plus-sized cocoa-complexioned sister with dark brown eyes. She wore her naturally curly hair in a short, well-kept afro and had a beautiful smile. "Special delivery!" she announced.

The basket was covered in green cellophane and secured with a huge black satin bow. Smiling, I instructed her to sit the basket on the corner of my desk. "Is it from my hubby?" I asked, standing and immediately opening the gift.

"I'm not sure," Katlyn said, shrugging her shoulders. "There's no tag."

I knew if the gift had been from my hubby, he would have included a card. Damon loved to surprise me, but he also loved to reap the rewards of my appreciation. "Strange," I said, "but thank you, Katlyn."

"You're welcome," she said. She flashed me her signature smile then exited the room.

The basket was filled with fancy-looking hair- and skincare products, everything from shampoos and conditioners to oils, lotions, and body butters. There were also two large scented candles that smelled like a mixture of vanilla and hazelnut. Each of the items had a nice light scent, and the labels read "Salon Déjà Vu" and stated that they were made of all-natural products with no alcohol. I figured it was the owner's way of marketing her business, and although I had never heard of the salon or the products, I was still thankful for the gift. I made a mental note to ask Mona, my hairstylist, about them when I went for my next appointment.

I was in the process of wrapping up my paperwork when Katlyn knocked again, this time to let me know I had a visitor. "Let him in, but only if he's tall and handsome," I teased, assuming my visitor was Damon.

"He's definitely both." Katlyn smiled, flashing her brown eyes at me.

I stood, ready to wrap my arms around my hubby's neck; however, I was surprised to see Kelly instead of Damon. Smoothing my hand down the front of my Chanel suit, I sat back down.

"So you base your visits strictly on how good-looking the visitors are?" he asked, shutting the door behind him. He was carrying two rolled papers in his hand, along with a small pink bag.

"No." I laughed lightly. "I just thought you were Damon."

"Sorry to disappoint you," he said, "but if it makes things any better, I come bearing gifts." He peeked over in the basket. "Not that you need any more of those, I can see."

"Not disappointed, just surprised," I said pleasantly. "And for the record, a woman can never have too many gifts! Now have a seat," I ordered politely. I observed that Kelly looked extremely nice in the midnight-blue button-down shirt and dark slacks he was wearing. "How did you get here?" I asked.

"I drove," he said, jingling his keys at me.

"What?" I asked.

"I'm teasing," he said. "Caught a cab."

"Not funny," I said, shaking my head.

"Shouldn't you be at home resting?" I questioned.

"Probably," he said, exhaling, "but I have work to do." He handed me the documents from his hand. "I had to put the design on two pieces of sketch paper because my pad wasn't big enough," he said, "but I think you get the idea."

I unrolled the sketches and studied them. They were designs for a Japanese garden for the backyard. "I love these!" I said sincerely.

"Really?"

"Yes, I honestly do," I said, studying every detail.

"I figure we could seclude the entire south corner of the property," he said. "We could put up some trellises for a few climbing plants, plant flowering cherry trees or Japanese maples…hell, we can even have a pond with koi fish!" he continued excitedly. "Umm, stones and boulders, paper lanterns…"

I smiled as he rambled on and on, trailing off on a list of all things Japanese. "I love it!" I said, interrupting him. "I just love it. So this is what you've been spending your resting time on?" I asked.

"Yes."

"It's a wonderful idea," I said, glancing over the designs again. "Once you're up to it, price everything and just let me know. I'll run it by Damon."

"I'll do that this evening."

"Aren't you tired?" I asked. "Wouldn't you rather spend your time relaxing right now, while I'm still allowing you to use your injuries as an excuse?" I teased.

"Are you kidding me?" He shook his head. "I'm bored out of my mind. Besides, the best way to get over an injury is to get back to work."

"Don't you have friends or someone special you could spend some time with?" I asked, rolling up the sketches and securing them with a rubber band.

"I associate with very few people," he said. "I find that the less friends a man has, the better off the man is."

"I feel the same way about women," I confessed. "The woman with a whole lot of female friends—"

"Has a whole lot of female problems!" Kelly finished.

I smiled and nodded my head, for he had taken the words right out of my mouth. "Exactly."

"Well, I should let you get back to work," he said, standing. "I just wanted to run my ideas by you and bring you this." He extended the bag he had been carrying when he'd walked into the office.

"What's this?" I asked, taking the bag from his hand.

"Open it."

Doing as Kelly requested, I opened the bag and found a beautiful porcelain angel figurine inside it. As I held it delicately in my hand, I smiled. "It's beautiful," I said sincerely. The angel was painted with a beautiful cocoa-colored complexion and pretty pink wings. She wore a pink and white dress and was barefoot, sitting on a rock, as if she was looking over someone or pondering peacefully. Staring at her face, my smile grew wider. "It's Jasmine!" I said in awe.

"Yeah. This guy I used to work with makes them," Kelly said. "I showed him a picture of Jasmine, and he handcrafted it to look like her. I figured she could be your little guardian angel, watching over you while you work."

The figurine was truly beautiful. I set it down on my desk and smiled again. "I love it, Kelly," I said. "Thank you!" I probably had thousands upon thousands of expensive gifts at home and in my office, but I was really touched by Kelly's. You can buy diamonds and gems at any mall, but what he had given me was rare, and it took time to create.

"You're very welcome." He smiled, revealing his beautiful white teeth. "I think she looks good right there on your desk."

"I do too," I agreed.

"You really like it?" he questioned, staring at me.

"Yes, absolutely," I said.

"I didn't know what to get the woman who has everything," he said, "but I wanted to show my gratitude for everything you've done for me."

"I don't have everything, Kelly," I said softly, "but I am blessed, and no matter what I have, I'm always very thankful for the little things." I meant every word I said to Kelly that day. Despite the fact that Damon and I are well off, I still take pleasure in the basics, and I still love receiving gifts, no matter what they cost.

"And I'm very thankful for you," Kelly said.

There was a gap of silence between the two of us as we looked into each other's eyes.

"More than you'll ever know."

Chapter 17

Damon

I wanted to make sure Kelly was on the up and up, handling his business properly, so I enlisted Lawrence to check him out. To my satisfaction, Lawrence hadn't caught him slipping once. After two weeks of nothing, I decided to give my investigation a rest. "Here's what I owe you," I said, sliding a plain brown envelope across my desk toward Lawrence. The envelope contained $25,000, a small fee to pay to ensure that the man sleeping right under my family wasn't some kind of pervert or a criminal.

Slipping the envelope off the desk, Lawrence smiled. "Always a pleasure doing business with you." He stuffed the envelope in the inside pocket of his Armani jacket and then reclined in his chair. "I'm glad your boy was clean."

"Yeah, you and me both," I said.

"But what I don't understand is why in the hell you allowed your wife to move his ass in yo' shit?" Lawrence shook his head. "You could have saved yourself some damn money."

"He's our nanny's nephew," I said nonchalantly. "The brother has been taking some hard hits lately, and Octavia feels sorry for him."

"The good thing is he's up and moving, and he'll be moving into his own place soon."

Kelly stated he was feeling better more and more each day. Although he still had a cast on his arm, he was up and working every day. He had started work on the project he had presented to Octavia, and it looked like it was going to be a nice addition to our property. When Octavia told me about Kelly's idea for the garden, I agreed to fund it, no questions asked. I could tell she loved it, and whatever she wanted, I was willing to buy. Although Kelly hadn't given me any problems and he was doing a good job, I still preferred him to be out of my guesthouse as soon as possible, even if it meant I had to pay for his new residence, something I'd already agreed to do.

"Something don't make sense though," said Lawrence. "If the brother has a degree and his work history checked out, why the hell is he planting daisies and water lilies for y'all? That shit just don't add up."

"The brother just wants to work," I said, "but you speak like you feel like there's more."

Lawrence leaned forward in his chair and shrugged.

"You saying you missed something?" I questioned.

"I didn't miss shit," he said, cocking his head to side. "What I am saying is that I been making shit happen for a very long time, and I know things don't just fall into place. There is always a mutherfucka like me hiding in the shadows, making it happen, and a lot of times we're making it happen for a mutherfucka like you."

I processed what Lawrence was saying and responded, "Well, I'ma chill for now. Like I said, it's one more week. Until then, I'll keep my eyes on him."

"All right," Lawrence said, nodding his head.

I was in a very good mood, especially since my day had started out on a very positive note. First, my wife woke me up with some good-morning head, and second, despite his reservations, Lawrence announced that Kelly's background check had come out clean. Plus, I'd arrived at work and discovered that our numbers had gone up and my money was making me even more money. Things couldn't have been better.

There was a tap on my office door.

"Come in!" I said.

"Mail call," Louisa said, entering through my office door. She handed me a stack of envelopes then quietly exited as quickly as she came in.

I shuffled the envelopes from one hand to the other until I saw "DNA Diagnostics Center" printed on the upper right corner of one of them.

"I've got to make a move," Lawrence said, standing. "Call me when you need me."

I nodded my head, silently acknowledging Lawrence's request while focusing on the envelope. Once Lawrence was gone, I ripped the envelope open and stared at the results in front of me. Tossing the printout on my desk, I shook my head. I ran my hand across my chin and tried to come to terms with what the results had to say about the rest of my life.

"Damon, you have a call on Line 1." Louisa's voice came through the speaker on my desk phone, and I knew without asking who it was.

"This is Damon."

"You got it?" Nadia asked excitedly.

I hadn't spoken to Nadia since we'd taken the paternity test in Atlanta two weeks prior. I knew she'd been waiting for the same thing I was, and now we both had our answer. "Yes," I said, taking a deep breath.

"I told you, Damon!" she squealed. "It says 99.9 percent."

"I know, Nadia," I said, clearing my throat, which suddenly felt like it was swelling shut. Loosening my tie, I reclined in my chair. The test results had obviously confirmed one of my worst fears: *I am Donovan's father.*

"I'll be in Atlanta this weekend," Nadia said quickly. "We should make plans for you to spend some time with *our* son. Also, we'll need to have a family meeting to discuss how we're going to handle visitation."

Family meeting? Visitation? Nadia's words bounced around in my head as I continued to stare at the test result, wishing that at any moment, Octavia would wake me up from what had to be a nightmare.

"I'd like to see Octavia again," Nadia rambled on. "I need to know the woman my son is going to be spending every other holiday with."

The mere mention of my wife snapped me out of my mental fog. "Nadia, I think we need to slow down for a moment."

"What do you mean?"

"I'm still trying to focus on the fact that I have a son," I said. "You're already asking for family meetings, discussing visitations, and…and what the hell do you mean you need to see my wife again?" I understood that Nadia was happy to have confirmation that I was her son's father, but the woman had clearly lost her mind if she thought Octavia was going to be down with us being one big, happy family. *How did I fuck up like this?* I asked myself.

"I assume you've told her," Nadia said from the other end of the phone. "You did tell her; didn't you?" she prodded.

"No, I most certainly did not," I said.

"Well, surely you have to tell her now, right?"

"I haven't decided what I'm going to do!" I snapped. Nadia had too many questions, and I didn't know all the answers. I did know that I wanted her to shut up with her interrogation so I could concentrate on the change that had just occurred not only in my life, but in Octavia's and Jasmine's as well, even if they didn't know it yet. "Who have you spoken with about this?" I asked, suddenly concerned that Nadia had been running her mouth.

"Well, no one," she said hesitantly.

She's lying, I concluded. "Nadia, don't play with me," I spat into the phone

"María," she said. "That's it, and she won't talk."

"How do you know?" I asked, assuming that for the right amount of money, Nadia's assistant would hum like a bird. *Why in the hell would María be loyal to Nadia?* I still remembered how Nadia spoke to the woman like she was beneath her.

"Her family is here illegally, Damon," Nadia informed me. "She won't say a word...or else."

I decided to take Nadia's word and have faith that she knew what she was talking about when it came to María. "Are you sure that's it? No one else knows?" I demanded.

"No one else, Damon. I-I promise."

"What about your grandmother?" I asked. I was sure that if Bernice knew, my grandmother knew as well.

"No way!" she whined. "I told them that someone else is the father."

This was of no relief to me because I was sure that if my grandmother had seen Donovan, she'd surely noticed the resemblance between him and my daughter. I could feel my anger raging more and more with each deep breath I took. "I don't believe you. If you told María, Nadia, then how can I believe you didn't tell someone else? For all I know, you might go spilling your guts to some damn tabloid...or worse!" I was snapping on Nadia out of pure frustration.

"They don't know!" she screamed. "And who else would I tell? Who else could be worse?" she asked, sounding like she was on the verge of crying at any moment. "Octavia? Who, Damon? Do you really think I'd tell her?"

"Yes, my wife!"

"I would never tell her anything you don't want me to." She sniffled. "But why haven't you said anything to her? I mean, doesn't she have a right to know?"

I wanted to tell her that for the first time in my life since I had become a man, I felt something I had never felt before—fear. I had done a lot of dirt in my life, and I was almost positive that I would do a whole lot more, but the only thing that shook me to my inner core was the fear of losing the only woman I had truly ever loved. "It's just...it's complicated," I stated simply.

"What's complicated about telling your wife that you fathered a child before the two of you were together?"

"We were together then, Nadia. We just weren't married."

"If I remember correctly, not long after you and I slept together, you busted her for screwing some other guy."

Nadia was speaking the truth, but I did not want to hear it. I didn't need her or anyone else to remind me of the way things had transpired at the beginning of my relationship with Octavia. The only thing that mattered was where the two of us were at that moment, and we were doing well—but now I had this to deal with. "I don't want to discuss my wife with you," I said firmly. "In fact, I prefer that you never mention my wife again. It's really none of your concern."

"She's going to find out sooner or later, Damon," Nadia stated. "No one can keep this kind of secret forever. It's probably best that you speak to her now, or it will hurt her more later when she finds out you kept it from her."

"Leave it alone," I ordered. "I'll handle my home and you handle yours."

"Fine!" she snapped. "Do whatever you want. I just need to know what your intentions are regarding our son."

Rubbing my hand across my head, I began to organize my thoughts.

Donovan was one of three innocent parties in our nasty little secret paternity triangle, and Octavia and Jasmine were the other two. I needed to protect Octavia and Jasmine, but I also knew I had a responsibility as a father to Donovan. It was neither right nor fair for him to suffer because of his parents' situation. Like some sort of sick twist of fate, I had been begging Octavia for another child with the hope of conceiving a son. *Apparently, God has a sense of humor,* I thought, though I didn't find it funny. The circumstances were less than ideal, but I had to find a way to make the best of it. I really had no other choice, circumstances being what they were. "This weekend may not be a good idea," I said.

"Why not?" Nadia sighed heavily. "Damon, this weekend is the only time I can get away. In fact," she said quickly, "I probably won't be able to get back down that way for another three or four months. We need to take care of it now."

"Fine. I'll see what I can do," I said.

"Perfect," she said sarcastically.

"How are you doing financially?" I asked. I needed to know that Donovan was being properly taken care of. I feel a certain way about men pushing luxury cars while their seeds sit there wondering about their next meal. I knew Nadia had an established career and was doing her own thing, but I felt it necessary to let her know that I was willing to do my part when it came down to providing for my own flesh and blood. I also wanted to defuse some of the obvious tension I felt and heard in her voice. I needed to keep her on my side so she wouldn't go off and do something stupid, like running her mouth to Octavia about Donovan.

"I'm good," she said. Her tone was no longer full of tears, nor was there any anger in her voice. In fact, she seemed happy—maybe even relieved— that I had asked. "I just want you to get to know your son. I know you can't be a full-time father," she said, "but I want you to be there for him as much as possible. I may regret saying this, since I know you already have a family of your own and everything, but I would like for us to make Donovan's childhood as stable and normal as possible. He's quickly approaching the age when he will be making memories, and I want those memories to be good ones, even if that means keeping all of this a secret."

I felt a certain relief in hearing those words from Nadia, and I wanted to believe she was telling me the truth. "Nadia, you know me," I said. "I'll do what I can to be the best possible father to Donovan."

"I believe you, Damon," she said, "and I know we will make this work."

***

I decided to take my wife out for a night on the town, first because I loved her, and second, because I felt guilty as fuck for what I'd discovered earlier that day. I chose to treat her to dinner at BB King's Blues Club in Memphis.

"Baby, it's a weeknight," Octavia said, looking over at me. She looked ultra sexy in her above-the-knee fitted off-the-shoulder dress. Her hair hung loosely at her shoulders, just the way I liked it.

"I know, babe, but we deserve this," I said. "Hell, *you* deserve it."

"No, you're right. *We* deserve this," she said, smiling at me.

"We do, babe," I agreed. "We do." I had been debating all day about telling her the truth, but to be honest, I knew before I opened the test results that I was not going to tell her about Donovan. I know it sounds crazy, but my true intention was to find a way to take the secret to my grave. I had convinced myself that it was possible and that with the right means—meaning money, in my case—I could maintain and keep my secrets concealed from Octavia forever. I know I was wrong on so many levels, but I had faith that things would work out if I planned and played my cards perfectly.

"You look so sexy tonight, boo," Octavia said, turning in her seat to face me.

I had chosen to wear a midnight-blue Versace sport shirt and dark gray slacks. I knew my lady loved to see me in blue, and I loved they way she looked at me whenever I wore it. "I had to bring it tonight," I said, pulling my Jaguar XF into the club parking lot. "A man can't get caught slippin' when he's married to a woman like you."

"You never slip, babe," Octavia said sweetly. "That's one of the many reasons I love you."

Sliding the gear shift up to park, I stared at her. "What are the others?" I asked.

Stroking my cheek lightly with her fingers, she smiled. "Because even though I have and get my own, you still provide for me. Because you would lay down your life before you allowed our daughter or me to be hurt. Because you loved me through all my bullshit and stayed with me even after I almost got the two of us killed. Because—"

"I get it, boo," I said, smiling proudly. She had stroked my ego and made my man hard from her compliments alone.

"One more," she said, holding up her finger.

"What's that?"

"Because I trust you," she said seriously, "and I never thought I could trust anyone the way that I trust you." The look in her eyes was so sincere, and I knew her words were true. It took all the strength in my body for me to keep looking at her; guilt is like a flesh-eating parasite. I was already starting to feel the effects of it as it began eating away at me.

***

The filet mignon and grilled mahi-mahi Octavia and I shared was cooked to perfection, almost as delicious as the meals she cooked for me at home when she had time. I teased her about that as the two of us slow-danced to the sounds of Will Tucker and the BB King All-Stars.

"I'm saying baby, the cooks almost got you," I joked.

"Lies! All lies!" She laughed, shaking her head. "I give credit where credit is due, but we both know I'm that fiyah, and I give your tongue multiple orgasms."

I pulled her closer to me and kissed her neck just below her earlobe. "Later, my tongue is going to give you multiple orgasms," I whispered.

She smiled brightly and laughed lightly. "Tell me something I don't know."

"I love you."

"Again," she said, cupping my face with her hands, "tell me something I *don't* know."

"I'm ready for dessert," I said, giving her a quick peck on the lips. "Are you?"

"I'm always ready," she said, coyly batting her eyes at me.

"I have a room waiting for us at the River Inn." Octavia had told me she had seen a special on the luxurious hotel while watching the Travel Channel. I had made her a promise that the next time the two of us were in Memphis, we would rent a room there. Both of our businesses had been doing well, but we finally had time to get away, so I made good on that promise.

"You know I have wanted to stay there since I heard about the place," she said, offering me another huge and beautiful smile.

"I know…and tonight you will."

"What about Jazz?" Octavia asked with raised eyebrows. "You trust Contessa to watch her overnight now? And Kelly?"

"I think Contessa would be just fine overnight with our baby girl," I said honestly, "but right now I don't have to worry about that because your parents are watching her. As far as Kelly goes, I've checked him out, and until he does something to make me doubt him, we're good."

"I can't believe you worked all of this out," she said. "I'm always the last to know."

"Baby, if I'd have told you, it wouldn't have been a surprise."

"True."

"So are you ready to go?"

She pulled me closer and slowly flicked her tongue across my bottom lip before giving me a full kiss.

"I take that as a yes," I said, leading her off the dance floor by the hand and then out the exit doors of the club.

***

The River Inn was a small luxury inn with no more than twenty-eight rooms and approximately six suites. The entire inn was done in a European décor, accented with Southern charm. There was a peaceful view of the Mississippi and a majestic beauty about the property. The penthouse suite reminded me of something out of a classic film, only with marble counters, plush carpet, and several other upgrades. After calling to check in on Jasmine, Octavia left me alone in the sitting room while she freshened up. I had vowed that the night would be only about the two of us, and I planned to make sure it worked out that way, right after I called to check my voicemail at the office.

The first message was from my father, telling me he hated that he had missed me when I'd stopped by the house but that we should catch up soon. At fifty-eight, Pops was still a man on the go, and he looked good for his age. If he and my mom ever divorced, he would have to fight the ladies off, young and old.

The next five messages were from Nadia. I felt a surge of frustration as she droned on and on about how happy she was that Donovan had me in his life then asked for a number outside of my office where she could reach me. "I noticed you changed your cell number over a year ago, but you need a second one where you can be reached after hours," she said.

The last two messages were her asking why I hadn't called back, saying "DJ," her new nickname for Donovan, wanted to talk to his daddy and tell him goodnight. I was ready to pop off on her ass until I heard his soft baby voice saying, "Goodnight Dad-dy. See you soon."

After hitting the end button on my Blackberry, I reclined on the sofa. If Nadia was attempting to pull at my heartstrings in an attempt to convince me to haul my ass to Atlanta for the weekend, she had succeeded, because I planned to be there to see my son.

"Hello, baby."

I was lost in my thoughts of Donovan when I looked up and found my very sexy, very naked wife standing in the doorway, just smiling at me with a come-and-get-it grin. Her skin looked like pure polished gold under the glow of the dimmed lights. "Well, hello to you," I moaned, readjusting my man through my pants. I was instantly hard at the sight of her, and I love that she has that effect on me.

She walked over to me slowly, swaying those hips of hers and licking her lips. "Dessert is officially served," she said seductively. Stroking my cheek gently, she tossed her long mane from one side to the other then spread her legs shoulder-width apart.

"And I am more than ready," I said, grabbing her by the hips and pulling her toward me. I ran my hand down her thigh then lifted her left leg up until her ankle was resting on my shoulder. Stroking her clit gently with my thumb, I watched as she tossed her head back and closed her eyes. The look of pleasure on her face made me crave more of her. Placing one hand underneath her toned, tight ass, I braced her as I grabbed her thigh gently then pulled her right leg up. We reclined back on the sofa until her naked, phat lips were positioned over mine. Inhaling her essence, I licked the hood of her protruding clit like it was a lollipop.

"Damon...mmm..." Octavia moaned.

My dick was pressing against my boxers, fighting to break through as I moved my tongue up, down, and around until finally sucking gently on her clitoris. Slipping my tongue down to her heated hole, I tasted her sweetness once before moving back up, then down inside her wet spot again.

"Yes...shit, yesss..." she moaned.

She rotated her hips as I pushed my tongue as deep as it could go inside her playground. The heat oozing from her pussy was electrifying, but it was no match for the rain that fell on my lips and tongue when she came. Her body shook as she moaned deeply and passionately. I unzipped my pants quickly and had barely pulled my joystick out when Octavia climbed off my shoulders and dropped to her knees. She plunged down on my hardness, locking her lips around me. She sucked me hard and strong, using only her wet, warm mouth while her hands squeezed and stroked my sac.

"Baby..." I gasped. My toes curled involuntarily as she plunged up and down on my stone-hard dick, each time taking more and more of me into her mouth and throat. I could feel myself on the verge of climax as I whispered, "Sit on it." In an instant, she was positioned on my lap. Her hot box felt like it was burning as she rocked and rotated her phat cat on my man until the only sounds we could hear in the room were the swishing of her wetness and my own moaning.

Chapter 18

Octavia

I made myself a pledge that if Damon's Atlanta office kept giving him problems, I was going to jump in my whip and make the four-hour drive my damn self and start regulating and kicking asses! After we finished making unbelievable love in Memphis, he sprung on me that he would be out of town for the weekend. I was not feeling my man being gone again, but at the same time, I had to respect his hustle.

Mama and Daddy called requesting to spend the weekend with Jasmine, so Contessa decided to go to Tennessee for the weekend to visit her son Jay, which meant I had nothing to do with my time. After cleaning my already dust-free home, thanks to Contessa Pledging every square inch and corner every chance she got, I took a shower and stretched across mine and Damon's bed. After staring at the vaulted ceiling for well over ten minutes, I decided to give my bestie a call to see how things were going on her escapade around the world.

"Everything is going well," Shontay said.

I could tell she was beaming on the other end of the phone.

"The people here are so beautiful, Tavia."

I listened as Shontay went on and on about her adventures in Africa and the jungle.

"Savoy and I actually went on a safari. The animals were so close to the vehicle that we could almost reach out and touch them." She continued, "You have got to come see this place for yourself. It's just...amazing."

"What the hell?" I asked. "Tay, I barely get close to wild animals in the zoo. There is no way I'm riding through their turf close enough for them to reach out and take a bite out of me or kill me with one of their claws." She erupted in laughter, but I was more than serious. If God intended for us to ride alongside wild animals, He would have named Damon and me Tarzan and Jane, and the last time I checked, I wasn't living in a tree house with a chimpanzee for a pet.

"Well, my adventure will be coming to an end in a couple of weeks," Shontay said, disheartened.

"You're coming back to the States?" I asked excitedly. I was happy that my girl was having the time of her life, but I missed having my sister around.

"Yes." She sighed. "But I have a major dilemma."

"Which is?"

"Savoy wants me to move to Atlanta, but my home is there."

"If I remember correctly, you sold your home," I reminded her. "So you're homeless, right? Rich, but homeless."

It was true. Shontay had put her home on the market when Kenny had refused to grant her a divorce and move out. Before Shontay's mother, Josephine, had passed, there was a span of several years when the two of them were not on speaking terms. During that time, Josephine had managed to score a winning lottery ticket. She had attempted to contact Shontay, but Kenny's trifling ass had blocked her number. Not only that, but he also hid all the letters she wrote to Shontay, and he stole several thousand dollars out of them—gifts intended for Shontay. After Josephine passed away, Shontay discovered the truth about why her mother wasn't able to contact her and that Kenny had known about her inheritance all along. Shontay finally made up her mind that she was done with Kenny and asked him for a divorce. Kenny agreed, on the condition that Shontay pay him half of everything she owned. Even though the home the two of them shared at the time had been somewhat of a family heirloom, given to Shontay by her grandmother, he refused to leave. The only agreement the two of them could come to was that the house would go on the market and they would split the profits from its sale. The house sold, but Kenny never received his half of the money; he was dead before the check was cut.

"You have a point." Shontay giggled. "But if I remember correctly, I have a nice studio apartment—better known as your guesthouse—waiting for me."

"Well, you *had* one," I teased.

"What do you mean *had?*"

"One of our employees is residing there."

"You gave my apartment to the hired help?" Shontay asked, laughing lightly. "Tell that broad she has to get her shit out of my place."

"I'll relay the message, but the broad is a dude," I said, "and I'm only joking—sort of. He's just staying there temporarily. In fact, this will be his last week."

"Who is he?" Shontay asked. "And what is so damn special about him that he gets to sleep in my bed?"

I took a few minutes to bring Shontay up to speed on Contessa and Kelly. I also enlightened her on the night I'd caught Kelly naked in the hot tub.

"So what is he working with?" Shontay asked, point blank.

"What do you mean?"

"C'mon, girl! His body. Is it banging? Is his dick hanging, swinging, or just barely leaning?"

I laughed, thinking back to the time when my best friend was too timid to discuss menstrual cramps, let alone the size of a man's penis. She had changed over the years, and her confidence was now off the Richter Scale. I was going to tell her that I hadn't noticed, but she cut me off.

"And don't tell me you didn't notice, because we both know otherwise."

"I really didn't get to see his man," I said, "but the rest of his body is nicely developed."

"Nicely developed? What the hell does that science textbook shit mean?"

"I could tell he takes care of himself," I said.

"Is he fine?" she asked loudly. "Can you tell me if the man is fine?"

"Why are you concerned? You're with the second-finest man I've ever seen."

"Just because I'm with Savoy doesn't mean I'm canceling all other men out of the equation."

"What does that mean?"

"It means Savoy and I have an open relationship. Although we're together, we will not rule out the fact that there might be someone with whom we may be more compatible."

"So you guys agreed to see other people?" I concluded.

"Right now, we're only seeing each other, but we've agreed to leave our options open."

I heard what she was saying, but it all sounded like a load of bullshit to me. *If you have a strong connection with someone and love them, why leave the door open? Doesn't that just invite problems or complications?* "Well, if you two like it, I love it," I said.

"Besides, we don't know what's going to happen when we return to the States," Shontay added. "After being with Kenny and being unhappy for so long, I think it's best that I take my time with my next commitment."

"I agree with you on that," I said.

"So what's up with you for tonight?"

"Well, Damon's in Georgia on business," I said, "and your goddaughter is with Mama and Daddy." I rolled over on my stomach and paused before saying, "So I guess I got nothing going on."

"Why don't you go out, Tavia?" Shontay asked. "I remember a time when you used to tear the club up."

"I don't know," I whined. "I guess marriage has changed me."

"Well, it should in some ways," Shontay said, "but it shouldn't stop you from being you. You just have to compromise on a few things and learn how to balance, but you still need your own identity and space," she continued. "Even lovers need a break."

***

After Shontay and I hung up, I decided to get my ass up and take it out for some shaking. Before leaving the house, I called Damon to check in, but the call went straight to voicemail. I concluded that he must have been in a bad coverage area, so I left him a message and was on my way.

I stepped into Club Hydro with my hair hanging straight over my shoulders, wearing a fitted one-shoulder, red, above-the-knee dress and red four-inch peep-toe stilettos. To accentuate the dress, I threw on a wide gold belt and a pair of long gold chandelier earrings. I looked ultra hot and felt super sexy. The only thing missing was my bestie.

Club Hydro was one of Shontay's and my favorite spots when we wanted to get our dance on. It had been well over a year since I had stepped foot in the place, and it seemed quite a few things had changed since then. The club was now strictly for ages twenty-five and older, and no athletic gear, baggy pants, or tennis shoes were allowed. One thing that hadn't changed was that they still played the best hip hop and R&B, and the bartender—a short, dark chocolate, chubby brother named James—made the best concoctions in the history of mixed drinks.

I sat at the bar sipping on one of my favorite drinks, something called a *panty-dropper*. I was trying hard to relax and enjoy the atmosphere, but all I could seem to think about were my husband and daughter. I decided I would have one more drink and then call it night. Sipping on my drink slowly, I sang along to Rick Ross's "Aston Martin Music" pumping through the club speakers.

"I don't take you for the wallflower type," I heard someone say from behind me.

"Kelly?!" I smiled, facing him.

He stood behind the stool where I was sitting, wearing an emerald-green button-down and jeans that were creased to perfection. Around his neck was a small platinum cross. He looked good. Slowly climbing on the stool next to me, he motioned for the bartender. "Double-shot of Hennessey please," he ordered, "and another...what are you having?"

"Um, it's called a panty-dropper," I said, slightly embarrassed, "but I was just leaving."

"Why?" Kelly asked, looking disappointed. "Have you been here long?"

"No, but I'm just not feeling it," I confessed. "I'm used to having my home girl with me."

"Why didn't you bring her?"

"She's in West Africa."

"Damn." Kelly laughed lightly. "That's a good excuse—the best I've heard yet."

"It's not an excuse," I said, smiling. "She's really in Africa."

"Well, where's Damon?" he asked, tossing his shot back.

"In Atlanta," I sighed.

"He's on the go a lot, huh?"

"Normally not back to back like he has been lately," I said, "but business called, and he had to handle it."

"So you're here all alone," Kelly said, shaking his head, "looking like *that*?" The expression on his face was unreadable.

"Like what?" I asked, playing dumb.

"Nothing," he said quickly. "Well, I'm here alone too. If you like, we can keep each other company."

I pondered his offer in silence.

Kelly looked at me with raised eyebrows then finally motioned for James to come over. "Another panty-dropper," he told him.

I shrugged my shoulders then smiled. There was no use thinking about it anymore; it was obvious Kelly had made my decision for me.

***

Twenty minutes later, Kelly and I were on the dance floor, moving to Esther Dean's "Drop it Low." I giggled and laughed at him the entire time we were moving because he had no rhythm whatsoever, but there was no shame in his game. Kelly held his head high and smiled like he was the shit on the dance floor. When Jamie Foxx's "Fall for Your Type" came on, I exhaled then turned to exit the dance floor.

"Where you goin'?" Kelly asked, gently grabbing my arm and pulling me toward him.

"To sit down," I told him. "You are not going to stomp all over my toes," I teased.

"I may have two left feet when it comes to dropping it like it's hot," he said, "but please believe I can slow-drag like a pro."

"Mm-hmm." I laughed.

"Trust me," he said, giving me a cocky smile. "I got you. Besides, you know I'm still on the mend. That's the only reason why my two-step was more of a flop."

"Hurt my toes, and I will dock your pay for a month," I said, slipping my arms up around his neck.

Placing his hands on my hips, Kelly smiled. "They're far too pretty for that," he said nonchalantly.

"True," I said, agreeing with him.

The two of us moved to the sounds of Jamie, and Kelly wasn't lying when he said he could slow dance. He was actually coordinated when it came down to slow tempos.

"So how did the two of you meet?" he asked.

"Who?"

"You and Damon."

The mere mention of how I met my husband made me smile ridiculously, like some silly schoolgirl embarrassed by a puppy-love crush. "I was sitting on my mother's porch one day, and he pulled up asking for directions," I said. "I was blown away when I saw him, so much so that I offered to lead him where he needed to go—and then some, because we ended up going out that night." I continued, "From there, things just seem to fall into place." Of course I conveniently left out the part about me screwing the dope dealer/killer by the name of Beau and all the strange occurrences that followed after Damon and I met and how Beau almost killed both us but Damon ended up killing him. I figured all those details would take away from our storybook romance a little.

"Almost seems too good to be true," Kelly said, staring at me.

"Don't get me wrong. We have our issues and problems, but the good outweighs the bad."

"Is that all that matters?" he asked. "The good outweighing the bad?"

"I think so."

"Or does it depend on the magnitude of the bad? What if things were really, really good all the time, but then one really, really bad thing happened?"

"I don't know," I said honestly. "I guess it depends on what that one thing is."

"Well, hopefully the two of you will never have to go through that," he said quickly.

"I sure hope not," I said, thinking of Damon. "I really hope not."

Kelly and I shared one more dance before we came to a mutual agreement that it was time for both of us to go.

"Have you had dinner?" Kelly asked as we approached my car.

"No…and I'm starving," I confessed.

"You wanna grab a bite?" he asked. "There's this little spot over in Providence that has the best pizza."

"Mellow Mushrooms!" I said, as I was familiar with the Italian spot since Damon had taken me there a couple of times. I absolutely loved the place.

"Yep, that's the place." Kelly smiled, rubbing his stomach. "I could go for their meatball appetizer."

It sounded so good, and my stomach was on red alert, growling like I hadn't eaten in days. The only problem was that I had a light buzz from the three panty-droppers I'd guzzled down, and all I really wanted to do was go home, throw on some shorts and a cami, and watch a good movie while talking to Damon. "I think I'm going to pass this time," I said.

Kelly looked disappointed that I had turned down his invitation. "I understand," he said. "It's just that I hate eating alone in public on Saturday nights." He gave me a sad puppy dog look that made me want to pat his head and call him a good boy.

I laughed lightly then remembered I had over 4,500 square feet of loneliness waiting for me; my immaculate home that I usually shared with my daughter and husband was empty. Bearing that in mind, I decided to offer a compromise. "I'll tell you what," I said. "I make a mean, straight-from-scratch pizza pie and some of the best cheesy bread you can sink your teeth into."

"Say no more." Kelly smiled and threw his hands up in the air like a suspect who'd been caught. "I'm sold."

I gave him a subtle smile as I pulled out my cell phone. Looking at the screen, I frowned: no missed calls or messages. Whatever had my hubby in Atlanta had him completely tied up. *Too damn tied up*, I thought, frowning even more.

***

"Where did you learn to cook like that?" Kelly asked, licking his lips.

The two of us sat at my kitchen island, finishing off our glasses of Moscato. After taking a quick shower and changing my clothes, I had made us a stuffed-crust meat pizza and garlic cheese sticks. I could barely finish half a slice; Kelly, on the other hand, had the appetite of a man who hadn't eaten in days. He gobbled down two whole slices without taking a breath in between. "My mama is a great cook," I told him. "I learned my way around the kitchen at an early age because of her."

"Do you ever cook in your own restaurant?"

"From time to time," I said proudly. "In fact, I take the time to teach each and every one of my cooks my own personal recipes."

Kelly nodded his head and smiled. "So the almost-as-good-as-sex cheesecake is one of your recipes?"

"Better-than-sex cheesecake," I said, correcting him.

"Well, as good as that dessert is, I beg to differ," he said, lowering his eyes at me. The way he was staring at me caused my stomach to flutter.

"Well, you have a right to your own opinion," I said, "no matter how wrong it is."

"Come on now," Kelly said, reclining in his chair. "Can you really compare cheesecake to sex? And I'm talking good sex," he continued, "the kind of sex that leaves your legs shaking and your mouth dry because you've been moaning all night." He paused and continued staring at me.

I didn't know if it was my alcohol high or what, but the way he was eyeing me seemed overtly sexual.

"The way your body warms slowly from the inside out because he's hitting it just right, and then when he hits that one special spot and he stays there pushing on your G-spot, making you wetter than you've ever been before and hotter than a summer day in Alabama…"

He stopped there, but the flutters in my stomach continued, sending waves of excitement further down, to my most delicate region. Yes, looking at Kelly and listening to his words had made my pussy wet. Clearing my throat, I tried to concentrate on the fact that he was my employee, the hired help, and the entire conversation crossed far too many lines. It was completely and utterly inappropriate. "Well, when you put it that way…" I said, climbing off my chair. I made my way over to the kitchen sink with my empty plate in one hand and his in the other.

"So you agree?" Kelly asked, joining me at the sink. He leaned against the counter, facing me. The two of us were close—close enough for me to smell the faint scent of Gucci Envy on his skin; close enough for his forearm to touch mine and send the fine hairs on my skin standing straight at attention like miniature soldiers; close enough that I could feel his warm breath, slightly tainted with alcohol from the Hennessey he had consumed earlier. We were so close that my nipples grew hard from his nearness, and in that moment, I knew we were too damn close!

"You do agree," he said, staring at me with his eyes low.

I looked in his eyes while clearing my throat.

He leaned toward me and slipped his hand in the warm, sudsy water I had drawn for washing dishes. He touched my hand sensually beneath the surface. "Let me help you," he said lowly as his hand caressed mine in the water.

I was seconds away from God-only-knew-what when the phone rang. Pulling my hands quickly from his touch, I moved hesitantly toward the cordless phone that was sitting on the island counter. I didn't bother drying my dripping hands; I was too thankful that the awkward shared moment with Kelly was interrupted, literally saved by the bell.

"Hello?"

"Baby?"

"Dame!" I said, looking back at Kelly.

He gave me a small smile, handed me a dry kitchen towel, then turned to face the sink again. Drying my hands, I watched him briefly as he resumed washing dishes in my place.

"I'm sorry I missed your call," Damon said, sounding extremely apologetic. "I was in a bad area, and my phone didn't have a signal. Then when I called you back, it went straight to voicemail."

"My battery died," I said, and that was the truth.

"Oh," Damon said. "Well, I'm sorry it took me so long to call you back. I had my nose buried in paperwork."

"It's okay, baby," I said, feeling slightly guilty that my man was working hard for our money while I was out shaking my ass with Kelly. "I just wanted to let you know I was going out for a little bit."

"Really? Did you have a good time?"

"Yeah," I said. "I also came to the sad realization that my life is a bore without you and Jasmine."

"I can say the same about mine," he said. "You and Jasmine are my life."

Smiling brightly, I excused myself to our family room. I wanted to speak to my husband in private, and I needed to remove myself from Kelly and the obvious sexual tension that was looming between us. "I should have gone to Atlanta with you," I said to Damon once I was out of Kelly's earshot. I plopped down on sofa to talk to my boo. "I could have visited Ilene, and the two of us could have gone shopping while you were handling your business."

"That would have been nice, babe," Damon said, "but we will make up for this time, I promise. The good news is that I won't have to take another trip for a while."

Hearing that made my smile grow wider, especially since I knew it would prevent me from getting into any further potentially compromising positions with Kelly. "Good," I said. "So how's the biz?"

"It's going well. You know how it is, boo—contracts, arguments, and…" He stopped speaking, and it sounded like he was covering the phone receiver to muffle something out. A few seconds passed and he resumed talking. "Sorry about that, hon'," he said.

"Are you at the office now?" I asked curiously, checking the time on my watch. It was one a.m. in Atlanta, a little late to be dealing with paperwork.

"No. I'm at the hotel," he said quickly. "I accidentally dropped the phone."

"Oh, I see."

"Anyway, I just wanted to call and tell you goodnight and say I love you," he said. "I'll be home tomorrow to show you just how much."

"I can't wait," I said. "I love you too, baby—always."

***

After ending my conversation with Damon, I returned to the kitchen to find the lights out and Kelly gone. I decided I'd had enough for one night, and it was time for me to retire to my bedroom. I climbed into Damon and my king-sized bed, wearing nothing but my birthday suit and a frown, an expression resulting from being naked, horny, and alone. I also had a million and one thoughts running through my head. The one that stood out the most was of Kelly and the sexual attraction, something I could no longer deny.

Chapter 19

Damon

After spending the day with Donovan at the park, followed by a visit to Chuck E. Cheese's, I discovered the kid was smart, full of energy, and very well mannered. I spent the entire day with him, attempting to make up for as much lost time as possible in twenty-four hours. When it came time for me to drop him off at the hotel with Nadia, he wrapped his arms around my neck and started to cry. I didn't have the heart to leave the kid in tears, so I opted to give him a bath and read him a bedtime story until he drifted off to sleep. I loved those father-son moments, and I was instantly caught up in them—so caught up that I didn't hear my phone ring when Octavia called. I came up with a quick lie that she believed, but it didn't make me feel any better about the situation. I was slipping quickly, and I knew if I didn't gain some control over my situation, I was going to be exposed. To make matters worse, I was almost busted on the phone when Nadia came waltzing into the room, talking to me while my wife was listening on the other end. Nadia did so even after I had told her I was calling to check on my wife. Granted, Octavia hadn't heard her (at least I guessed and hoped not), but I had a strong feeling that Nadia did it on purpose.

"Why would I do that, Damon?" she asked, rolling her eyes. "I told you

I respect your decision to keep our family a secret."

Nadia had begun referring to the three of us as "our family" at every opportunity. Earlier she had insisted upon accompanying Donovan and me on our outing, but I told her firmly that I was there to visit with my son and only my son. I didn't want her getting too comfortable around me, and I didn't want to delude her into thinking that there was an ounce of hope that the two of us would someday get back together. After pouting and trying to throw a bullshit line at me about Donovan not being familiar with me, she finally gave up.

I peeked in on Donovan one last time before going back to my hotel. I was satisfied to see that he was still sleeping peacefully. I slipped out of the room and back into the living room of the suite to find the lights dimmed and Nadia sitting on the sofa wearing nothing but a smile. There was an open bottle of *Rémy Martin* sitting on the coffee table in front of her, along with two glasses, one of which was half-empty.

"María is gone," she said, standing and walking up to me.

I allowed my eyes to drop from hers just long enough to scan over her body and then back up again. I felt a rising inside my pants and wanted to readjust my man, but I refused to allow Nadia the pleasure of seeing me do so.

Nadia stopped directly in front of me, so close that one wrong move or even a simple twitch of my hand could mean my fingers ending up in the wrong place. "DJ is asleep," she tempted, "so it's just us—just you and me." She had the audacity to reach out and slowly stroke the side of my face with her fingertips.

"Actually," I said, taking her hand in mine, "I'm leaving too."

"Marriage has made you soft, Damon." Nadia took a step forward, pressing her breasts against my chest and sending a rush of blood to my ever-hardening dick. Smiling victoriously, she reached down and cupped my crotch with her hand. "Well *some* parts of you have gone soft," she said seductively. "I knew it! You want me, don't you, Damon?"

What Nadia failed to realize was that I—like the majority of straight men in the world—am naturally physically attracted to beautiful women. My man rising to attention had nothing to do with Nadia at that moment and everything to do with the fact that there was a beautiful naked female standing there in front of me. It was really no different than a porn-induced hard-on, period; a chick in one of those films might have sucked off and ridden a dozen brothers in one day and probably reeks like sweat and dried cum, but as soon as a man sees her naked ass, his dick responds whether he wants it to or not. It doesn't mean he wants her, and it sure as hell doesn't have anything to do with love. "I want you to..." I began, jerking her hand away from my body.

Nadia's eyes lit up.

"I want you to stop thinking this is going to happen. We have a son," I said. "That's all—no more and no less."

The light that had illuminated her eyes just seconds earlier slowly dimmed, and an unflattering shade of red moved across her face. Her expression told me she was not only embarrassed but also pissed off. Nadia was silent as I walked past her and out the door.

***

The next morning I stopped by Nadia's suite to say goodbye to Donovan. I was greeted at the front door by María.

"Good morning," she said with a smile.

"Good morning, María." I entered the suite and scanned it with my eyes, corner to corner. Donovan was sitting Indian-style on the living room floor, wearing his SpongeBob pajamas and watching cartoons. I was relieved that there was no sign of Nadia, as I didn't have the patience to deal with her. I placed my hand on top of Donovan's curly locks and gently pulled his head back. "Hey, big man," I greeted, then kissed him on the forehead.

Donovan gave me approximately ten seconds of his attention, then turned his gaze back to the TV screen.

"Would you like some coffee?" María asked me.

"No thank you," I said. "I have to go. I just wanted to see Donovan before I left."

"When will we see you again?" Nadia asked from behind me.

I turned around to look at her; she looked like shit run over twice. Her hair was sticking out all over her head, and her eyes were bloody red. *Too much liquor,* I thought to myself. "I'm not sure at the moment," I said honestly. I knew if I made my visits regular weekend events, problems would arise with my real family, and I wasn't about to take any chances.

"Well, what is DJ supposed to do?" Nadia snapped. Clearly, she'd developed an attitude in an instant, and I could tell she was ready to argue.

I, on the other hand, was not in the mood for her tantrums and had no intention of listening to her rant.

María quickly moved over to Donovan, took him by the hand, and led him out of the room. I concluded she was used to Nadia's melodramatic bullshit.

"Donovan will be fine," I told her. "I'll call him, and I'll make a trip out to L.A. as soon as I can."

"But—"

"No buts," I said, cutting her off. "This is how it's going to be for now. I'll call you tomorrow, before I head back home." I stopped at the front door, pausing to look at her. I wanted to make sure she understood where we stood.

Nadia's expression told me she was not happy with my response to her question, but at that moment, I was too tired to give a damn.

"Expect a package in the mail in a couple of days," I told her.

"What kind of package?" she asked sourly.

"A credit card," I advised her. I had already made preparations and ordered an additional American Express card for Nadia under one of my corporate accounts. I knew Donovan had needs, and as his daddy, I was responsible for supplying them. The account was one I rarely used but I kept open in the event that I needed to handle some private business. It was in my name, but I had Nadia added as an authorized user. I figured giving her the card would be less hassle than sending her a check every month, and that way, I wouldn't have to worry about her calling me to ask for money.

"A credit card?" Nadia's mood appeared to lighten instantly at the thought of spendable plastic.

I decided to defuse any bright ideas she had before her thoughts began to spiral out of control. "It's to be used strictly for *Donovan,*" I ordered. "Do you understand?" I asked.

"Of course, Damon," she said nonchalantly. "I told you, I don't need your money."

"I'll keep that in mind," I said, "and you should remember that too." I opened the hotel door and began to walk out, but then I turned to look at her again. "Please don't make me regret this decision, Nadia."

The Lies We Tell For Love

***

I decided to pay my parents a visit. I needed to talk to someone, anyone who understood me without judgment, someone I could trust. That someone was my mother.

"Two weekends in a row?" Mama purred, giving me a big hug. "To what do I owe the pleasure?" she asked as she pulled away to look me over the way mothers always do.

"Can't a man visit his mama?" I asked lightly.

"Of course you can," she said sweetly. "Are you hungry?"

"No, I'm good," I said, "but thank you."

The two of us decided to sit on the balcony adjacent to the great room of my parents' home.

"Your father is going to hate that he missed you," she said. "Again."

"Where is he today?" I asked.

"He went out on the lake with some buddies of his," Mama said, rolling her eyes. "It's a monthly ritual." Mama's facial expression told me she did not approve of my father's extracurricular activities, and that reaction surprised me somewhat. I had never known her to be concerned about my father having his own time or spending time with his colleagues and friends.

"He worked hard for many years before he retired," I told her. "I guess this is his time to relax and have a little fun."

"Fun?" she said, sucking on her teeth. "When grown men have too much fun, they find themselves in too much damn trouble."

I didn't comment because I knew all too well that what she was saying was true. My one night of fun with Nadia had me wading in a sea of worry.

Before I had time to respond, the smile on her face faded into a look of concern. Stroking my cheek with the tips of her fingers, Mama studied my expression. "Something is wrong," she concluded.

I wanted to tell her everything, but I had no idea where to start. Clearing my throat, I pondered how to let my mother know all the dirt that had been going on in my love life. "Have you ever kept a secret from Dad?" I finally asked.

Laughing lightly, Mama nodded her head. "Of course I have, darling," she said. "I've lied to him too. In fact," she added, "every time he discovers something has been added to my wardrobe, I tell him I bought it last year."

"Not that kind of secret or lie," I said, folding my hands together. "I'm talking about a life-altering secret that could possibly destroy what the two of you share, just break it in two—the kind of secret that requires you to calculate your every move and guard your every word," I said, exhaling lightly.

Mama looked at me in silence, her gray eyes wide with what I felt was concern and curiosity.

"We all have something in our past that we may deem as being unnecessary information for our present," she said. "However, it is up to each of us to decide if withholding that information will have a devastating impact on our future."

I pondered her words.

"Is there something you would like to tell me?" she asked, crossing her legs.

Leaning forward in my chair, I paused briefly. "I—"

"Excuse me, madam," said Isabella, my parents' maid, stepping onto the balcony. Isabella had worked for them for years, and she had more privileges and perks than any maid I've ever met. When my mother went shopping, she always bought Isabella something, and every year Mama treated her to an all-expense-paid vacation. In my eyes and my parents', Isabella was more family than hired help.

"Yes, Isabella?" Mama asked, still looking at me.

"Sorry to interrupt," Isabella said, "but you have a visitor." I watched as Isabella raised her eyebrows at Mama.

Mama instantly rose to her feet, as if the two of them had shared some kind of telepathic message. "Excuse me, DJ," Mama said, kissing me on the cheek. "This will only take a moment."

I wondered who could have been at the door and why it required my mother's urgent departure. I sat on the balcony alone for a few seconds until my stomach began to growl and I decided to raid my parents' refrigerator. I was making my way through the great room when I heard my mother's voice.

"How dare you come to my home!"

"I wouldn't have had to if you would have returned my calls!"

I wanted to drive my fist through a wall when I heard Nadia's voice.

What the hell is she doing here? My heart pounded fiercely as I marched to the front door.

"Stay away from Damon," Mama snapped.

"What's going on here?" I asked, stepping up beside Mama. Nadia stood on the steps of my parents' home, looking like a mouse caught in the talons of a hawk. I noticed she was holding a check in her hand. I stared at her, silently letting her know that she had committed the ultimate fuck-up by coming to my parents' home.

"Nothing, Damon darling," Mama said quickly. "Nadia and I were just—"

"I need to speak with Nadia in private," I said, cutting her off.

"Damon, there is no need for that," Mama said. "Nadia was just leaving."

"I know she is," I said, stepping past my mother, "but I need to speak with her alone before she goes." Before Mama could protest, I had my hand wrapped around Nadia's arm, marching her toward the driveway where she had parked her rental car.

"Damon, you're hurting me," Nadia whined as I pulled her along with me.

I stepped around the driver side of the Honda Accord and pushed her against the door. I knew I was being rough with her, but any desire I had to be a gentleman flew out the window when I saw her standing face to face with my mother. Shooting my eyes toward the door where Mama was still standing, I waited until I saw her shut the door, leaving Nadia and me alone. "What the fuck are you doing here?" I asked, redirecting my eyes and all of my anger at Nadia.

"I-I…" she stuttered.

I had forgotten all about the check until Nadia began fidgeting with her hand, which she held tightly at her side. Reaching down, I snatched the check from her hand before she could blink twice. The check was one of my mother's, made out to Nadia in the sum of $50,000. I grabbed her by the neck and pressed my palm firmly against her throat, squeezing tightly. "What in the hell is this?!" I asked.

"Your mother was kind enough to make a donation to a nonprofit organization I'm attempting to start," Nadia said nervously.

I laughed at the thought. My mother would rather piss on Nadia then give her a drink of water, and there was no way she would be "kind enough" to donate so much as a penny to anything involving Nadia. I knew in my heart that something was wrong. "Tell me the truth, Nadia!" I yelled. "What are you doing here?" I demanded.

Nadia's face was turning red as tears began rolling over the rims of her eyes. "I am telling you the truth!" she cried. "Ask her!" Grabbing my wrist with her hands, she gasped lightly.

I could feel the pressure leaving my body, flowing through to my hand, grabbing the air from Nadia's body. I wanted to choke the life out of her the way her antics were doing to me.

"I caann't breeeathe!" she gasped.

In that moment, it was as if I blacked out and all my restraint and awareness of my surroundings left my body. I continued to squeeze Nadia's neck until a voice deep within me told me to let her go. It wasn't until I felt my mother's hand on my shoulder that I realized the voice belonged to her.

"Let her go, DJ!" she commanded.

Regaining my awareness of what I was doing and where I was, I slowly loosened my grip.

"Let go," Mama repeated.

Obeying my mother's request, I released my grip on Nadia's neck. Sliding down the side of the car, Nadia cried while clutching her neck. I bent down and grabbed her by the arm to pull her back up. Nadia leaned against my body, breathing in and out quickly. I could feel her heart beating rapidly as she struggled to catch her breath. I stepped away from her, then looked at my mother. Her expression was un-readable.

"What is this?" I asked, holding out the check.

My mother took the check from my hand and then looked at Nadia, then me, then back at Nadia again. "It's our family donation to Nadia's organization," Mama said. I watched as she extended her hand to Nadia; the whole time, she never took her eyes off her. "Our first," Mama continued, "and our last."

Nadia quickly snatched the check from my mother's hand, then opened the car door. She eased down into the driver seat, then looked up at me. The expression on her face was one of fear and anger.

Looking at her neck, I could see the imprint of my own fingers. I had lost control and done the one thing I thought I would never do—I had put my hands on a woman. "Nadia, I—"

"I'm fine," she said quickly. "Thank you, Ilene." Nadia shut the car door with fury, and I stepped back to watch her as she started the car engine and quickly pulled off, burning rubber.

I was still trying to process the events that had taken place with Nadia when I rejoined my mother on the balcony. She sat with her legs crossed and a glass of wine in her hand. Standing next to her, I remained quiet for a moment, then asked, "Since when did you start supporting Nadia?"

"I don't support her," Mama said, staring straight ahead. "That check is for a very good cause."

"Is that the only reason?" I asked. "Is there something you're not sharing with me?"

"That and the fact that I want her to stay as far away from you as possible," Mama finally confessed.

"So you're paying her to do so?" I sighed.

Nodding her head, Mama looked up at me. "I love you, Damon," she said, "and I would do anything for you—anything to protect you from hurt or harm."

Squeezing her shoulder gently, I said, "I love you too, and I know I would do the same for you." I wanted to tell my mother that I loved and appreciated her for what she thought she was doing for me, but the truth was that it was now impossible for Nadia to stay out of my life. The two of us had a child together, and no matter how my mother or I felt, we were all connected and would be for the rest of our lives.

***

After my father returned from his day on the boat, the two of us sat out on the patio, playing catch-up. "How is marriage?" he asked.

"It's good." I smiled. "How is it for you?"

"Same thang, different day," he said, "but I wouldn't change it for anything in the world."

"Not even a younger, prettier woman?" I teased.

"Hell no!" Dad laughed. "At least with your mother, I know what to expect. It'd be hit and miss with anybody else. And let's face it…I don't have that much time on my hands."

"How have the two of you made it this long and managed to stay happy?"

"Man to man?" he said.

I nodded and watched my father as he scratched his head.

"It hasn't always been easy. There are some things that come naturally, like loving your mother, and there are other things like being understanding and keeping the fires going. You gotta practice those things daily."

"I don't think Octavia and I will ever have a problem with the heat," I said, smiling. "Our attraction to each other is mutual, and we have very healthy appetites."

"That's good, son, but in every marriage or long-term relationship, there are going to be times when things just seem to fizzle out," he said. "It's easy to promise faithfulness, but the test comes with practice."

I heard every word my father was speaking, but I had my mind set. There was no way I could ever see myself being unfaithful to Octavia.

Chapter 20

Octavia

I enjoyed being around Kelly and thought he was a great guy, but the truth is, I didn't need any unnecessary distractions in my life. Nevertheless, Kelly was going to be around, at least until his work at my home was finished. After our inappropriate moment in the kitchen the night before and my personal acknowledgement that I was attracted to him, I decided to let him know how I felt and where I stood. I took a deep breath then exhaled while knocking on the door of the guesthouse.

Kelly opened the door wearing nothing but jeans that hung low on his hips, allowing a slight peek at his goody trail. His eyes traveled from mine down over my physique then back up. I was wearing a sleeveless fitted wrap dress that showed just a hint of cleavage in the front. Although the dress went down to my ankles, the way Kelly was looking at me made me feel like I was almost naked. I cleared my throat, a habit I have whenever things made me uncomfortable.

"May I come in?" I asked.

"Of course you may," he said, stepping back to let me in.

I stepped inside the guesthouse and observed how neat Kelly had kept the place. That made me very happy, because one thing I can't stand is a man keeping his place dirty, particularly when that place belongs to me.

Kelly shut the door behind me then looked at me carefully.

"Pink is your color," he said, staring at me.

"Thank you," I said.

"I love your hair down," he said, "but you look extremely beautiful with it up as well."

I touched my hair nervously and then smiled. I had chosen to pull my hair up into a bun, leaving a single curl out to frame my face. "Okay" was the only word I could manage to get out. The two of us stared at each other for a brief moment until I remembered why I had come to see him. "I, uh, I have something for you," I stammered, handing him the envelope from my hand.

"It's not a pink slip, is it?" he asked, raising his eyebrows.

"Um, no," I said, folding my hands together. I observed his expressions as he read over the papers I had given him and waited patiently until he was done.

Once he was done, he folded the paperwork and slid it back in the envelope. "A lease?" he asked, smiling at me. He seemed happy about the gift I had given him, and I was relieved.

Kelly put out so many different signals that I had no clue as to how he would react. I assumed he was ready to transition out on his own, and the Lord knows I was ready for him to go. That morning after calling my husband to tell him I love him and calling my parents to check on Jasmine, I had called my former landlord, Jayson, and asked for a favor. "Yes," I said, "I figured you were ready to get out on your own and have your own space."

"Oh you did, did you?" he asked.

"Yes," I said, smiling slightly. "It's a beautiful community located off Jeff Road."

Kelly nodded his head as he slowly walked toward me.

"They have a pool and a nice clubhouse, as well as a fitness center," I continued. "The apartment has a huge walk-in closet, a garden tub, and all stainless steel appliances." I went on giving him the details of the property, sounding like a realtor attempting to sell a listing. "It's a fairly new community, but the manager is an old friend of mine," I advised him, "and he agreed to put you on the lease, in spite of your credit issues—as long as you didn't have a criminal history."

Kelly smiled.

"I paid the deposit and the first six months of your rent."

Standing in front of me, Kelly held up his hand. "Why don't we talk about what this is really about," he said.

"Meaning?"

"Meaning you and I both know what's going on here," he said softly. "Octavia, I—"

"What's going on is that we had an agreement," I said, cutting him off, "and you have been doing a great job with your side of our bargain. Now it's time for me to live up to my end."

"I know you feel the same attraction for me," he said with confidence, "as I feel for you. That's what this is really about," he continued, "isn't it?"

"Kelly, this is about business and nothing more," I lied.

"Bullshit, Octavia," he said. "You're just as attracted to me as I am to you. Last night, I know you felt what I was feeling," he continued, "and I know you wanted what I wanted."

"Last night we had too much to drink," I attempted to reason with him, "and we both crossed the line."

"Crossed the line?" He laughed lightly. "This is crossing the line." He reached out, grabbed me by the arm, and pulled me into his body. In one swift-smooth movement, he wrapped his arms around me and silenced me with his lips before I could take another breath or mumble another word.

His lips were warm and soft as his tongue parted my lips and found mine. I felt his hand as it moved up my neck to my hair. I felt the bun I had tightly secured crumble as my hair fell over my shoulders. I felt his heart pounding inside his warm chocolate chest as his lips devoured mine, causing the warm place between my legs to throb almost unbearably. In the pit of my stomach, I felt a tingling as I let go, allowing our lips and tongues to satisfy each other. The lust burning inside of me begged me to wrap my arms around him and go further, to allow my hands to follow the trail of fine, dark hairs that disappeared below the waist of his jeans. The burning within me encouraged me to touch the hardness in between his legs that I could now feel pressing against me, through our clothes. The lust I felt was egging me on, daring me to go further. But still, the desire in my heart to remain true to Damon pulled me back, dragged me back from the hell that would have been created if I'd succumbed to that lust; it commanded me to walk away. I pulled away quickly, pushing Kelly away from me. My heart felt like it was beating a mile a minute as I tried to gather my thoughts. I took deep, quick breaths, attempting to slow my heart rate.

"Every time I'm near you," Kelly said, breathing heavily, "I want to do that."

I stepped around him and stood with my back to him, not wanting him to see the effect that our kiss had on me. "You can pick up your keys Monday morning," I said, still struggling to catch my breath. "When I come home from work, I expect you to be gone."

Chapter 21

Octavia

My hubby returned home bearing gifts and promises that he had no plans of traveling out of town for business anytime soon. Although the ring Damon gave me—a two-carat genuine heart-shaped sapphire stone surrounded by diamonds on a platinum band—made me very happy, knowing my man was going to be home to hold me made me ten times happier. When I announced that Kelly was no longer living in our guesthouse, Damon didn't ask questions; he just kissed me and said, "Good."

Kelly managed to avoid me at all costs. He didn't arrive at the house until after I left for work and made sure he was gone before I returned home. I was more than content with that. It was hard enough facing Damon, knowing what had transpired between Kelly and me, and I did not need the added stress of looking at the man with whom I had disrespected my marriage and love.

Since I now had two establishments to run, I promoted one of my employees, Amel, to act as the general manager of The Ambiance. Amel had been my employee for nearly four years and had proven herself trustworthy and loyal. Don't get me wrong…there was a time when I thought Amel was on a one-way path of destruction.

After I cut Beau off, he had begun to date her. The two of them met one day at the restaurant while Beau was having lunch with Damon. Beau met Damon when he approached him, pretending to be an investor. When I say that Beau was obsessed with me, I'm not bullshitting or stroking my own ego. The man was determined to have me, by any and all means necessary. As part of his plan, he forged a business relationship with Damon, and the two of them began spending time together. The day the two of them were having lunch, Amel saw Beau for the first time and instantly developed a crush. From the outside, I couldn't blame her. Beau had flawless dark skin and a nicely toned body. He had that bad-boy swag, coupled with a certain element of charm that caught everyone's attention. However, on the inside the brother was straight crazy. At first Beau acted like Amel didn't exist, but it didn't take long for him to change his mind and begin spending time with Amel, with the hope that it would bother me. It did bother me but not because I was jealous. It bothered me because I knew he was playing with Amel's emotions and using her to try and get back at me. The thought of sweet, innocent Amel being played because of me made me feel like crap inside. In Amel's eyes, however, Beau loved her, and she was sure all the extravagant gifts he bestowed upon her were expressions of that love. At the time, Amel was a nursing student who only worked part time for me. One day I noticed that not only was she wearing $200 weaves and carrying Gucci handbags, but she was also pushing a brand new Cadillac Escalade. I knew I was paying her above average for her line of work, but I wasn't paying her that damn well. When I questioned her about it, she happily informed me that her new man, Beau, gave the items to her. As it turned out, the gifts weren't the only thing Beau was giving her. He also introduced her to heroine.

Amel's performance at work began to go to Hell in a Gucci handbag, and her attitude with the other employees became downright nasty. I confronted her about it, and she politely told me to kiss her ass and that her man would take care of her even if I fired her. Those weren't her exact words, but that's what I took from our conversation.

If it hadn't been for Amel's mother contacting me in regard to Amel's whereabouts, I never would have taken it upon myself to go to her home, and I never would have found out she was on drugs, though I had my suspicions that something was going on with her. I convinced Amel to get help, and she checked herself into rehab and got the treatment she needed before it was too late. During Amel's time in rehab, the police were tipped off (with the help of my father) on Beau's illegal dealings, and his home was raided. Amel still stood by her man until she read in the *Huntsville Times* that when Beau's home was raided, he was in the company of a female by the name of Nicole Hathaway. Nicole, a.k.a. "Nikki," who just so happened to be Amel's best friend.

Amel finished her treatment, and when she came home, I had a job waiting for her.

I was sitting in my office going over the profit and loss statements when Amel knocked on my office door. "It's open," I said, looking up briefly.

"Hey, boss lady." Amel smiled , poking her head into the room.

"Hello, Amel," I said, smiling. "Come in." I watched her as she sat down in the leather chair directly across from me. Looking at her, I smiled, thinking about how far she had come from that terrible day when she'd confessed to using drugs. Her almond-colored skin was smooth and glowed lightly. Her hair, which she now wore in a natural fro, was thick and full. She had even gained a few pounds over the years. Standing at five-six and weighing somewhere around 135 pounds, she carried her weight well in her cream dress pants and mint-green silk button-down shirt. She had even stepped up her shoe game and was wearing a pair of four-inch gold open-toed signature Coach heels.

Flashing her pretty eyes at me, Amel smiled innocently.

I was all too familiar with the smile. "What's up?" I asked, knowing that her schoolgirl grin meant she had either done something she shouldn't have without my approval or she had some juicy gossip she couldn't wait to share.

"I sorta kinda booked The Ambiance for a wedding reception," she said softly.

My first thought was, *Hell no!* The first and last wedding I had catered had turned out to be a life-changing event for me, and I wasn't even the bride! The dresses and decorations the bride had selected were hideous and are forever implanted in my memory, and also, it was at that wedding that I unfortunately met Beau. "You know how I feel about catering receptions," I said calmly.

"I know you vowed you would never, ever do another one again." Amel sighed.

"Never," I repeated.

"Right," Amel agreed, nodding her head, "but I think this one is different."

"Does it involve a daddy's girl who has to have everything perfect for her special day?" I asked sarcastically. "The day she's dreamt about since she was a little girl and can't believe it is finally happening, so she must have everything perfect?"

"Well no," Amel said, laughing. "She's a mama's girl if anything, but all the rest of what you just said is true."

"Then the answer is no," I said quickly.

"But there is something you should know."

"Mm-hmm," I said, shaking my head. "I don't care if she offered you a million dollars, we're not going to do it."

"Come on, boss," Amel begged, clasping her hands together.

It was then that I noticed the diamond glistening on her ring finger.

Smiling brightly, she wiggled her left hand out in front of me. "Not even for me?" she asked. The smile on her face stretched further.

I grabbed her hand to admire the rock. "You?" I asked happily.

"Yes!" she giggled. "Tarik popped the question!"

Tarik was one of my former employees, one of my ultra-fine employees. At six-eight, he had mounds of muscle and a milk-chocolate complexion. He worked for me as a bouncer until he opened his own private security service. He and Amel had been dating for about a year.

"Congratulations, Amel!" I said, genuinely happy for the two of them.

"Thank you," she said. The smile remained on her face as she went into detail about Tarik's proposal and their plans to have a private ceremony on the lake, followed by a large reception at The Ambiance. "That is, if you will allow it," she said. There was evidence of doubt and hope in her voice.

Looking at her, I smiled. "You know I will make an exception for you," I said. "Just let me know the date and time."

"Great!" Amel sounded relieved. "We're planning on about 100 people for the reception, and we want the full catering package. Just name the price, and I'll write you a check for the deposit."

"Okay," I said, pretending to hit the keys on the adding machine sitting on my desk. "Hmm...50 percent of zero is, uh...zero."

"What?"

"Amel, I'll do it for free," I said. There was no way I was going to charge her. She was my right hand at The Ambiance, and I loved her.

"Octavia, I can't let you do that." She had tears in her eyes as she looked at me.

"You don't have a choice in the matter," I said. "Just give me your menu, the date, and the time."

"Oh, thank you, Octavia," Amel said humbly.

"No…thank you for allowing me this opportunity to do this for you and Tarik," I said sincerely. "Is there anything else I can do?" I asked. I was willing to help Amel in any way possible. She had turned her life around and was on her way to a beautiful new beginning with Tarik. I was happy for her and wanted to show my support emotionally and financially, in any way I could.

"Just one more thing," Amel said, dabbing at the tears that had made their way down her cheeks.

"Name it."

"I want you to be at the wedding," she said. "I mean, will you be my maid of honor?"

I was honored but completely surprised by Amel's request. "Are you serious?" I asked, smiling.

"Tarik is my best friend," she said, "and besides my mother, you are the only female I trust and have a genuine love for. So yes, I'm very serious," she said.

"I would be honored," I said sincerely.

After a peaceful silence, she said, "I keep asking him why he loves me," and she shook her head as if she couldn't believe it.

"Why wouldn't he?" I asked, leaning forward in my chair. "You're beautiful, intelligent, and one of the sweetest people I know."

"And a former heroine junkie," Amel said sadly. "Tarik could have any woman in the world."

"But he chose you," I said. "That's all that matters. Your past is your past. Look at you today and just imagine where the two of you will be in the future. Amel, stop asking that man why he loves you and start celebrating the fact that he does." I was speaking words that I once had to tell myself. I could not—or, better yet, didn't want to—believe Damon truly loved me. What I discovered, however, is that when we stop questioning love and doubting whether or not we're worthy of being loved, everything falls into place and goes according to plan. "And stop reminding yourself and Tarik of who you used to be," I added.

Nodding her head, Amel smiled slightly. "Okay," she said.

"Promise?"

"Promise." She rose from her seat and began walking toward the door. "I almost forgot," she said, turning to look at me. "A woman came in a couple days ago. She asked Tabitha if she could speak with the manager. When I went out to speak with her, she told me she wanted to compliment us on the service and the food."

"That was nice," I said, always happy to hear positive feedback from our patrons. I knew if he or she took the time to tell us how much they enjoyed dining at The Ambiance, they would take the time to tell their friends or colleagues the same.

"Yes, it was," Amel said, "but after that, she started asking me strange questions."

"Like what?" I asked curiously.

"She asked me about Beau and how he died," Amel said flatly.

It had been nearly three years since Beau's death, and I couldn't imagine why anyone would be asking about him. "Hmm. Do you think it was someone who used to be friends with him?"

"I did, but then she asked me something else."

"What?"

"About the incident at the grand opening of The Ambiance 2."

That sent my radar up. After Kenny's and Donna's deaths at The Ambiance 2, reporters swarmed both of my establishments. If it hadn't been for HPD repeatedly stating that the three deaths were in no way connected, I'm sure my businesses would have gone under. I assumed that whoever had questioned Amel was from the media and was trying to get their big break by finding a flaw in the system.

"Don't worry about it," I said, rolling my eyes. "She was probably just a reporter, trying to get some juicy gossip."

"True," Amel agreed.

"See, Amel? That's why I tell you to leave your past in the past," I said, exhaling. "No matter what you do or where you go, there will always be someone who is more than happy to remind you of where you came from."

Chapter 22

Damon

I hadn't seen Donovan in weeks, and I have to admit that I missed him. I wished I could have both of my children in the same home, but that seemed impossible. I had spoken with him over the phone almost every day, and each time I felt more and more like shit—not just because I had assumed the role of a part-time father, but also because I was concealing the truth from my wife.

I tried to nonchalantly bring up the subject of men having children with other women just to see where her head was. After that conversation, I felt even more torn about telling her the truth.

The two of us were lying in bed when I brought it up. "Babe, a colleague of mine and I were talking about marriage and communication," I said.

"Um, men discussing marriage alone?" she joked. "Was this a woman-bashing session?"

"Naw, never that," I said. "Anyway, we were talking, and he was telling me about a dude he knows who found out he has a daughter by a woman he used to mess with."

"Okay," she said, looking at me.

"Well, the dude is married now, but his little girl is something like eight."

"How long has he been married?"

"Four years," I said, "and the baby's mother didn't tell him about the baby until around six months ago. He had no idea he had a child by her."

"That's trifling," Octavia commented. "So now she wants to pop up with their daughter?"

"Well, the woman claimed she didn't know for sure that he was the father," I said.

"Do you think she's lying?" she asked.

"According to him, they had a DNA test done, and he's the father."

Her eyes were wide. "Wow," she said. "How did his wife take the news?"

"That's the issue," I said. "He hasn't told her yet. That's why he wanted to talk to me about it. He isn't sure what to do."

"What?" Octavia was wearing an expression of utter disgust. "How could he not tell her?"

"Well, he says that before the two of them got married, she expressed some, uh, well less-than-appealing views about men having outside children."

"I can understand that," she said. "I mean, I thought Kenny was the scum of the Earth for having a child with Alicia. But the truth is, I didn't like how the situation played out. Shontay found out over the telephone. I mean, yeah, he cheated, but he could have put it on the table. How in the hell did he think he was going to be able to keep that kind of secret?"

I had forgotten the entire story behind Kenny and Alicia and how the news of Kenny fathering Alicia's child was unveiled. According to Octavia, Shontay had her check a number that Kenny was calling daily, and Kiya, Kenny and Alicia's daughter, answered the phone. Kenny was there and took the phone from her. That was how Shontay discovered Kenny had a child; she heard Kiya call her husband *Daddy*. At that point, Kenny had no other choice but to fess up.

"Think about it," Octavia continued. "Telling her would have been bad, but waiting for…wait, how long has he known now?"

"Six months."

"Waiting for six months is ten times worse," she continued. "There's probably been 100 different opportunities for him to tell her, yet he hasn't. She'll probably flip out and question everything he says from here on out, and I can't say as though I'd blame her."

The Lies We Tell For Love

"You're probably right," I said, pulling her into my arms. I took a deep breath then slowly exhaled. I didn't comment any further, seeing as though it was totally unnecessary.

As for Nadia, she kept her conversation with me brief. I could hear in her voice that she was still pissed about what had taken place at my parents' home. Granted, putting my hands around her neck was the wrong thing for me to do, but her agreeing to stay away from me while knowing she would never be able to do so was just as wrong.

Since returning home from my visit with Donovan, I had been spoiling Octavia with gift after gift. I didn't mind in the least, as she is worth every dime and then some. I had another surprise planned for her that I could hardly way to give her, a gift I had been promising her for a while. I had finally decided to take the time to make good on my promise. I was in my office wrapping up details of a business deal when I received a surprise visit. "Come in," I said, after hearing a knock on my office door.

"Sorry to disturb you," Louisa said as she opened the door, "but you have a visitor."

I glanced at my Rolex and saw that it was a quarter till four p.m. I knew I had to be out of my office no later than four thirty so I could pick up Octavia's gift before five. "Who is it Louisa?" I asked patiently. I had fulfilled all my appointments for the day, and I was clueless as to who could be there to see me.

"A very charming young man." Louisa smiled. "He says he works for you."

"What's his name?" I asked, looking down at my watch. I always tried my best to make time for my employees, but at that moment, I was completely focused on my wife, trying to make sure I'd be able to surprise her like I'd planned.

"Kelly." Louisa smiled like she'd hit all six numbers and the damn Power Ball on top of it. "Kelly Baker."

I wondered what Kelly could possibly want and why he suddenly felt the need to pay me a visit at work. "You can let him in," I said.

A few seconds later, Kelly strolled into my office, dressed like he was heading to an office of his own. He had on a dark suit and a dark pair of Stacy Adams. "Thank you for seeing me," he said, extending his hand to me.

"No problem," I said, offering a firm shake. "Have a seat. I see the cast is off," I said, observing that Kelly's cast and sling were now gone.

"Yes, I just left the doctor," he said, sitting down across from me. "It feels a little funny, but it's good to have two working arms again."

"I know it is," I agreed.

"Listen, I know you're busy," Kelly said, leaning forward in his seat. "I just wanted to tell you that I had a job interview earlier and I got a job. After I finish the garden at your home, I will be teaching at Monrovia Elementary."

"Congratulations!" I said sincerely.

"Thank you," he said, bobbing his head. "I appreciate that. I also want to thank you for your hospitality and everything you and your wife have done for me."

"You're welcome," I said, "but to be honest, all the credit should go to Octavia."

Kelly looked away for a second then said, "Yeah, she is something special—a very kind-hearted woman. She's a rare find in this world."

It wasn't Kelly's words that sent my radar up, but the way he was saying them. He sounded far too jealous for my taste. "The world is full of good women," I told him. "You just have to find yours."

"Maybe," he said. "How did you do it?"

"What do you mean?"

"How is it that you lucked out and found that one?" he questioned. "She's so beautiful, talented, and giving."

"I guess I was in the right place at the right time," I said. Leaning forward, I clasped my hands together on the desk in front of me.

"Almost sounds too good to be true," he said, running his hand over the hair on his chin. "I mean, Octavia told me the story of how you two got together, but it almost sounds like a fairytale. It's so…perfectly calculated. Shit!" He laughed. "In my mind, for something to go down like that—I mean, to find that happily ever after—a man would almost have to make it happen himself."

My conversation with Lawrence ran through my mind. *Is there something more to Kelly that we missed?* "I believe a man has to go for what he wants," I said calmly. "If you leave things to chance, you can end up empty-handed and assed out."

"Hmm. I'll have to remember that," Kelly said in a tone that sounded slightly threatening. "Go for what you want? Yeah, I can do that." He stood and adjusted his jacket. "Anyway, I better get going," he said. "I won't be around for a few days, if that's all right with you."

"That's fine," I advised him. "Is everything okay?"

"Oh, everything is good," he said. "I'm just going to dip out of town for a minute and visit an old friend. I figure I better do it now before my schedule gets too hectic."

"Understandable," I said.

"Well, thank you for your time, and please tell Octavia I apologize."

"Apologize? For what?" I asked.

"Oh…" he said with raised eyebrows. "For not telling her first about my new job."

"Why don't you just tell her yourself?" I asked curiously. He and Octavia had a much closer connection than I had with the man, so it seemed odd for him to suddenly ask me to serve as the middleman and relay messages.

"I just felt it would be too uncomfortable hearing it from me," he said. "She'll know what I'm talking about." He turned and walked to the door.

"Kelly…"

He stopped at the door with his hand on the knob but didn't turn around.

"There's one thing about going after what you want," I said. "Just make sure that whatever it is, it's not already another man's prize."

He nodded and mumbled, "I'll try to keep that in mind."

I sat at my desk staring at the door after he exited. My last statement to Kelly was more of a warning than just friendly advice.

***

After picking up Octavia's gifts, I called to let her know I was heading home. I was still tripping off my conversation with Kelly, but I was not going to allow that to ruin my mood or what I had planned for my wife that night. "I'll be home shortly," I said over the phone.

"Okay, baby," Octavia said in that sexy, enticing voice of hers. "I'll be waiting in the dining room. Dinner will be done by the time you get here," she added.

"Baby, you didn't have to cook," I said. "We could have ordered in."

"I'm happy to cook for you," she said. "You know I like my man to have home-cooked meals."

I was thankful for that because the woman knows her way around the kitchen. However, I understood that she had a career and was a mother and was good at being both. I was delighted to come home and find my meals on the table, but I never wanted her to think it was mandatory. "You are the best, baby," I said. "I love you, and I'll see you when I get there."

"Love you more," she said.

I walked through the door carrying two dozen long-stemmed red roses in one hand and a gold envelope topped with a big red bow in the other.

Dinner was waiting for me in covered dishes on our dining room table, where Octavia was sitting, dressed in a pink lace negligee that was nearly transparent and hugged her body like a glove. I took one look at her, and my man began to get hard. "Are those for me?" she asked sweetly.

"Only if you tell me that that," I said, pointing at her, "is for me."

She stood and walked around the table toward me. I noticed she was wearing pink platform heels. Her legs looked like they belonged on a runway—long and sculptured without an ounce of fat. "All yours," she said. Cradling my face in her hands, she pressed her soft lips to mine. Then she pulled away and smiled sweetly

"Where's Contessa?" I asked.

"At Kelly's for the night," she said. "Jasmine is upstairs sleeping, so the two of us can be as bad as we like."

"Sounds good," I said with a naughty smile.

"I'll take those now," she said, reaching for the roses and the envelope.

"You can have these," I said, handing her the flowers, "but this has to wait until after dinner." I teased her by holding up the envelope and wiggling it at her.

Poking her lip out, she frowned. "Fine," she said, easing the negligee up to reveal her bare clean-shaven pussy. "You can't have any of this until after dinner either then."

I reached down to cup the warm place between her legs with my free hand. "How do you know I wasn't planning on having this for dinner?" I asked.

"Oh, so I guess the smothered pork chops, turnip greens, macaroni and cheese, and fresh baked biscuits I made will all go to waste," she said, shrugging her shoulders.

My stomach immediately began to growl, as anxious to have some of that as my dick was to have some of her. "There is no sense in that," I said quickly. "You know me, baby. I'm always up for seconds—or at least for dessert."

She pushed my hand away playfully and laughed. "That's what I thought," she said.

***

Good food and good conversation with a beautiful woman makes for a perfect evening, but good food and good conversation with a beautiful woman you love is priceless. After dinner, Octavia and I cuddled in our family room, talking about our day. Octavia lay with her head on my shoulder, stroking my chin with the tips of her fingers.

"Kelly came to see me," I told her.

"Really?"

"Yep. Said he had just left a job interview with the school system," I said. "He got the job. He told me to tell you that after he finishes the garden, he will be working at Monrovia."

"Wow," she said. "That's great."

"Yeah, it is," I said, tightening my arms around her. I was waiting for her to further comment, but she never did.

"He's going to be out of town for a couple of days," I informed her. "Visiting some of his people."

Octavia nodded her head but remained quiet.

"He also asked me to apologize to you."

"For what?" Octavia asked, clearing her throat.

"Not telling you himself," I said. "He said he thought it might be too uncomfortable and that you would know what he meant. So what did he mean?" I asked.

Octavia cleared her throat again. It was the second time she had cleared her throat in less than five minutes. I knew from experience that the only time Octavia ever clears her throat while speaking is when she is nervous. The wheels inside of my head began to spin. I wanted to know what about our conversation about Kelly had my wife on edge.

"I don't know," she said. "Maybe because I'm the one who hired him or something like that."

"You're probably right," I said. I decided not to address my concerns with Octavia. I had my way of finding out anything I needed to know, and if there was something Octavia wasn't telling me, I would find out in due time.

"Well, I'm glad he is going to have a career in his field," she said. "Contessa will be proud." She looked up at me then smiled. "Almost as proud as I am of my wonderful husband."

"Aw, thank you, baby," I said sincerely. I slid my hand down her legs and began to rub and massage her thighs gently.

"Mmm," she moaned. "That feels good."

Pulling her up onto my lap, I slid my hands over her round ass. Her skin was as soft as cotton and as smooth as silk. "I bet I can do something that feels even better," I said, kissing slowly along the curve of her neck.

"I know you can," she whispered, stroking the top of my head, "but first…" Pulling away, she stared at me with her beautiful brown eyes. "First I want my other present."

Laughing, I thrust my hips forward, pushing my hardness up against her open legs. "You don't want this present?" I teased.

Octavia slipped her hand down in between us and massaged my rod through my pants. "Oh, I plan to unwrap that shortly," she said seductively, "and I'll handle it with the utmost care."

"Promise?" I asked, squeezing her breast gently. I watched as her chocolate nipples grew hard with my touch.

"That's a guarantee," she moaned.

"Go grab it off the table." I barely had the words out of my mouth before Octavia was off my lap and running barefoot back to the dinning room. I chuckled as I watched her. She looked like a little girl on Christmas morning, excited about a present under the tree.

A few seconds later, she returned with the open envelope in her hand, waving the two airline tickets in the air. "Paris!" she squealed, jumping up and down.

"Yes, baby." I laughed lightly. "Paris."

Her face was beaming with excitement, and seeing how happy she was made me happy. She ran back over to the sofa and climbed back onto my lap. She gave me a long, passionate kiss on the lips that made my pulse race.

"I love you, Damon," she said, looking into my eyes. "You are so good to me."

"You deserve nothing but the best, baby," I said, running my fingers through her hair.

"You are the best," she said. "You're better than I could ever imagine a man being, and never could I have imagined that I would be this happy. I'm so lucky," Octavia said. She looked at me, and I could see tears welling up in her eyes. Octavia has always been strong, and few things make her cry. If I remember correctly, the only time I'd ever seen her shed tears was when we had unbelievable make-up sex after a short break up when Beau sent me that sex tape, and also when she held our daughter for the first time. Although, she shares her thoughts and feelings with me often, Octavia seldom ever cries while expressing herself. Seeing her tears and feeling the truth in the words she expressed further fueled my desire to protect her from all hurt and harm.

"I'm the lucky one," I said, stroking her cheeks with my fingers. "Never forget that," I said. "Never forget that you and Jasmine are my world and that without the two of you, I'd—"

"Shh," she said, cutting me off. "I know, and we're not going anywhere," she promised. "The three of us will always be a family, and you are stuck with me for life."

"Life?" I said, smiling.

"Yes, life," she laughed, "without parole." She kissed me again, this time slipping her tongue in my mouth and finding mine.

The two of us kissed until we were practically out of breath.

"Why don't you lock up down here?" she suggested. "Then meet me upstairs in the bedroom."

"Sounds like a plan," I said. I held onto Octavia as I stood. She wrapped her legs tightly around my waist, pressing herself against my dick. The action caused my man to jump slightly. I gently eased her down onto the floor then adjusted myself through my pants.

Smiling, Octavia lowered her eyes. "I'll be waiting," she said. "Just the way you like."

"And how is that?" I asked, although I was quite aware of what she meant.

"Buck-naked, with my legs spread," she said seductively.

The image alone made my dick harder. "Promise?" I asked.

"Guaranteed."

"Give me two minutes to set the alarm and lock it down," I told her. "Then I'll be upstairs to put it down."

"Promise?" she asked, batting her long lashes at me.

"Guaranteed," I told her.

I watched as she turned on her heels and began walking toward the staircase with her wide hips swinging from side to side. When she reached the stairs, she turned to look at me then slowly eased the negligee she was wearing up her hips and over her head, revealing her perfect naked body. She blew me a kiss then winked at me before strutting up the staircase. All I could do was shake my head and smile.

After ensuring that all the doors were properly locked and secure, I walked into the kitchen to make sure the patio door was locked. Once I saw that it was, I punched my pass code on the alarm keypad and flipped down the flat-screen monitor that was concealed underneath one of the kitchen cabinets. I had spent over $100,000 on the high-tech security system that ran throughout my home, and I made sure I was getting my money's worth. All the cameras installed outside my home appeared to be working fine, with the exception of one on the south side of the property. There was a picture there, but it was slightly fuzzy. I made a mental note to check it out the first chance I got, but at that moment, all I wanted to do was get upstairs and inside my wife.

***

Two hours later, Octavia lay with her head on my chest, running her fingers along the curve of my biceps. Running my index finger down the curve of her naked back, I closed my eyes.

"Amel and Tarik are getting married," Octavia said, breaking the silence.

"That's good," I said sincerely. "Tell Amel I said congratulations."

"I will," she said, yawning lightly. "She asked me to be her maid of honor."

"You accepted, right?" I asked.

"Of course," Octavia said quickly. "I also volunteered to pay for the reception."

Kissing the top of her forehead I smiled. I wasn't surprised at all. In fact, I wouldn't have been surprised if Octavia had ended up paying for the wedding. My wife is like that—always a giver who would do anything to help another person out. "That was sweet of you, babe," I told her.

"I figured it was the least I could do." She sighed. "Amel is a great employee, and she's been through a lot, so I just—"

"You weren't responsible," I said, cutting her off. I already knew where she was going with the conversation. Octavia felt guilty, as if she was responsible for what happened between Amel and Beau, but the truth is that Amel was a grown woman, and her decisions were her own, as were the consequences that resulted from them.

"I know, babe."

Octavia turned on her side so that her back was facing me.

I rolled over and wrapped my arms back around her so that my chest was pressed against her warm, naked back.

She looped her fingers through mine then yawned again. "Oh, I guess there's some member of the media trying to get her next big break," she said, laughing lightly.

"What do you mean?"

"Amel said a woman came in to The Ambiance asking questions about Beau."

"Maybe she heard through the grapevine about Amel's engagement to Tarik," I said nonchalantly, "so now she's trying to dig up old wounds." Octavia had advised me that Tarik was starting to do security for some major players, from rappers to ball players. He had branched out from being just a local name and was now making connections across the country.

"I didn't consider that factor," she said. "I guess because Amel told me she also asked about the incident at The Ambiance 2. And when I say *incident*, I mean—"

"The shootings?" I concluded.

"Yep."

"Did she give Amel her name or show ID?" I asked. I still had little to no concern about the fact that someone was curious about the murders. I had covered my ass and covered it well. I figured that whoever was snooping around must have been new to the city and didn't have the right connections. By "right connections," I mean they weren't linked to anyone who worked for the city or state. If they were in the loop, they would know better than to even attempt to ask questions about the nights Beau and Kenny died, so I had to assume that whoever the person was, it was just an innocent civilian who liked to gossip.

"Nope," Octavia said. "She didn't give her name or anything. Just came in for lunch and asked to speak to the manager. Amel said she went out to speak to her, and the woman complimented her on the food then started with her questions."

"You're probably right," I said, kissing her on her neck. "She was probably just some amateur-ass new reporter, looking for a scoop—hoping to blow up by finding a flaw in the system or some form of conspiracy."

"I'm sure that whoever she is, she'll soon discover that we have nothing to hide. Not a thing." She sighed.

Chapter 23

Damon

My morning had started out with a bang. I was awakened to the warm sensation of my wife's lips wrapped around my man, followed by what felt like the best nut of my life. After that, Octavia told me it was a freebie and she needed no pleasure in return. When I asked what I had done to receive such royal treatment, she smiled and held up the tickets to Paris that she'd kept on the bedroom nightstand.

"Remind me to surprise you more often," I teased.

The two of us took a quick shower together, shared breakfast, then went our separate ways.

I had a few client consultations scheduled for the morning, and I planned to take the rest of the afternoon off and spend some family time with my wife and daughter. However, the first thing on my agenda when I arrived at my office that morning was to make a phone call to Lawrence. I was just getting ready to make the call when Louisa buzzed me to let me know that I had a call from American Express on Line 1. After verifying my identity with the customer service supervisor, Angela, I finally got the chance to ask her about the reason for her call. As it turned out, Nadia had attempted to make a $30,000 purchase using my card. I didn't give a damn what she was trying to buy; I was just relieved that I had set up alerts requiring major purchases over $500 to be approved by me. After I ended my call with Angela, I picked up my desk phone and dialed Nadia's number.

"Helloo!" She sounded like she was singing on the other end of the phone.

"Look, Nadia, I told you specifically that the AmEx card was to be used only for Donovan," I spat without even bothering to say hello.

"Yes, and that's all I've spent it on," she said. The happiness I heard in her tone changed instantly.

"Really? What the hell could Donovan possibly need that cost thirty grand?"

"It's actually thirty plus," she said, exhaling a sigh as if she was annoyed with having to explain herself. "I was going to pay the difference in cash, but since you refused to approve the purchase, I guess I'll be jumping on public transit with *our* child."

"What's wrong with the car you already have?"

"Nothing," she said, sucking her teeth. "I just want a new one. Is that a problem?" she asked.

Nadia was really getting on my nerves from the other end of the phone. I decided I'd better wrap up the conversation before things took a wrong turn. "Not at all," I said calmly.

"Great. So you're going to approve the purchase." She stated, not asked, and I could hear the victorious smile in her voice.

"No."

"What?"

"I'm not buying you a car, Nadia. I'll buy a car for Donovan when he turns sixteen, but you're on your own."

"Are you serious?"

"Hell yeah I'm serious," I said. "What would make you think I owe you a car when you already have a perfectly good one?"

"Humph. I bet if your wife requested it, you'd do that for her," she snapped. "Hell, you'd probably buy the whole damn dealership."

True, I thought to myself, *but we're not talking about my wife.* "I'm not going to argue with you about this," I said firmly. "If you want the car, you can pay for it out of your own pocket."

"Damn it, Damon! If I had that kind of money, I would have already paid for it!" she yelled.

"Well, you don't and I won't," I said.

"In that case, don't worry about it," she said, sucking her teeth from the other end of the phone. "I'll just get the money from Donovan's grandmother."

My heart rate increased instantly. "Wait…what did you just say?" I asked, clenching my fist.

"From his grandmother," she repeated loudly. "Ilene."

Click. She hung up before I could respond.

I had lost my focus and forgotten my reason for calling her in the first place; now my mind was set on letting her know exactly how I felt about her threat to contact my mother. I dialed her number again and immediately got her voicemail. I wanted to go completely in on the message and let her know exactly what would happen if she went through with her threat, but I knew that was not my best option, as I didn't want that shit recorded. I decided to hang up, wait for a few minutes, and try to call the trifling ass again.

"What?" she snapped.

"Don't you ever threaten me again," I said through clenched teeth. "And stay the fuck away from my mother, or—"

"Or what?" she dared, cutting me off. "Or what, Damon? You know, you talk big shit for a muthafucker who has so much to lose," she continued. "Maybe I should reach out to your wifey instead. I'm sure she would love to know the truth about who she's really married to."

There was a sarcastic tone in her voice that just grated on my nerves, and it was in that moment that I knew what I had to do. Nadia could have very well been bluffing, but it was a chance I was not willing to take. It was time for our secret to be revealed. "Do whatever you feel you need to do, Nadia," I said. "As a matter of fact, you don't have to bother telling my wife anything. I'll tell her my damn self."

"Oh, really?"

"Yes," I said. "I can't keep hiding Donovan like he's some kind of disease. My son doesn't deserve that," I said sincerely. "Octavia will be angry, but I know our love is strong enough for her to forgive me."

"Congrats," Nadia said even more sarcastically. I could hear her clapping from the other end of the phone, rubbing it in. "Good for you. But will she be willing to overlook your other dirty little secrets?"

"And exactly what are you referring to?" I asked.

"You think because you have money that you can make all the bad shit just disappear?" she taunted.

"Again, what the hell are you referring to?"

"L.A. is a big city, Damon," she said, "until you become *somebody*. Then you find out exactly how small the social circle of the elite really is."

Sitting forward in my chair, I listened in silence.

"Speechless? You?" Nadia asked, laughing lightly. "That's right, Damon. People talk—especially women."

"If you have something to say, just spit it out," I ordered. "Why don't you tell me whatever it is you think you know and quit playing games?"

"Well, for starters, I know that Alicia Green is more than a helpless damsel you rescued from distress."

"Alicia and I went to school together years ago," I said casually. "So what?"

"Damon, you and I both know that's not all there was to it. Don't lie." Nadia laughed.

"You don't know shit," I said angrily.

"Hmm. I don't? Are you sure about that?" she taunted. "Tell me, Damon, is that a chance you're really willing to take?"

"I've been taking chances all my life, Nadia," I said. "What's one more? If I were you, I'd be very careful when it came to picking my battles," I warned. "And I'd be even more careful about who I started a war with." continued, "Money doesn't make all the bad shit disappear, but the right amount of it can get rid of the wrong people."

Silence.

"I'll see you soon," I said, breaking the pregnant pause.

"Soon?" Nadia's tone changed. The arrogance and sarcasm had been replaced with what sounded a lot like fear.

"Yes," I said. "Soon. I'm coming to get my son," I added.

Click.

I hung up before she could respond simply because there was nothing left for the two of us to discuss. Nadia felt the ball was in her court, and truth be told, she was right because she had my son and my secret in her arsenal. It was time for me to gain control of our situation and put the ball back in my own damn hands.

"Hello?" Octavia answered.

"Hey, baby," I said, looking at my watch. "I'm going to have to cancel our lunch date."

"Aw!"

"I know. I'm sorry, sweetheart," I said. "Something came up, and I have to take care of an issue with a client, but I'll definitely be home in time for dinner."

"Mm-hmm," she said, smacking her lips. "You owe me...and Jazz."

"I know," I said. "How about I treat my two favorite girls to Ruth's Chris?" I asked.

"Let me think," she said. It took her less than three seconds to come back with an excited "Okay!"

"I love you, baby."

"I love you too," I said before ending the call.

***

Lawrence stared at me from the other side of my desk. Smiling, he erupted in laughter. I had just brought him up to speed on everything that had been going on with Nadia and the fact that she and I had a son together. I had completely forgotten about Kelly, for at that moment, I had bigger issues to contend with. "I just want to know how you expected to pull this off?" Lawrence asked, shaking his head.

"Pull what off?"

"Keeping wifey from finding out about your illegitimate child," he said, leaning forward in his chair. "I mean, don't get me wrong, 'cause you're good, but damn, man!"

I knew Lawrence was right, but I didn't have the time nor the patience to dwell on where I'd gone wrong with the situation with Nadia. The only thing I was concerned about was keeping my family together. I knew telling Octavia about Donovan was going to be a chore all its own, and though I was sure she was going to pop completely off, I felt in my heart that she would ultimately forgive me. I had bigger problems to worry about. If Nadia really did know more than I thought she knew and decided to get brave and start running her mouth, things were going to come out about me that I was sure Octavia would be unable to forgive. "Can you handle this or not?" I asked impatiently.

Lawrence stood and adjusted his jacket. He offered me a small smirk and a nod. "Have you ever known me to turn down an assignment?" he asked as he walked to the door. "Consider this shit done," he said before exiting.

Chapter 24

Octavia

It was "pamper me day," which included my mid-month trip to the Hair Tip to see my stylist, Mona. She was the salon owner and had been doing my hair for almost nine years. She had several other qualified stylists working for her, but I refused to allow another stylist to touch my hair. Mona did a great job, never overbooked herself, and never kept me waiting. As long as she continued that kind of customer service, I would always remain one of her most loyal customers. I sat in Mona's styling chair flipping through the latest edition of *Black Hair* magazine while Mona trimmed the ends of my dripping wet hair.

"So Shontay's still out gallivanting around the globe?" Mona asked.

"Yes, ma'am." I laughed lightly. "And she's loving every minute of it."

"Good for her."

"I know that girl deserves it," I said, thinking about my bestie. I hadn't talk to her in weeks, and I was sure she would have been back in town by now. I made a mental note to give her a call just to see how things were going. "Oh, I wanted to ask you about some products," I said, suddenly remembering the items I had in my bag. I reached into my purse and pulled out the bag where I had placed the shampoo and oils in from Déjà Vu Salon. "I received these as a gift," I told Mona. "Are they really all natural?"

I needed to know before I used the items. The last thing I wanted was to wake up with my hair all over my damn pillowcase.

Mona removed one of the bottles from my hand and nodded her head. "Oh, this is the new top-of-the-line stuff," she said happily. She opened the bottle and took a big whiff of it. "Damn, girl, this smells good."

"So it's on the up and up?" I asked.

"Hell, yeah!" Mona exclaimed. "You are looking at fifty bucks a bottle right there."

"Really?"

"Yes, ma'am," she confirmed. "Hubby knows how to spend," she said.

"Well, these didn't come from my hubby," I informed her. I told Mona that the basket was sent anonymously and that I assumed the salon owner was just looking to do some marketing.

"Girl, the chick behind these products is the next Paul Mitchell," she said. "She is banking. I seriously doubt she would send her products to anyone for free. And if she is doing that, where in the hell is my gift basket?"

"Who is she?" I asked.

"Name's Lena Jasper," she said. I watched her as she dug through a stack of magazines that were lying next to her station. "I hate when these broads borrow my ish and don't return it!" she huffed. "Who has my copy of *Today's Black Woman?*" Mona yelled Standing with her hands on her wide hips, she scanned the room with her eyes.

"My bad, Ms. Mona," said Jade, Mona's nail technician. I watched as Jade walked across the wooden floor, swinging her lean hips from side to side, until she reached the station where Mona and I were.

Jade was a beautiful Latino woman with emerald-green eyes and something I could only refer to as a J-Lo ass. She always wore her silky black hair in cornrows, straight to the back. She licked her lips and winked at me. Jade had been making passes at me on the low every since Mona had hired her three years earlier. Mona kept her around because she was the best nail tech in the city and could do nails by hand or with a drill. Plus, she was the bomb when it came down to designs. I had to give her credit for her work, but the trick worked my last nerve with her lesbian come-ons. I have no problem with how people choose to float their boats, as long as they don't try to put their tongue on mine uninvited. For the longest time,

The Lies We Tell For Love

Jade claimed to have a live-in boyfriend, but she finally came out of the closet eight months before this. I just so happened to be in the salon the day she made her big announcement.

"Excuse me, excuse me," she said, standing in the middle of the room. "I have a confession to make."

Everyone stopped what they were doing to focus on Jade and her big confession.

"I'm a lesbian," she said proudly.

We all looked at her like we were waiting for her to say something else. When she didn't, everyone continued working, back to business as usual. There were no comments, whispers, or even gasps of shock. Why? Because people don't stop to make news out of shit they already know!

She handed Mona the magazine then looked at me through the glass. "Looking good, Ms. O," she said, shamelessly licking her lips again.

Cutting my eyes at her, I gave her a smirk. "Keep on with that, and I'll tell your wife," I said.

"What my wife and your husband don't know won't hurt them," she said with a coy smile.

"When Hell freezes over, Jade," I said.

"So you say, O...so you say." Jade laughed, then strutted off.

"Leave Octavia alone!" Mona snapped, flipping through the magazine, "and stop borrowing my books if you're not going to return them." Mona chuckled and looked at me. "That girl is determined to get at you."

"She is determined to get her ass kicked then," I said.

Mona found the page she was looking for and handed it to me. "See? Lena Jasper," she said, crossing her arms across her breast. There was an article in the beauty section of the publication, featuring an up-and-coming stylist in Los Angeles who was taking the West Coast by storm. "That heifer is getting paid," Mona said, tapping the page with her fingernail. "She is so hot she refuses to be photographed."

According to the article, Déjà Vu was a full-service salon, offering everything from hair and nail care to skincare and makeup. The salon was the biggest of its kind, rated number one in the area since its opening a little over a year ago. In less than a year, the salon had already doubled what it took to open. In addition to her salon, Lena planned to open a boutique within the next year.

I sat there trying to remember where I had heard her name before. I thought maybe Mona had mentioned her before and I had forgotten, but I still couldn't understand why anyone would send me a gift that was valued over $500, according to Mona. It made no sense, but I was going to enjoy the freebies anyway. I planned to use each of the products, and if I really enjoyed them, I would be sure to order more.

***

Damon seemed incredibly tense that night as the two of us lay in bed. When I inquired about his day, he simply advised me that it had been a little rough. "Is there something I can do to help alleviate the stress?" I asked, running my hand across his bare chest.

"Not tonight, bay," he said. "Let's just lie here."

I agreed, but I was extremely concerned. Whenever Damon and I were in the same city, with the exception of one of us being under the weather, there was only one week out of each month when we didn't indulge in something sexual. Other than that, making love or engaging in oral sex was something we did on a daily basis. Daily! It didn't matter if one of us was snoring with one eye open. We enjoyed each other every single day. "Are you feeling okay?" I asked, worried about him.

"Yeah, baby," he said. "I'm fine."

What the hell? I touched his forehead nonchalantly just to see if he had a fever. He felt fine to me. Damon wasn't sick, and Mother Nature hadn't come calling on me yet, so I had no idea what could possibly have had my hubby so distracted that he wasn't in the mood to touch me. It wasn't like him at all. Flashbacks of my moment in the guesthouse with Kelly invaded my mind. *Is it possible that Damon knows something? Certainly, he would have said something to me by now. Oh, God…if he knows, maybe he's so hurt that he's just speechless? Confess, Octavia,* the little voice in my head whispered to me. *Shut the hell up!* I whispered back to that bitch. She was trying to get both of our asses in hot water! I decided to leave well enough alone. I was 100 percent certain that Kelly was not going to rat either of us out. Besides, it wouldn't be much longer before he'd move on to live and work elsewhere. I planned to ride it out. *After all, he'll be out of our lives soon enough, right?*

Chapter 25

Damon

I hadn't heard from Nadia, nor had I been able to get in contact with her since the last time we'd talked. I decided one sure way to get her to contact me was to cut her credit card off. I had yet to tell Octavia about Donovan, and I didn't have a damn clue what I was waiting for. Maybe there was a small part of me that was hoping Nadia would break the news and take some of the pressure I felt off me. It was a straight bitch move, but I'm man enough to admit that. I knew there was no way the information would sound better coming from the other woman, but at the same time, I had held the secret inside for far too long. My mind was set on what I had to do, but then Lawrence came to see me unannounced.

For the first time since I had been doing business with him, he wasn't dressed in a suit. Instead, it was a khakis that were creased to the tee and a money-green Ralph Lauren polo shirt with white and green Air Max. I was going to joke with him about finally tricking some unsuspecting woman into going out with him, but the look on his face told me the news he had for me was no joking matter. "What you got for me?" I asked.

He handed me a large manila envelope then reclined in his chair. "First of all, your baby-mama doesn't reside in L.A.," he informed me bluntly.

"What?"

"Nadia relocated to Atlanta more than a year ago," Lawrence advised me.

I could understand her wanting to move, especially with the direction her career was going. What I couldn't figure out was why she lied about it. "What else you got?" I asked. I was anxious to see what else Nadia had been up to, but I was completely unprepared for what Lawrence had to tell me.

He opened the envelope and slid out some documents and several photographs. He handed them to me and shook his head. "I would have gotten back to you sooner," Lawrence advised me, "however, I wasted two days in L.A. looking for the bitch, only to discover her ass moved across the country."

I could feel my anger boiling inside of me as I read over the papers Lawrence provided, everything from copies of Nadia's petition for child support to records of another paternity test. Of course the paternity test showed that the other man was not the father.

"Look at the pictures," Lawrence urged. "I have a name and address for the blonde in the first photograph."

"I don't need her name," I said angrily. "I already know the bitch." Staring at the pretty blonde female in the picture with Nadia, I reminisced about the day we'd meet. Her words echoed through my head, *"Right this way, Mr. Whitmore."* Lawrence had captured pictures of her having lunch with Nadia and the two of them shopping. They looked like they were having a wonderful time—all at my expense, I was sure. "Give me her address," I demanded. "I'm going to go pay her a visit."

"Which one?" Lawrence asked. "Baby-mama or ol' girl."

"Both," I said. As I glanced through the last three photographs and clenched my fist. The other pictures showed her in what appeared to be a heated argument with a woman. For a moment, I thought my eyes were playing tricks on me, but the pictures were vivid and clear.

"I told you shit don't just happen, D," Lawrence said lowly.

"I see that," I said, running my hand over my head.

"You need some help handling this?" he offered. "I got a new client I'm meeting up with in the A this week anyway. I'd be more than happy to help you clean this up."

I shook my head. "No, just get me a car," I said, "nothing flashy. That's all I need." As I stared at the pictures, I began planning my next move. "I got this," I said, "Yeah, I got this."

***

I was in my own zone for the entire drive home. I had so many questions that needed to be answered, and I was overcome with emotions after what I'd learned from Lawrence. The biggest emotion of all was anger.

I was almost finished packing when Octavia walked through the door. The smile on her face quickly dissipated when she saw my open bag lying on the bed. I was expecting her to throw me some attitude at any moment about having to go out of town again, but she didn't. Instead, she stood with an unreadable expression on her face. "Damon," she said slowly, "where are you going?"

"I have to go Atlanta for a few days," I explained. "There is a major problem at the office."

There was something in Octavia's eyes that looked like relief. "Oh," she said. "Okay,"

"Baby, what's wrong?" I asked, extending my arms to her.

She walked over into my embrace; wrapping her arms tightly around my waist. "It's just…well…after the other night, when you didn't want to have sex," she said, "I thought something was wrong between us. And now I come home and find you packing your bags," she rambled.

Cradling her face in between my hands, I looked into her eyes. "Babe, I was tired and stressed out the other night," I reassured her. "That's all it was. We are going to have those moments, but that doesn't mean I want you any less."

Her honey-brown eyes were wide and clear as she looked at me, not uttering a word.

"I love you, Octavia," I said. "Leaving you is the one thing you never have to worry about from me."

She smiled the smile I had grown to love. "I love you more," she whispered to me.

Lowering my head, I kissed her lips slowly. I wanted to treasure every second of the moment the two of us were sharing because I knew in my heart that once I returned from Atlanta, the life we knew and shared would never be the same.

Chapter 26

Octavia

When I came home and saw Damon packing his bags, I wanted to throw myself at his feet and beg him not to leave! Okay, maybe I'm being a little dramatic, but it felt like my heart was going to drop to my toes. There was a look of anger that I had only seen once before, the day I came home and found him watching the video of me and Beau. When I saw that expression, I immediately thought he knew about Kelly. Maybe I should have known better, but it takes a lot of brain power to keep a secret from your spouse. Add that to all my day-to-day work and responsibilities, and it's easy to panic at the first sign of anything. I was feeling so guilty about Kelly that I didn't even bother to trip when Damon advised me he was going out of town—yet again. Now that I think about it, I was somewhat relieved that I would have a few days to get my mind right and some time to sit down with Kelly.

The garden Kelly had created was breathtaking. There were trellises covered with ivy and jasmine and beautiful green shrubs and azalea plants. Kelly had planted two flowering cherry trees and even a Japanese maple. There was a small pond in the middle of the garden that would later be home to some koi fish. A few minor details still had to be handled, like the koi pond and the stone path leading from the main house to the garden, but for the most part, the overall condition of the place was beautiful. There was a bench made of solid oak that you could sit on and watch the fish in the pond, as well as a small watering fountain. Kelly was on his hands and knees arranging stones around the pond when I approached him. "It looks absolutely wonderful," I said, standing behind him.

"Thank you," he said. He stood facing me. "I'll have it completed by this afternoon." Dusting his hands off on his jeans, he scanned the area with his eyes. "I wanted to create a place of harmony and serenity," he said, "a place where you can come and be at peace—just you and your thoughts."

"I like it," I said.

"Good, because I had you in mind while I was creating it," he said, staring at me. "Your smile, your eyes, everything about you."

Kelly's voice was low and seductive, and I suddenly felt uncomfortable in my place of peace. "I think we should talk," I said quickly. I sat down on the bench, then waited as Kelly took a seat beside me. "I need to make sure the two of us are all right with what happened," I said, looking at him.

"You mean the kiss?"

"Yes."

"If you're asking me if I'm going to tell Damon," he said, laughing lightly, "you don't have to worry about that."

"That wasn't what I was asking," I said. "I'm going to tell him myself."

Kelly looked surprised. "Why would you want to tell him something that will just make him angry or suspicious?"

"Because Damon and I don't keep secrets between us," I said confidently, "and I'm not going to be the one to start."

Kelly's eyes grew wide. "No secrets?" he asked with raised eyebrows. "Are you sure about that?"

"Positive," I said.

"As long as you're sure," he said. "I hope nothing ever falls in your lap that contradicts your theory."

"I'm sure it won't," I told him. "I know my husband, and when it comes to honesty and loyalty, he is nothing less than the truth."

***

Damon promised that I could choose any week I wanted for us to take our trip. I decided that since I had time on my hands for once, I would start making preparations. One of the things I wanted to make sure I had was a global phone. I knew I was probably going to be too busy making love to my husband in Paris to call anyone, but considering that we are parents, I wanted to make sure I could call home and check on Jasmine with no problems. I sat in our home office on the phone with Verizon Wireless, discussing my upgrade options. After ten minutes of the customer service representative giving me more information than I knew what to do with (half of it being things I did not understand), I opted to go online and look at the available devices and plans myself. I knew the rep had a time limit on her call, and I've personally never liked being rushed to make a decision. I logged into mine and Damon's account and started browsing through their available Smartphones. I found one that caught my eye, a global Blackberry, and I jotted down the name and model number. I'm a hands-on kind of woman, and I usually never make a purchase without trying an item out first, but at least when I went into the store, I would know what I was looking for and the features I intended to use. I was preparing to log off of our account when something—most likely my overactive curiosity—led me to look over our phone bill. My husband has always been a talker and not a texter, so it somewhat surprised me when I saw that he had message usage. Another woman might just assume her man was texting a client and leave it at that, but I'm not that woman. I pulled up the details and waited for the page to load, showing me the number, date, and time. The messages were received a few weeks prior, when Damon was in Los Angeles, all from a number I didn't recognize. I would like to say I left well enough alone, but of course I didn't. Instead, *67-1-760-555-5555 was recited over and over in my head until I dialed the number.

The phone rang several times before voicemail picked up. "You've reached Lena. I'm sorry I missed your call…"

I placed the cordless phone back in its cradle and couldn't help but wonder why the name "Lena" was suddenly popping up every damn time I turned around. The day I'd heard it at the salon, I couldn't remember why it sounded familiar, but now Lena Jasper was all coming back to me. I hadn't *heard* it before; I had *seen* it because Lena Jasper was the name written on the check I found in my husband's jacket. I was willing to bet both of my businesses that the Lena on the voicemail was Ms. Jasper. Her voice made her sound like a walking slut-bucket just waiting for a drop! Damon had been noticeably nonchalant about her, as if she was nothing more than a tenant, and when I'd asked him about the products from Déjà Vu, he'd acted like he'd never heard of the shit before. *If she's nothing but a tenant, why would she feel so relaxed sending her landlord's wife a present? How many landlords have tenants who send expensive gifts to their wives? Not a damn one I can think of!* I decided it was high time for me to find out a little more about Ms. Lena Jasper and exactly what her connection was to my husband.

I Googled Déjà Vu Salon in Los Angeles. My search popped up over ten articles about the salon and Lena herself. After ten minutes of reading and researching, I found a piece of information that almost knocked me out of my chair. When the salon opened a year earlier, it had been financially backed by an independent investor. Even though the investor's name wasn't listed, he wasn't anonymous to me. When I read that he or she was linked to Gold Mortgage, I knew the investor had to be my husband.

"Déjà Vu. How may I assist you?"

"I'd like to make an appointment," I said, tapping my fingers on the desk.

"With whom?" The receptionist sounded entirely too happy for my blood at the moment.

"Lena Jasper," I answered.

"Are you a new client?"

"Yes."

"One moment. Let me check Ms. Jasper's availability."

I sat with the phone pressed to my ear and my temper churning slowly. Kelly's words echoed in my ear: *"No secrets? Are you sure about that?"* I wasn't so sure of anything anymore.

Chapter 27

Octavia

I called Damon and advised him that Amel and I were going to Memphis to look for wedding dresses. Of course it was a lie, but most alibis are. I trusted Contessa with Jasmine, but in the event that something happened, I felt that Mama and Daddy would be better suited to watch their grandbaby while I took an overnight trip. I planned to be in L.A. no longer than forty-eight hours, just long enough to meet that Lena chick, catch a nap, then fly back home. I sat in the waiting room of Déjà Vu Salon, anxiously awaiting my name to be called—actually for the pseudonym I had given them. I had a ton of scenarios running through my head as to how my meeting with Lena would play out. Although several of them included me beating her down to the floor with a can of oil sheen and a flat-iron, I was optimistic that the two of us were going to survive my visit without any blood or hair being shed.

I glanced around the room, admiring the details. The salon had wall after wall of floor-to-ceiling mirrors and hot pink and black tiles checkered on the floor. In fact, hot pink appeared to be preferred color scheme in the establishment—the employees' polo shirts, the stylists' smocks, and the styling chairs were all the same shade of electric pink.

"Victoria!" I heard Joni call.

I rose, acknowledging that I'd heard her call "my" name.

"This way," she guided, smiling happily.

I followed her through the waiting room and down the hall to what she explained was the VIP room. When I'd made my appointment, I'd specifically requested the VIP section. I wanted to have plenty of privacy with Lena in the event that she might say something to me that I didn't want to hear and I'd have to go pop-to-the-crazy.com on her ass.

"Ms. Jasper will be right with you," Joni advised me before exiting the room.

The VIP room had one styling station and one shampoo bowl. According to the information Joni had provided me over the phone, it was reserved for clients who preferred complete privacy. When Joni advised me that the room was $100 an hour to rent, in addition to whatever services were rendered, I knew it was intended for clients whose money was long. I stood by the styling chair, waiting for Lena and trying to decide what I was going to say to her and how I was going to say it.

"You must be Victoria."

I turned on my heels and finally saw the woman behind the name. She was tall, with deep, dark skin and a nice body. She wore a dark designer suit with a short jacket and wide-leg pants that showed off just the right amount of her leopard-print wedge shoes. I had to silently give the woman credit for her sense of high fashion. Her hand was extended to me, but when she saw who I was, she immediately dropped it back to her side. "Octavia?" she said. She spoke my name like I was a ghost who had walked out of her dream and landed smack dab in the middle of her reality.

I returned the favor and looked at her like she was the Ghost of Whores from the Past and had just come back to haunt me. "Alicia!" I said in disbelief.

***

Alicia, who I now realized also went by "Lena," suggested that the two of us go somewhere to talk over a cup of coffee. I told her that was fine, as long as the coffee shop had a bar where they served wine! My nerves were completely shaken, and I needed something a whole lot stronger than Juan Valdez. We ended up at a little bistro restaurant a couple blocks down from her salon. It was a sunny October day, so we opted to sit out on the patio.

The Lies We Tell For Love

I stared across the table at her, taking her new look in. It was as if she'd gone through a complete makeover. I'm not just talking about hair, makeup, and clothes, but also a complete reconstruction—a reprogramming. Lena was sophisticated and articulate, as well as pretty—a far cry from the ratcheted Alicia I'd first met years ago in a rundown motel room. I dropped my eyes down to her breasts for a second then back up again. *I wonder how much she paid for those?* I thought to myself. *Or did Damon invest in those too?* Suddenly my anger trumped my curiosity, but I managed to hold my tongue for a while longer.

We sat in silence until the waiter returned with a bottle of Moscato and two frosty wine glasses.

"I think the two of us are way past the point of friendly greetings," I said, the first to speak, "so why don't you just tell me what in the hell is going on with you and my husband!"

Lena took a casual sip from her glass and looked at me. "There is nothing going on, Octavia," she said. "Damon and I are just friends."

"Just friends?" I questioned. "When did the two of you become *friends?*" I demanded, throwing quotation marks around the word in the air as I spoke it.

"Octavia, I really think these are questions you should ask Damon," she said.

"Oh, I plan to," I said, "but right now I'm asking *you,* woman to woman, exactly when did you and my husband become friends?" I was also wearing a designer suit and heels, but I'd have no problem getting dirty or knocking blood from Lena's mouth!

Lena took a deep breath then exhaled. "Damon and I have known each other since we were teens," she confessed, "but we lost contact with each other until just before Kenny's death."

"What?" I asked.

"Octavia, you asked for the truth," she said, "woman to woman, and the truth is exactly what I'm about to give you."

I relaxed in my chair and crossed my legs. "I'm listening," I prompted.

"Damon and I met in Atlanta, during my freshman year in high school," she explained. "We dated for a little while, until my family relocated to Huntsville."

I closed my mouth and opened my ears as Lena went on, telling me her side of the story.

She advised me that Damon had put a private investigator on her tail after I told him how much drama she was causing in Shontay's marriage. Apparently, that was when Damon discovered who she was and remembered her from school. "He approached me with a business proposition," she said. "If I agreed to leave town, he said he would help me start a new life here." She confirmed that Damon fronted her the money for her business and also placed her and her daughter in their current home. I had to respect the fact that her decision to change her name was fueled by her desire to keep what happened that night at The Ambiance 2 from effecting her career. She advised me she left her daughter Kiya's first name the same, but everyone called her by her middle name, Janai, and her surname was now also Jasper.

"Did Damon proposition you before or after you agreed to help Shontay?" I questioned.

Lena looked surprised that I had remembered that little detail. When Shontay was on the mission to rid herself of Kenny, she had gone to Alicia and asked her for her help in setting Kenny up. I playfully called the entire scheme "Operation Shakedown," but the truth was that I knew from the very beginning that pulling Alicia into the plan was a bad ideal. "Their offers were almost simultaneously," she said. "What does that matter?" she asked. She seemed offended that I had asked, but I couldn't have cared less.

"It matters because my best friend broke you off a little change," I reminded her, "and because you accepted my husband's offer. It matters because it seems you are just in too deep with the people I love. And in addition to that, you're sending me gifts?" I asked, shaking my head.

"Gifts? What are you talking about? What gifts?"

"The little basket of goodies from your salon," I advised her.

"I didn't send you anything," she said. "I would never betray Damon's trust like that."

Her loyalty to my husband bothered me, and I planned to make sure she understood she was once again riding for the wrong man—a man who would never be hers. I kept these thoughts to myself for the time being, but I did share my curiosity with her about who would have sent a basket of her products to me.

"I don't know," she said. "Maybe it's just a coincidence."

The Lies We Tell For Love

"I don't think so," I said. "I'm willing to bet whomever it was wanted me to find out about your friendship with my husband, and I can't be pissed with them," I said, looking her square in the eyes. "There are some things a woman deserves to know. Are you sleeping with my husband?" I stared Lena directly in her eyes, anxious for her reply.

"No," she said.

"And why should I believe you?" I questioned. "If I remember correctly, you had no problem sleeping with a married man not so long ago."

Lena looked slightly offended by me bringing up the past, but like I said, I couldn't have cared less. It was the truth, and the truth doesn't change, even if people do. "You should believe me," she said, sucking on her teeth. "You know your husband, and we both know he would rather die than betray you."

I searched her eyes with mine, looking for a drop of deception; I found none, though I did see something that resembled jealousy flickering there. "Now that you have your new start," I said, leaning forward, "I feel it's time for the ties you had with my husband to be broken."

Lena looked at me with raised eyebrows. "I told you we are just—"

"Just friends," I recited. "I know. However, much like your previous life, there are some things better suited for the past." I reached into my purse and dropped a 100-dollar bill on the table for our waiter. "Anyway, I have a flight to catch," I continued. "I'll make sure any loose ends you and Damon might have are wrapped up immediately."

"Octavia, don't you think the decision to end our friendship should be left up to Damon?"

"Of course," I informed her. "I'm just preparing you in advance for what's coming next."

"And exactly how do you know that's how it will turn out?" she asked, though her confidence looked slightly shaken.

"Because, as you said earlier," I said sarcastically, "I know my husband."

Chapter 28

Damon

*L*awrence had a car waiting for me, a Chevy Malibu, at my office when I arrived in Atlanta. I'd been parked on the curb outside the townhouse of Nadia's friend for only an hour, but it felt like days. Finally, Gia pulled up, just the woman I had come to see. She climbed out of a black Chevy Tahoe, dressed in dark jeans and stilettos with a white t-shirt with "Who's Your Daddy?" in big red letters on the front—a dramatic change from the uniform I had first seen her in that day at her job. I watched as she removed her handbag and several shopping bags from the trunk then strolled up to the door.

Once she was inside, I made my approach. I pulled the hood of my sweatshirt down over my head. The attire I had chosen for the mission, oversized sweats and steel-toed boots, was completely out of character for me, but these weren't normal circumstances. I rang the doorbell and waited impatiently for her.

When she finally answered, she swung the door open with a big smile plastered on her face, until her eyes locked with mine. "Is there... something...I can help you with?" she stuttered.

"Let me in," I ordered softly.

"Do I know you?"

I didn't have time to play games, so I lifted my shirt up to show her the .45 I had tucked in the waistband of my pants. Her pale face seemed to turn whiter. "Let me in," I demanded again.

Backing away from the door slowly, she did as I ordered.

I quickly stepped inside the foyer and locked the door behind me.

"Listen," she said nervously, "my boyfriend will be home any minute, so—"

"You and I both know you live alone," I said, staring at her. "And even if you didn't, do you really think I would care at this point?"

She shook her head. "No."

"All right, so why don't we cut the bullshit? Tell me everything I want to know," I said calmly.

"I..I..I..don't know what you're talking about," she stuttered.

I grabbed her by the arm and pushed her, forcing her to sit down on the small leather sofa. "Well, allow me to introduce myself," I said, pulling the gun out of my pants.

Her brown eyes grew bigger as I aimed the barrel of the gun at her face.

"Now do you remember me?" I watched as tears began to fall from her eyes, leaving tracks down her cheeks.

"Damon?" she whispered. Her lips quivered as she said my name.

"I thought so," I said. "Now, I want you to tell me what your connection is to Nadia Jones."

"We don't have one," she said slowly.

I respected her loyalty, but it was not the time for her to be loyal to anybody but me and that weapon of mine. A person has to choose their battles, but when you're staring down the barrel of a loaded gun, you'd better make sure you choose correctly. I was two seconds away from doing something we both would regret. I kept my eyes locked with hers as I pulled the pictures Lawrence had given me out of the side pocket of my pants. I dropped them onto her lap and cocked the gun.

Gia jumped slightly in her seat as she moved her eyes from the gun to me then back down to the gun.

"This is your last chance," I told her. "You can tell me the truth the first time, so we'll both walk away unharmed, or you can continue with this little game of yours, and I can put a hole in your head."

Her tears began to overflow.

"You decide," I told her. "What's it gonna be?"

"Okay," she sobbed. "Please…just don't…please don't hurt me."

I took a step back, putting distance between the two of us. I lowered my weapon to my side and took a deep breath. "I'm listening," I prodded.

"Two years ago, Nadia came into the office and said she had some questions," she began to explain. "I answered them, and she went on her way. A couple days later, my car quit on me down the street from my job, and Nadia just so happened to be passing by. She gave me a ride home and called AAA to come tow me. We struck up a friendship that very same day. I was in a very bad place financially, and Nadia offered to help."

"Right. Now get to the part that involves me," I ordered. I wasn't in the mood to listen to the damn fairytale behind their friendship. I wanted to know what her friendship with Nadia and her position at the DNA Diagnostic Center had to do with me—nothing more and nothing less.

"That's it," she said. "There is nothing else. I know it was a conflict of interest for me to be involved with the testing, especially with Nadia being my friend, but I administered the test anyway."

Gia's story seemed far too convenient for me, damn near contrived. "You think I believe that?" I snapped. "There's something you're not telling me. I want the truth, and I want it now!" I raised the gun back up, aiming it at right at her face.

Gia threw both of her hands up in the air.

I brought the gun back down to my side.

"Okay," she said. "Okay! Originally she offered me ten grand to tamper with the results, to make it out that someone else was the father, but when she called me to schedule the appointment, she told me she'd changed her mind. That's it, Damon," she pleaded. "I promise."

"Why would Nadia want someone else to be Donovan's father?" I questioned.

"Because she was offered money," she said. "That's why."

"Money? From whom?" I asked.

"Your mother."

Gia continued to explain that my mother had approached Nadia and offered her money to claim that another man was Donovan's father, but Nadia apparently loved me too much to do that. I had to tune Gia out as I attempted to decipher what she was telling me.

"Nadia loves you, Damon," she rambled on and on.

I felt my muscles tighten and my hand shake as I raised the gun and squeezed the trigger. The *bang* from the shot jerked me back from my mental blackout. Gia sat on the sofa in a pool of what I presumed to be urine. Her breathing was heavy, then shallow as she stared at me in horror. The shot I'd let off had made a mess of her wall. Running my free hand over my head, I processed everything I'd just learned. "If you tell anyone about this—"

"I won't, I won't! I promise," Gia pleaded. "I won't say a word to anybody."

I gave her one more glance before pulling the hood back on my head and walking out the door. I sat behind the wheel of the car pounding my fist on the steering wheel. I had to get back to my office, trade the rental Malibu in for my Range Rover, get to my hotel room to change clothes, and make one more stop. I was hoping the woman I was going to see could shine some light and clarity on the situation because I had more questions than answers.

"Talk to me," Lawrence answered.

"Listen, I just left the blonde," I told him as I drove toward my parents' home. "I had to get a little out of character, so—"

"Is she dead?" Lawrence seemed somewhat enthusiastic about the possibility. The man has a sick sense of humor.

"No," I said quickly, "but I need you to make sure she keeps her end of the bargain and remains quiet about my visit."

"Consider it done," he said. "What about baby-mama?"

"I have a stop to make before I head in her direction," I advised him. The more I thought about it, the more I was sure Gia had probably jumped on the phone to warn Nadia of my visit. "Tell you what," I suggested, "why don't you go ahead and pay her a visit, too, but don't go in until I get there?"

"I got you," he said, and we hung up.

Chapter 29

Octavia

*I*n life and love, there comes a time when we realize our mate has been untrue. It could be something as simple as lying about a phone call or something as grand as having a sexual affair. No matter how big or how small the infidelity may be, it evokes painful emotions within. I was disappointed by the information Lena had provided me. She had given me a play-by-play of how Damon had given her the helping hand she needed to launch her career. The things Damon had done for her, such as giving her a townhouse, were things that shouldn't have shocked me in the least, because my Damon has always been a giver. He's always believed that for every million you earn, you should strive to give back to at least a million people. If I hadn't been so hurt by the whole thing, I would have been proud of him. However, he made one mistake—he lied to me. Lena told me she hadn't slept with Damon, and I believed in my heart that she was telling the truth, but there was a yearning in her eyes that told me she was thirsty, and she wanted a nice, tall glass of my husband. I was in no way concerned about this because despite the disappointment I felt toward him at that moment, I still loved and wanted him and I'll be damned if I'll ever let another woman lay a finger on my man.

I made it back from L.A., and my first stop was by my parents' home to pick up Jasmine. My mother told me she wanted to talk to me about something, I told her I needed to talk to her as well. The truth was that I needed some motherly advice. Mama and I sat out on her front porch, reclining on her swing. She was dressed in a soft pink peasant blouse and cream skirt that touched just below her knees. I had thrown on a pair of fitted jeans and a red fitted Victoria's Secret shirt and white Nikes for the plane ride. My hair was pulled neatly on top of my head, tied with a red satin ribbon. I was in a dress-down mood, but I refused to look completely thrown off. Even in the midst of a storm, a woman must keep it sexy! I decided to see what Mama wanted to talk to me about before bombarding her with my drama.

"I'm happy you met Damon," Mama said after asking me about my trip to what she thought was Memphis.

"I am too," I said. No matter how I felt about his secrets, I still considered him one of the best people who has ever entered my life.

"I sleep peacefully knowing you have someone to love and protect you," she said, taking my hand in hers, "someone to be the man to you that your father is to me."

I looked away so Mama wouldn't see my telling expression.

"I'm so proud of the woman you have become," she continued. "The wife, the mother."

"Well, I learned from the best," I said, looking back at her.

"I love you, baby." She smiled.

"I love you too."

There was silence between us for a moment, as I meditated on her words while thinking about Damon.

"Octavia…" she said softly, gulping slightly.

"Yeah, Mama?"

"I-I have cancer." Her words were spoken soft as cotton, but the impact they had on me was as heavy as a brick wall tumbling down on my spine.

I looked at her, gauging her expression. There was peace on her face and serenity in her eyes. To be honest, it sent chills down my spine and goose bumps across my skin. "What did you say?" I asked her slowly. I wanted her to repeat her words, but not for fear that I hadn't heard her correctly. I heard her clearly the first time, and I knew Mama was not the type to make what would be a cruel, heart-wrenching joke. In that moment, though, I needed her to have some ill, twisted sense of humor. I needed those words to be a lie. I needed that very moment to be nothing but a bad dream that I was awaiting God to wake me from. However, when Mama squeezed my hand tightly and looked at me with compassion in her eyes, I knew before she repeated herself that what I'd heard the first time was real.

"I have cancer," she repeated. "Breast cancer."

"Are you...are you sure?" I stuttered slowly.

"I've been going back and forth to the doctors and specialists for the last month," she informed me. "I didn't want to tell you until I was 100 percent sure and until I believed it myself. It's true, Tavia," she said gently, "and I've accepted it."

In that moment, I wanted to pull her into my arms, stroke the top of her hair, and tell her everything was going to be all right. I wanted to tell her I was there for her and that she was going to beat that awful disease. I wanted to be the strongest woman in the world and let my mother know that there would be no tears and no sadness because that ugly, life-altering parasite had chosen the wrong woman to mess with and that we were going to win this fight. I wanted to do and say all of those things people say to each other in those moments, but I couldn't. Inside of me, there was a wall of pain and unstable emotions. When I attempted to part my lips and offer my mother encouragement, that wall came crashing down on the inside, and my tears overflowed on the outside. I felt weaker than I had ever felt in my life. The physical pain I'd experienced during the birth of my daughter was like a pinch on the arm compared to the emotional pain I felt at that moment. I slid from my place on the swing and, like a child pleading their parent not to go, I wrapped my arms around my mother's knees and cried out in sorrow. I felt my mother's hand as she stroked my hair, and I heard her voice as she told me without reservation that everything was going to be all right. Still, though, I continued to cry, allowing my tears to saturate the soft material of her dress and dampen her skin. I felt like I was letting her down in that moment, and I knew I was being selfish, but I didn't care. Cancer had invaded my mother's body. Cancer had come into our lives and violated the only person other than my daughter that I loved more than myself. *How dare this disease touch what was given to me?* I was having a selfish moment, and although I knew in my heart that my mother's illness wasn't about me, I could not get over the agony of knowing where this new, unsolicited journey in my mother's life might lead and where that would leave me. In that moment, as the knot in my throat felt like it would choke me, I went from being a grown married woman with responsibilities to nothing more than my mother's baby. I was her child, and I could not bear the thought of her leaving me. "Why?" I managed to choke out. "Why?"

"You know better than that," Mama said, sliding her hand under my chin.

I lifted my head so that my eyes were locked with hers.

"We don't question God," she warned me. "We take whatever He gives us, and we pray. We pray for understanding and for the strength to accept that which He has given—the good and the bad. Then we thank Him. We thank Him for the chance to learn and for all that He has blessed us with. We tell Him that if He does not do anything else for us, it's okay because that which He has already given us is much more than we've ever deserved."

"I love you, Mama," I said, wiping my face with the back of my hand, "and I appreciate everything you have done for me and the woman you are."

"Thank you, love," she said, wiping her own eyes.

"What can I do for you?" I asked. "How can I help?"

"Pray," she said. "I haven't given up Octavia, and neither should you. We will do what we can to make the best of what we have, and we will remember it is not over until He says it is over."

I forced myself to smile while continuing to hold on to her lap.

"Now," she said, "what was it you wanted to talk to me about?" she asked.

I pulled myself back up on the swing next to her. "Nothing," I said. "Nothing at all." I chose not to tell Mama about my problems because in the grand scheme of things, they no longer mattered. When something so big as what my mother was going through enters the scene, all the petty little things go out the window.

***

My drive home seemed longer than usual as rain pounded fiercely against my windshield. I was trying hard to focus on the road in front of me, but my visibility was extremely low in the downpour, and the thoughts running through my mind were keeping me from being able to concentrate. If I had been alone, I would have continued to drive, but Jasmine was in the back, sleeping peacefully in her car seat, and I refused to risk my daughter's life. I drove a little further and stopped at the first gas station I could find. I pulled into the parking lot and killed my engine. Leaning against the driver side door, I stared out the window. My tears resurfaced, and I began to cry again. I pulled my Blackberry out of the console and dialed Damon's number. I attempted to call him twice, only to get his voicemail both times. "Please call me," I pleaded on his recording, "and if it is at all possible, please come home. I need you." I wanted my husband there with me to hold and comfort me. I sat in my car waiting for the rain to ease up, and finally my phone rang, but it wasn't Damon.

"Where are you sweetheart?" Contessa asked with concern oozing from her voice.

"Ms. Contessa…" I cried.

"Charlene told me," she said. "I know, baby. I know."

I could not manage another word, so I just cried softly.

"Where are you?" Contessa asked again. After I told her my location, she said, "Stay there."

Thirty minutes later, there was a tap on my car window. I let the car window down and saw Kelly standing in the rain. "Unlock the door," he ordered.

I did as he requested, and in less than twenty seconds, he'd pulled me out of the car and had his arms wrapped around me. I didn't protest or resist. Instead, I succumbed to the strength of his embrace, allowing him to comfort me and do what my husband couldn't do at that moment.

***

Contessa looked relieved to see Jasmine and me when we came through the front door. I inhaled the scent of Pine-sol and lemon Pledge and noticed that the house was spotless, as always. Contessa immediately took Jasmine out of my arms then kissed me on my cheek and said, "I'm here if you want to talk."

"Thank you, Contessa," I said. "If you could just keep an eye on Jasmine for a couple of hours, that would be a big help."

"Of course." She smiled. "I'm going to lay her down for her nap and then I'll be in my room if you need me."

"Okay." I watched Contessa carry Jasmine up the stairs leading to the second floor of my home.

"I'm going to go get your bags out of the car," Kelly said gently. "Where would you like me to put them?"

"Anywhere will be fine," I said while pressing the send button on my phone to call Damon. I slightly held my breath, hoping that this time, I would hear my husband's live voice rather than his recorded greeting on his voicemail. I was again disappointed and forced to leave another message begging him to call back or come home. I walked to the kitchen, retrieved a bottle of Fiji water from the refrigerator, and plopped down at the table. My mind was reeling with thoughts of death and sickness and worries about nearly everyone in my life, myself included. *Where is Damon?* In the paranoid state I was in, I began to fear that something may have happened to him. *What if he's lying in some gutter or alley, hurt or even dead?* I suddenly felt terrified and shaky as hell. Looking at my watch, I saw that it was four thirty p.m., which meant it was only five thirty in Atlanta. *Maybe he's still in his office or in a meeting.* I scrolled through my contacts and found the number for the Nomad Atlanta office. The answering service advised me that the office was closed and no one was in the building. I slammed my phone down on the table, and my heart rate began to increase more and more with every passing second. I made my way to the cabinet where Damon and I kept our liquor. I retrieved an unopened bottle of Hennessey Privilege and a glass.

"I left your bags in the foyer," Kelly said, entering the room.

"Thanks," I said, opening the bottle. I could feel Kelly's eyes on me, but I ignored his stares and filled my glass. I tossed the drink back and swallowed hard, flinching slightly from the burning sensation moving down inside my chest and hitting my nervous stomach like a lead balloon.

"Hey," Kelly said, walking up to me, "are you all right?"

I dismissed his question and continued to pour.

"You need to slow down," Kelly commanded, touching my elbow.

I stepped away from him and glared at him, right in the eyes. "Don't tell me what I need right now," I said firmly. "You have no idea what *I* need."

He looked from me to the bottle in my hand. "Maybe not, but I know how it feels to find out someone you love is sick," he said. His eyes were full of compassion and tenderness. "I also know getting twisted is not the answer."

It was obvious he was trying to help, but I didn't want his assistance at that very second. "I don't want to talk about this right now," I said, shaking my head. "Especially not with you."

"You need to talk about this now," he said.

I poured another shot, followed by another, then refilled the glass again.

Kelly shook his head.

I rolled my eyes at him and started walking toward the patio doors.

Kelly took quick strides toward me and finally stepped in front of me, blocking my path.

His attempt to stop me only further fueled my anger. "Move!" I snapped, stepping past him.

"Fine!" He yelled behind me as I walked out onto the patio, "Get drunk, Octavia! But I promise you that when you sober up, your problems will still be here, plus one more."

"Oh yeah?" I asked, turning around to look at him. "What's that?"

"A fuckin' hangover," he snapped.

"I'm a big girl," I told him. "I can hold my own."

The rain outside fell lightly upon my head as I walked down the stone path leading to the garden. Easing down on the bench, I replayed the day's events over and over in my head. I poured myself shot after shot. It felt like my life was spiraling out of control, spinning as fast as my drunken head. *How is it that one moment you can be so high on life and love, but in the next, you're so damn low?* I wanted to rewind the last forty-eight hours of my life and replay everything that had taken place, including my conversation with Lena. I wanted a do-over, a chance to make it all flow and work the way I wanted it to, but I knew no matter how much I wished for a second chance, that was not an option.

I looked up and saw Contessa marching down the lawn. She was holding an umbrella in one hand and carrying a coat in the other. When she finally reached me, she hovered over me like a mother hen guarding her chick. "You're going to be sick," she stated. "Here…put this over your head."

I looked away, not wanting her to see the tears that were forming in my eyes. I didn't argue, though, as she wrapped the jacket around my shoulders and pulled the hood over my head.

"Do you want me to call Charles and Charlene?" she asked.

I shook my head. "No, just give me a moment," I requested, barely able to recognize my own voice.

"Okay, darling," she said nervously, glancing at the glass in my hand.

"I'm fine," I said.

She smiled slightly and turned and walked away.

I took another shot to the head. I could already feel the effect of the cognac, and I knew the end result from that little binge of mine was not going to be a good one, but I didn't care. I looked in the pond and noticed that Kelly had filled it with fish. I smiled at the blurry orange and white and black creatures swimming around. As if echoing the hard rains and cloudbursts that were falling from the sky, the emotional levees I held on the inside finally broke again. Closing my eyes, I reclined on the bench, pulling my knees up to my chest as my tears flowed freely.

"Octavia…"

I heard Kelly's voice calling me, but I couldn't respond. I was practically choking on my own tears.

"Shh…it's all right," he said to me.

Lifting my head, I saw Kelly standing in front of me. I closed my eyes as another round of tears made their escape. "Leave me alone," I mumbled. "Please." I felt too weak to argue with him, and I was too numb to protest.

"Not a chance," he said.

"Why not?" I asked, crying.

"Because," he said, looking at me tenderly, "I care."

"Hold on," he ordered, picking me up in his arms.

***

Inside the guesthouse I stood, dripping water all over the floor.

Kelly stood in front of me, drying my hair with one of the fluffy towels I kept stocked in the linen closet. "Sit down," he said.

I did as he requested but chose to refrain from breaking my silence.

"Are you trying to catch pneumonia?" he questioned. "Do you want to be sick?"

I looked in his eyes. "No," I answered matter-of-factly. "What I want is for my life to go back to the way it was a year ago," I slurred, "back when my mother was healthy, when I could trust the words my husband spoke to me. That's what I want. Can you give that to me?" I cried. "Can I buy that? How much money do you think that shit will cost, Kelly? How much?"

"Octavia, when I found out Ciara was sick, I wanted to push down mountains to make her well!" he yelled. "I would have died for her to have life, but that is not how it works! All the money in the world cannot change the plan," he said, lowering his voice. "Some things are just meant to be, and others are not," he continued. "I know it doesn't seem fair, but it's reality."

I took a deep breath and exhaled through my lips. "I feel like I'm losing control," I confessed. "Mama and Damon—"

"What about Damon?" he asked.

Kelly looked genuinely concerned, so I poured my heart out, telling him about Lena and how I couldn't reach Damon on the phone. "At first I thought he may be hurt or something," I whined, "but what if it's someone else. What if...?" I couldn't bear to say the words.

Kelly sat down on the bed next to me and pulled me into his strong arms. "It's all right. It's all right." He ran his hands across my hair before leaning in and gently kissing my forehead.

Tilting my head back I searched his eyes, hoping they held all the answers.

Kelly lowered his head, pressing his lips to mine. He pulled away, then eased down on his knees. I watched as he removed my shoes one by one and then did the same for my socks. He patted my feet dry with the towel and ordered me to stand up. "Take your clothes off," he said, "and get under the covers."

I watched him intently as he turned his back to me. I unbuttoned my jeans then eased them down my hips to the floor, followed by my panties. I shivered slightly as I removed my shirt and sopping wet bra. I quickly climbed under the soft sheets and pulled them up around my neck to thwart the goose bumps that were invading my skin.

Kelly laid my wet clothes out on the back of the large chair in the corner of the room. "I'll go have Auntie get you some dry ones," he said.

"Kelly," I called.

He turned around slowly and looked at me.

"Lie with me?" I said.

I saw the look in his eyes, that look that told me the fine line we had drawn in the sand after our kiss was in danger of being crossed. I saw in his eyes that if he did lie down with me, being that close without touching me was not something he could promise. And, yes, I saw in his eyes that he wanted me. But to all those things I said, "So what?" In that moment, there, alone with him in my lowest moment, I dismissed all reasoning.

Chapter 30

Damon

"*I* want you to explain this to me," I demanded, sliding one of the photos Lawrence had provided me across the table to my mother. I planned to confront Nadia about the info Lawrence provided me, but first I wanted to know why Nadia and my mother were arguing in the other photograph.

Running her fingers through her hair Mama stared at the picture. "You hired a private investigator?" she asked calmly.

"Yes."

"Why?"

"Because I wanted to know what Nadia is up to," I said honestly.

"You're talking about the child, I suppose," Mama said, staring at me.

"Donovan," I said. "How long have you known about him?" I asked, leaning forward against the table.

"Since before he was born," Mama said. She had a blank expression on her face. "I remember she came to visit one weekend when your grandmother and Bernice were here to see your father. She was around six months pregnant at the time."

"So Grandmother knows too?" I asked, shaking my head.

"She knows about the child, Donovan," she said quickly, "but Nadia told her someone else is the boy's father."

"And she believed that?"

"Of course she did." Mama laughed. "Odessa believes everything that comes out of that little bitch's mouth. Nadia told her and Bernice that another man is the boy's daddy, but the first opportunity she got, she pulled me to the side and proudly told me that her unborn son was going to be my grandson."

I watched Mama as she slid back from the table and then walked over to the kitchen window. She looked like she was lost in her thoughts, consumed with her emotions.

"I offered her $50,000," she explained, "to go away and find another man to name as Donovan's father. I told her to pick anyone she wanted, just as long as it wasn't you."

My conversation with Gia replayed in my head. *She was telling me the truth.* "Why?" I questioned. "Why would you do that?"

"To protect our family," she said, "from the scandal and from that wretched wench. Nadia has always been bad news, Damon, and her having a child by one of our own would only make her worse."

"You should have come to me from the very beginning," I advised her. "I could have handled it."

"I'm sorry," she said solemnly.

"Does Pops know?"

"No," she said, looking over at me.

"I have been hiding this from Octavia," I admitted. "I've decided to tell her the truth. I can't keep sneaking behind her back and lying about my whereabouts. Donovan is my son, and Octavia is my wife. We're family, whether we want to be or not."

Mama looked at me and frowned. "Damon, you're…" She stopped what she was going to say when Isabella entered the room, carrying the cordless phone in her hand.

"Sorry to disturb you," she said, "but there is a phone call for Damon."

"Who is it?" I asked, slightly annoyed that my conversation with Mama was being interrupted.

"A Mr. Kelly Baker," Isabella announced. "He says it's urgent."

"Who is Kelly?" Mama questioned.

"Our nanny's nephew," I informed her before taking the phone from

Isabella. "This is Damon," I said into the receiver.

"Hey, I'm sorry to disturb you," Kelly said, and there was something in his tone that instantly told me something was wrong, "but I think you should know…"

I allowed Kelly to finish then finally advised him I was on my way home. "I'm getting on the road right now," I said before hanging up. I handed my mother the phone and began walking toward the front door.

"What is it, DJ?" Mama asked, following behind me.

"Octavia needs me," I said, opening the door and running down the front steps.

"Damon, I'm not finished talking to you," Mama said from the doorway.

"I'll call you," I said, opening my car door. "I love you." I climbed into my car and shut the door just as I heard Mama say she loved me too. I had left my phone on the charger inside my truck. I removed it from the cradle and saw that I had five missed calls and three messages.

"Damon, it's me, Lena. Look, Octavia was here, and she knows everything. I'm sorry."

I went on to the next message. It was from Octavia, and she was crying and sounded completely distraught. "Fuck!" I cursed, pulling out of my parents' driveway. I decided not to call Lena back. I would deal with what Octavia had to say when I got home. Kelly advised me over the phone that Octavia was heartbroken and had received some terrible news. I had to get home ASAP for damage control, I assumed the news was from Nadia and that the bitch had told Octavia everything.

***

It was close to midnight when I arrived home. I was nervous, anticipating what was waiting for me when I got there. My home was completely dark, with the exception of the night light in Jasmine's bedroom. I placed a kiss on my daughter's cheek and went to my bedroom. I opened the door and saw Octavia sleeping, which relieved me a bit. In my mind, I had expected her to be sitting up waiting for me, ready to pop completely off. I didn't want to wake her, but I needed her to know I was home and there for her. After removing my clothes, I pulled the covers back and climbed into the bed next to her. She was completely naked under the sheets. I wrapped my arms around her and snuggled against her warm, bare skin.

She shifted slightly in her sleep. "Kelly?" she mumbled

I paused, feeling something burning inside of me—anger and confusion from hearing my wife calling another man's name in her sleep. The room was completely quiet until I heard the sound of her breathing heavily.

Chapter 31

Octavia

I awoke to Damon lying next to me and what felt like a small body of water with hundreds of tiny fish swimming inside of my head. I had the worst hangover of my life and felt like at any moment, I was going to lose the contents of my stomach, which consisted of nothing but the cognac I'd guzzled. "Damon?" I said lowly. My throat was dry, and my eyes felt like they had pounds of luggage underneath them.

"I'm awake," he said, opening his eyes and sitting up next to me.

"What time did you get in?"

"Around midnight," he informed me. "I'm sorry I missed your calls. I left my phone in the car on the charger."

I didn't feel like examining his explanation, so I decided to take him at his word, at least for the moment. "We need to talk," I said, sitting up slowly in bed. I reached over on the nightstand and grabbed my robe. I didn't know how it got there, but I didn't care. I was just grateful that I did not have to get out of bed right away. Considering all the swimming that was going on in my head, walking was the last thing I wanted to attempt.

"Octavia, I'm sorry," he began. "I should have told you from the very beginning, but I didn't know how."

I had pushed the situation with Lena out of my mind until he started with his apology. "Listen, you should have told me the whole story about Alicia or Lena or whoever the hell she wants to be," I said cooly while slipping on my robe. "I was disappointed and mad that you didn't trust me enough to tell me that you and her used to be an item and that you felt obligated to help her." I exhaled slowly. "We will address that, but right now I have something to tell you—something about Mama."

Damon gave me a quizzical look. "Mine or yours?" he asked.

"Mine," I said, swallowing hard.

"What about her?"

"She...Mama has cancer," I said. "Breast cancer."

Damon looked completely thrown off by the news. He closed eyes briefly and rubbed his hands over his head. "Octavia, I'm so sorry," he said, looking at me, with his voice trembling slightly.

I gave him a recap of my conversation with Mama and told him everything she'd disclosed to me about her condition.

"Why didn't she tell us sooner?" he asked. "She and Charles have been going through this alone for a month?"

After running my fingers through my disheveled hair, I shrugged my shoulders. "She didn't want to worry me until she knew for sure that the diagnosis was true." I looked at him and continued, "And—let's be honest—you've been on the go so much..."

I watched as he climbed out of bed and walked slowly over to the door, dressed in nothing but his silk boxers. For a minute, I thought he was going to walk out of our bedroom mid-conversation, but he didn't. Instead, he turned around and gazed at me. "You were upset on my voicemail because of your mom?" There was a glimmer in his eyes that looked like relief.

"You thought it was about Lena?" I sighed. "I was bothered by that. I'll admit that. I mean, imagine how you would have felt if some strange man's name kept being linked to me? If you received anonymous gifts and—"

"What gifts?" he asked.

I had already told him I didn't want to discuss Lena at the moment, but he seemed dead set on the idea, and it seemed like as good a time as any. I told Damon the story of the gift and how I found out that his company was backing Déjà Vu. I mentioned the text messages I'd seen on our phone bill. I made sure I explained that I was online looking to upgrade my phone and that it led to me checking our usage because I didn't want him to think

I was just snooping. I gave him every detail of my trip to L.A. and my meeting with Lena.

"So instead of going to Memphis, you flew out to California?" He looked surprised.

"Yes. I had a gut feeling and a whole lot of unanswered questions," I stated, "and I was determined I would get to the bottom of all of them."

He smiled. "You are definitely something," he whispered.

I moved to the edge of the bed. "When it comes down to my family or the ones I love, I can be the wrong something for the right someone," I said seriously, meaning each and every word. You never know what you're capable of doing until the wrong force of nature pushes you outside of your element.

"Lena means nothing to me," Damon said, and he sounded convincing. "Not like that anyway. I love her, but only as a friend, Octavia—nothing more and nothing less."

"I believe you," I reassured him, "but the problem is that she doesn't feel the same way."

He walked back over to the bed and sat down beside me.

"She has feelings for you, Damon," I continued., "and it's not just friendship. She loves you in a completely different way."

"She told you that?"

"She didn't have to," I said, exhaling. "It was written all over her face. And," I added quickly, "I've already advised her that the two of you will no longer be able to maintain a friendship." I was waiting for him to say the wrong thing or display the wrong expression, but he didn't.

"I have no problem with that," he answered. He reached over and took my hand in his. His hand felt cool and soft, which was a total relief considering I felt like my body was inside a toaster oven. I interlocked my fingers with his.

"Yesterday, I felt like I was having a breakdown," I said truthfully. "I was such a wreck, and then when I couldn't get in contact with you, I thought something happened," I rambled. "I mean, there was a time when you always answered or got right back with me whenever I called. You never…" I abruptly stopped and stared down at the floor.

"Look at me," he instructed.

I lifted my eyes, turning to look at him.

"I know I have been unavailable a lot lately, and I have an explanation for that—"

"No, don't explain," I told him, placing my fingers gently on his lips to hush him. "Whatever it is or whatever it was, let's leave it in the past."

Damon looked like he was about to protest.

Raising my hand in the air, I shook my head slowly. "Please, Damon." In a small way, I sounded as if I were begging him. The truth is, part of me was. I could not take any more unexpected news at that moment. "I just got some of the most shocking news ever yesterday. Today, let's just be a family and focus on us and loving each other."

He stroked my cheek lightly with his thumb. "Of course," he said.

"There is one thing I do need you to do for me right now," I advised him.

"Name it."

"Can you get me some coffee?" I asked. "Please? Or else just knock the hell out of me, whichever comes first."

"Hmm. I think I'll get the coffee," he said, laughing lightly.

Although my head was still hurting, it felt good to hear Damon's laughter, and it felt damn good to hold his hand.

"Are you hung over?" he asked, staring at me.

"That's putting it lightly," I confessed.

He lowered his eyes, a clear indication that he did not approve.

I may have my drinks from time to time, and get a decent buzz going every now and then, but never have I ever been completely out of control. That horrible night was the first time, and the way I felt the morning after meant it would be my last. "I know," I said, feeling ashamed. "I shouldn't have."

"No, you shouldn't have," he scolded gently, "but *I* should have been here to take care of you."

"Yes, but you're here now," I said.

"I got on the road as soon as I spoke with Kelly," he said.

The mere mention of Kelly's name brought flashbacks of the night before. *Oh shit,* I thought. I felt a tingling sensation in my tongue and a burning in the back of my throat. "I'm sorry!" I grabbed my stomach with one hand and covered my mouth with the other before hurrying into the bathroom. I barely had the toilet lid lifted before I began to vomit.

Chapter 32

Damon

After running Octavia a warm bath, I carried her back to bed, gave her a warm washcloth to cover her eyes to help with the swelling from all her crying the night before, turned off all the lights, and told her I was going to get some Aleve from the drugstore for her. I told her to stay in bed while I was gone. Downstairs, I slipped in the living room and found Contessa reading to Jasmine.

"How is Octavia?" Contessa asked, looking completely concerned about my wife's wellbeing.

"She'll be okay in a few hours," I said, picking Jasmine up.

My little girl wrapped her arms around my neck and gave me a hug.

"She just needs some rest."

"I'll fix her something to eat a little later," Contessa volunteered.

"Thanks."

"I'm glad you're here, Damon," Contessa said. "I've never seen her like that, and it scared me."

I could only imagine how Octavia's disposition was when she'd come home after everything she'd found out about Lena and her mother and the whole nine yards. If I'd have had the chance to do it all again, I would have let Lawrence handle Nadia and Gia and stayed my ass at home. "I'm glad you were here for her," I told her. "Thank you."

"Well, I didn't know what to do," Contessa said, pushing her glasses up on her nose. "I called Kelly, and he came to the rescue."

"What do you mean?" I asked, waiting on her explanation.

"Well, when Charlene called and told me the news about her...well, her sickness," Contessa said hesitantly, "she asked how Octavia was doing. I told her Octavia hadn't made it home yet." Contessa scratched her head. "I got worried at that point and called to see where Octavia was. It was raining really bad, and I knew she had the baby with her and was probably upset. I was worried that something bad had happened. I called Octavia, and she didn't sound right." She continued, "She told me she pulled over at a gas station. She was crying so hard, Damon. I didn't think she should drive, so I told her to just wait there."

"And you sent Kelly?" I concluded.

"Yes. Kelly followed her and the baby home."

I had a gut feeling that the story didn't end there. "Was Octavia drunk when she got here?" I questioned.

"Oh, no that didn't happen until later." Contessa sighed. "I told you she wasn't herself."

"You did," I said, practically hanging on Contessa's every word.

"Well, she was sitting out in the garden in the rain, drinking away, shot after shot," she said, shaking her head. "I went out and put a jacket on her and tried to talk to her, but I couldn't get through to her. She just wouldn't come inside or put the bottle down. Kelly told me he would take care of her, so I went back upstairs to check on Jasmine and then went to my room. Well, I must have dozed off, because Kelly woke me up later and asked me to check in on her every once in a while."

"Where was Octavia then?" I questioned.

"Upstairs in your bed," she said, "naked as the day she was born."

That didn't really surprise me, as Octavia sleeps in the nude 70 percent of the time. There were several blanks in Contessa's story that needed filling in, but it was obvious that Contessa didn't have the answers. "Again, thanks for your help," I said, placing Jasmine down on the sofa. "I'm going to run out for a second. Do you need anything?"

"No. I'm fine, sweetie. Just glad to have you home."

"Don't worry," I said, kissing the top of my daughter's head. "I won't be leaving anytime soon, and if I do, I'll make sure my family is with me."

***

I grabbed my keys off the table in the foyer and exited out the patio doors toward the five-car garage. I stopped in my tracks when I saw Kelly exiting the guesthouse. *Why the hell is he still here?* I decided to wait for him to find out.

"Glad to see you made it home, man," he said, stopping in front of me.

"Thanks, for calling."

"No problem," he said.

"So you stayed here last night?" I asked.

"Yeah. I didn't want to leave Octavia in the condition she was in," he said, "I mean, someone had to be here."

His response got under my skin slightly, but I decided to let him slide. "Contessa told me how you came to my wife's rescue," I said pleasantly. "Thank you."

"It was my pleasure." He gave me a cocky smile—a smile that indicated there was something else he wanted to say. It was a smile that made me want to beat the breath out of him.

"Well, Daddy's home," I said. "Your services are no longer needed."

"No problem, man." He laughed, rubbing his hands together. "I think my job here is done. I'd better get going." He walked toward the patio doors. "I need to get some rest. I was up all night, just in case your family needed me. Now I've got to get my mojo back, I've got a date with a special lady tonight."

I followed behind him. "I'll let you out," I said, ignoring his comment about his plans for the evening.

The two of us walked through my home in silence. The tension was thick and hot enough to fuel a war. Outside in the driveway, I watched as Kelly climbed into Contessa's Toyota Camry. I hadn't noticed the car parked in the driveway when I'd arrived home that morning due to the lights on the front side of our property being off. I wondered why, if Kelly was in the guesthouse, he hadn't heard me pull in. *If he was so concerned about my family's wellbeing and "being there," why the hell didn't he come out to see who was pulling up on the place? Then again, maybe he did know it was me and didn't want to speak to me. But why in the hell didn't he just leave?* "Hey, by the way…" I said, standing outside of the car door.

"What's up?"

"How did you know to call me at my parents' home?" I questioned nonchalantly.

"Octavia gave me the number," he explained. "She figured you were there since she couldn't reach you at your office."

"I see," was my only response.

"Well, take care, man," Kelly stated, cranking up the car. "Tell Octavia I'll drop off a check next week to reimburse her for the deposit on my apartment."

"Don't worry about it," I told him. "Consider us even."

He gave me a cocky grin. "I figured you would say that."

I watched as he pulled off, zooming around then down the circular driveway. I could feel someone watching me, and I looked up and saw Octavia standing at our bedroom window. I watched as she ran her fingers through her hair and turned and walked away. I knew in my heart that something had transpired between Kelly and my wife; I just didn't know what it was, and a small part of me was wondering if I would be able to handle it when I figured it out.

***

I was pulling out of the parking lot of CVS, engulfed in my thoughts of Kelly and what may have taken place between him and my wife, when the sound of my Blackberry ringing interrupted my thoughts. I slid my device out of the console and glanced at the caller ID: an unknown caller. "This is Damon," I answered.

"It's me. Can you talk?" Lena sounded completely on edge.

"Yes," I said, "for a minute."

"Damon, I had no idea that Octavia was coming to see me," she began to explain. "She scheduled an appointment under a false name."

"It's cool," I said reassuringly. "Octavia told me everything."

"So you're not upset?" she asked. Lena sounded like the burden of the world had been lifted off her shoulders.

"No," I said. "I'm glad she knows. She handled the information a lot better than I expected."

"So the two of you are okay?" she asked, sounding like she was smiling on the other end of the phone.

For the moment, I thought, pondering how it was going to go down when Octavia finds out about Donovan and Nadia's sneaky, trifling ass.

"Well, Janai can't wait to see her Uncle Damon again," Lena said happily. "When will you be back to visit?"

I thought about my conversation with Octavia, and her words echoed in my ears: *"She has feelings for you, Damon, and it's not just friendship. She loves you in a completely different way."* Lena never gave me any indication that she wanted to be more than friends. Unlike Nadia, she never threw herself at me or treated me like anything other than a brother. However, as a man I know it's sometimes impossible for some women and men to be friends without one of the parties catching feelings. I wasn't willing to take any chances. "I'm sorry, Lena, but I won't be back to visit," I said, slowly breaking the news to her.

"What do you mean?"

"I think, considering the circumstances and our previous history, that it's best if we—"

"History? Damon, we were just kids!" She laughed lightly. "That was so long ago."

"I know," I said, "but I promised Octavia that we will put distance in our friendship."

"Distance? We live how many miles apart?" she joked. "I'm on the other side of the country. How much farther apart can we get?" She laughed.

I laughed a little myself, but I needed to stand my ground. "I know," I said gently, "but you know what I mean. You're doing great for yourself, and my townhouse is now yours," I reminded her. "If you have any problems or complications at the shop, like repairs and such, all you have to do is call the property manager, Julian."

"Wow." She exhaled. "I wish I had known the last time I saw you was going to be the last time."

"Hey, we never know when our paths might cross," I said, trying to lighten the mood.

"You're right," she agreed. "You know, I'll be doing some hair shows in and around the South, so you and Octavia will definitely have to come."

"We'll keep that in mind," I said, but in my mind, I could only think,

Hell no!

"And just for the record, Damon," Lena said abruptly, "I wasn't the one who sent Octavia the gift basket." There was a certain amount of sincerity in Lena's voice that made me believe her.

"I know you didn't," I said, "but I'm sure I know who did." I was thinking of Nadia. "Anyway, it's over now. What's done is done. I better go," I told her, wrapping up our phone call.

"Okay," she said happily. "I love you, Damon."

"Take care, Lena," I told her before hanging up.

***

Drunk or sober, I felt Octavia was one of the most beautiful women in the world, but I was thanking God that she looked 200 percent better when I returned home. Her hair was combed and pulled back in a thick afro puff. The bags under her eyes were gone, and she had a smile on her face. All of these things were a big plus. She was sitting up in bed wearing one of my button-down dress shirts. I look good in my clothes, but Octavia looks a whole lot better in them—and out of them, for that matter. "How you doing?" I asked, laying the CVS bag on the nightstand next to the bed.

"Better," she said. "Contessa made me some tea, and it knocked the life right back in me."

"What kind of tea?" I asked, sitting on the edge of the bed.

"She said it's some old home remedy, guaranteed to cure a hangover."

"It looks like it worked." I laughed.

"Definitely." She sighed. "And I'm glad it did. For a minute, I was catching it. Felt like shit," she added. "And looked like shit."

"You looked nothing like yourself," I commented, "but even on your worst days, you still look better than shit."

She flashed me her beautiful smile. "You really know how to make a woman feel good about herself," she said.

"That wasn't flattery," I told her. "It was the truth." I watched as she stretched out across the bed so that her head was resting on my lap.

"I love you, Mr. Whitmore."

"I love you, Mrs. Whitmore," I said, rubbing her back slowly.

"Did you happen to see a stray diamond earring lying around?" she asked.

"No, why?"

"I lost one of mine," she said.

"So we'll buy you some new ones," I told her, stroking her hair.

"You're the best."

"So are you."

"I was thinking," she said, rolling over so to face me, "we could give our trip to Paris to Mama and Daddy."

"Really?" I asked.

"Yes," she said, biting her bottom lip. "I think it'll be a nice getaway for the two of them after Mama recovers from her surgery." Octavia explained that her mother was scheduled for a mastectomy in two weeks.

"I tell you what," I said. "Why don't we keep our tickets and buy a second pair for the two of them?"

She sat up and stared at me in disbelief. "Really?" she asked, staring me in the eyes.

"Yes, really," I said, pulling her into my arms.

"You're the best."

"But you're better," I replied before pressing my lips to hers. She responded eagerly, and we kissed slowly until she finally pulled away.

"That reminds me," she said, snapping her fingers. "Ilene called while you were out."

I had forgotten all about owing Mama a phone call. "Damn. I forgot I told her I would call her," I said. "I was over at the house with her when Kelly called me yesterday."

"How'd he get Mama Ilene's number?" Octavia asked.

"I thought he got it from you," I said, but I decided not to tell her that Kelly himself had told me that.

Octavia frowned, shaking her head. "There are some things from last night that I can't remember detail for detail, but I'm positive I didn't give the number to him."

"You sure?" I asked. "You were uh...a little tipsy last night."

"Tipsy? Hon', I was straight drunk off my ass!" she said, rolling her eyes. "I'm woman enough to admit that, but I'm positive, bay, that Kelly didn't get the number from me."

"Well, maybe he saw it on the caller ID or something," I suggested, but my instincts were telling me yet again that I should have heeded Lawrence's warning that there was possibly more to Kelly, right from day one.

"Maybe," she said, sounding a bit suspicious herself.

"So what can you remember from last night?" I asked casually.

"Well, I got super wasted." She shook her head.

"How'd you get in bed?" I questioned. Part of me wanted to come straight out and ask, *"Did you screw Kelly?"* but I would not allow that part of me to dictate my conversation with Octavia. I repeated what Contessa told me and then asked again, "How'd you make it to bed, boo?" I asked lovingly. I was being cool and calm with my questions, but I was anxiously anticipating her answers.

"Let's just say I gave 'crawl into bed' a new meaning last night."

"One that you never want to repeat again?" I asked.

"You know it," she agreed with me.

"Did anything happen between you and Kelly?" I finally blurted out.

Octavia sat up straight and stared at me. Her honey-brown eyes locked with mine. "What? Why would you think that?" she asked.

"Well, this morning when I got into bed with you, you called his name."

Octavia's eyebrows went up slightly. "Baby, I'm sorry," she said lowly. "I remember talking to Kelly a lot about Mama and how his daughter Ciara died. Maybe I was having a dream about the conversation or something."

"You're probably right," I agreed with her.

"One thing I'm sure of," she said assertively, "is that nothing happened last night between me and Kelly other than conversation."

I decided to leave well enough alone and push the images of Kelly and my wife out of my mind. I trusted Octavia, and I knew if there was anything to find out about her and Kelly, it would eventually come to light. Until then, there was no sense in making unfounded accusations.

***

I returned my mother's call and filled her in on what was going on.

"Send Charlene my love," she told me. "Octavia and Charles too."

"I will."

"Your father and I will be there next week to visit," she informed me. "I haven't seen Charlene since Jasmine was born. We are long overdue for a reunion."

"Sounds good," I said sincerely. "Maybe we can crank up the grill."

"Perfect, darling," Mama purred. "Your father and I will bring a covered dish."

"Wait…Mama, you're cooking?"

"Um…no!" she said sarcastically. "I just said I'll bring the dish. Isabella will prepare whatever's going in it."

I chuckled. "I should have known."

"It's either Isabella or Publix," she offered. "Take your pick."

"Don't worry about either," I told her. "You and Daddy just get here, and Octavia and I will handle the rest."

"That sounds even better," she said.

***

That night I sat with Jasmine lying on one side of my chest and Octavia's head nestled on the other. I thought about Donovan and where he would fit into the picture if he was there with us. Earlier Octavia, Jasmine, and myself had enjoyed dinner with Charlene and Charles at their home. It was there that I informed Octavia's parents that my mother sent her love and that she and my father would be in town the following week. Both Charlene and Charles seemed happy to hear it, but nothing could top their expression when Octavia announced that we were sending the two of them on an all-expense-paid trip to Paris.

I was watching the six o'clock news with my two favorite girls lying next to me when I saw Gia's face on the television screen. According to the reporter, the girl was found at DNA Diagnostics, hanging from a third-story window. "Officers say they do not suspect foul play," the anchorwoman reported. "Miss Gia Diamante looks to be the victim of suicide."

"That is so sad," Octavia commented, stretching her legs out in front of her. "I wonder what she was going through that made her feel like she had to take their own life."

I wasn't there, but I was willing to bet money that Gia's death was far from a suicide. "I don't know," I said. "People often feel like they have no one to talk to."

"True." Octavia stood and stretched. "I'm going to go give Sleeping Beauty her bath then lay her down." She bent down and kissed me on the lips before lifting Jasmine off my chest. "Be back in a little bit."

I waited until the coast was clear before I called Lawrence.

"Talk to me."

"When I said to make sure she remained quiet, I didn't mean murder," I whispered into the phone. "Damn, man. Is that your only solution?"

"It's the best way to guarantee they're going to keep quiet," Lawrence said, yawning into the phone, "but why don't you tell me who we're talking about."

"The blonde," I said.

"Oh. Look, I know this is hard to believe," Lawrence said, "but it wasn't me."

"What?"

"Nope. She was gone by the time I got to her crib," he said. "I waited for a minute, but when there was no sign of her, I headed over to your baby-mama's spot."

"What happened there?" I asked quickly.

"Well, I waited for an hour for the tramp," he said sarcastically. "After seeing no movement, I went to her door. Her assistant, Mindy or Mary or—"

"María," I said, helping him out.

"Yeah, that's it. María said Nadia had been gone for a few days," Lawrence told me. "MIA."

"What?"

"That's what I said." He blew into the phone. "She said she got a phone call and packed up and kicked rocks."

"So you have no idea where the crazy bitch is?" I said, stating the obvious.

"Not a damn clue," Lawrence advised. "If I didn't know better, I'd swear she knew we were coming."

I pondered the idea for a brief second. "What about my son?" I questioned.

"That's the good news. I *do* know where your boy is," Lawrence advised me.

"Where?"

"In New York, with his great grandmother."

Chapter 33

Octavia

I was looking forward to seeing both of my in-laws, but I missed Ilene the most. She's a diva and dramatic as hell from time to time, but I love her to death. Amel and I were coming along slowly but surely with the plans for her wedding and reception, and I was enjoying every moment. Without a doubt, I was in need of some girl time, considering my bestie was still who-knows-where and had suddenly developed a bad case of I-can't-call-nobody syndrome. I needed to hang out with a friend, and Amel would have to do. The two of us had just completed the seating arrangement chart for the reception when Katlyn knocked, announcing I had a visitor.

"I'll talk to you later." Amel smiled and headed out the door.

"Talk later," I said to Amel. "You can send them in," I advised Katlyn, who was standing at the office door.

A minute later, Kelly strolled through my door, wearing a cream tailored suit, soft pink shirt, and gold tie. He was carrying a dozen long-stemmed roses. I hadn't heard or seen him since the night of my drinking binge, so it caught me a bit off guard. He came in and sat down without an invitation, then smiled at me and laid the roses across my desk.

"You shouldn't have," I said seriously.

"Aw, it was nothing," he said, staring at me.

Once again, his gray eyes felt like they were penetrating me, and I suddenly wished I had told Katlyn to leave my office door open. Is it safe to say I didn't trust myself with Kelly? Absolutely! "Again, you shouldn't have," I said.

"I just wanted to come by and see for myself how you are doing."

"I'm good." I smiled. "Thank you for your concern."

"I care," he said, leaning forward in his chair. "I told you that."

"I appreciate everything you've done for me," I told him nicely. "However, I think it's best if you and I refrain from contact from here on out."

"Why? Are you afraid?" he asked.

"No," I lied. "Not at all." The voice in my head was screaming, *Hell yes!*

I watched as he smiled, then began to clap his hands. "Bravo, Bravo," he said. "You are a very good actress, Octavia."

"I-I don't understand."

"You can pretend all you want," he told me, "but we both know the chemistry between us is only going to get better." Kelly looked extremely confident.

"Better? How?" I asked.

"The more we see each other, the stronger the connection," he said. "You can try to deny it. You can tell yourself you're so in love with your husband that you would never touch another man, but we both know that's a lie."

I was frustrated and annoyed with Kelly's choice of conversation. "What do you want from me, Kelly?" I asked impatiently.

"It's simple." Kelly stood and adjusted his jacket.

"And what's that?" I asked.

"I want you, Octavia," he said, turning to walk to the door. "And say what you want, but we both know you want me too."

I watched as he strolled out of my office with an arrogant swagger and closed the door behind him. Reclining against the leather chair, I closed my eyes, allowing the memory of what took place between Kelly and me in my guesthouse to flood my mind.

"Lie with me," I said.

Kelly stretched out on the bed next to me, lying on top of the covers.

The Lies We Tell For Love

I closed my eyes and took comfort in the heat his body was providing as he lay next to mine. Five minutes later, I was on my back, staring up at the ceiling, with Kelly running his fingers up in between my thighs. His hands were warm and soft as he spread my legs. I kept my eyes closed, wanting to focus on nothing as I felt Kelly's tongue against my clit. He pulled gently on the hood before wrapping his lips around it tightly. I felt a tingling sensation as he made circles around my hot button with his tongue. He pushed my legs further apart, then pushed his warm, wet tongue in and out, in and out of me. Grinding my hips slowly, I moved my warm slit up and down against his tongue. He grabbed my ass firmly and rotated his tongue up, down, in, and out. I could feel the heat penetrating from the inside of my body out. I opened my eyes and saw him fumbling slightly to open the condom and slide it onto himself. I could feel him positioning himself between my legs. I closed my eyes, again, trying hard to relax, but my body refused to cooperate.

"Are you okay?" he asked.

"I'm fine," I said. "I don't know what's wrong."

"Relax," he said. "Just relax." He attempted yet again to enter me.

I closed my eyes, and the only face I could see was Damon's. "Wait," I said.

I leaned forward against my desk, snapping myself out of my daydream. After I stopped Kelly that night, I'd thrown my clothes on in a drunken stupor and stumbled my way into the house and upstairs to my bedroom. I didn't have sex with Kelly that night, but I knew what had taken place between us was not on the list of acceptable behavior for a married woman. Now, Kelly had made it blatantly obvious that he had no intention of giving up. I sat there weighing my options. I could tell Damon and risk creating a severe rift in my marriage, or I could keep my mouth closed and live with the guilt. Staring at the honeymoon photo of Damon and me that I kept on my desk, I sighed. "I'm sure the guilt will pass eventually," I said to myself.

Chapter 34

Kelly

"Where have you been?"

I had barely walked through the door before Nadia got in my face. I slid my jacket off my shoulders and tossed it on the back of the armchair sitting by the door. *What happened to women greeting their men at the door with a hug or a kiss? Hell, greet me at the door buck-naked with your mouth closed, but save the who, what, and when for someone else.* I kicked my shoes off before walking over and plopping down on the sofa.

"Where have you been?" she repeated.

"I ran by The Ambiance for a minute," I told her.

Nadia frowned instantly. "That bitch must piss perfume," she mumbled.

I didn't want to hear her whining but I decided to humor myself. "What do you mean?"

"Octavia," Nadia snapped, rolling her eyes, "First Damon and now you!"

"I don't know what you mean," I teased.

"Kelly, we had an agreement, and the agreement was not that you would bring your ass to Huntsville and fall in love."

"First of all, I'm not in love with anybody," I corrected her. "I'm just playing my cards right—something you obviously forgot to do." I looked at her and frowned. Nadia was beautiful and had book-smarts, but when it came down to common sense, she was lacking that shit big time. She had the perfect hustle, a child with Damon Whitmore. She could have been set for life, but instead of enjoying the ride and luxuries of being baby-mama with one of the most successful brothers in the United States, the tramp had to go and get greedy: demanding to be a family with the man's wife, popping up at his parents' crib, and trying to use his credit card to purchase cars—a bunch of real stupid shit! Nadia stood with her hands on her hips. She was wearing a tank-top and knit leggings that showed her every curve. She was on hiatus from performing, and I noticed she was starting to pack on a few pounds. I wondered if she noticed the fully equipped gym located just ten feet down the hall. Really, she had no excuse. She wasn't working, and she didn't have to chase after Donovan, so there was nothing to stop her from maintaining and keeping herself in top-notch shape.

She switched over to the sofa and sat down next to me. "I thought we had an agreement, Kelly."

"We do," I reassured her.

"Okay, so what in our plans justifies you running up behind the Bama Barbie?" she questioned, referring to Octavia.

"I'm not running up behind anyone," I said. "I'm merely playing my cards right." I looked over at her, giving her a look of straight disgust. "If you had your mind right and were on top of your game—"

Nadia's expression told me she was ready to pop off at any moment, and she wasn't about to let me finish that statement. "If I wasn't on top of my game, you would not have this shit you have right now, Kelly!" she snapped. "My being on top of my game is what got you here!"

I wasn't going to argue with her. I was in a very good mood, a very happy place in my life. Besides, there was some truth in her words. Nadia's name was on the rental house we were standing in, as well as the one I utilized whenever I was in Atlanta. Also, if I had never met her, I would have never met Octavia. "Okay, Nadia," I said, walking down the hall to my bedroom with her hot on my heels.

"Kelly, do you even care about my feelings?" she asked.

Inside my bedroom, I eased down on the bed while she stood in front of me, waiting for an answer. *Hell no, I don't care about your feelings,* I thought, but I said, "Of course I do." I smiled at her. "You found me, remember, baby?" It was true.

I remember the day we met like it was only seconds ago. It was a hot July day in Huntsville, the day my life would finally change for the better. I was down on my knees in the middle of the floor of the Student Center at the University of Alabama in Huntsville, scraping gum off the carpet. I had been doing little odd jobs on campus to keep a little bit of money in my pocket. The truth is, there is nothing wrong with my credit. I don't have any bills past or present. However, I was having trouble maintaining stable income. Shit, I was having problems getting a job, period. I had plenty of experience doing all sorts of things, but my past criminal history outshone my work history. Screw what they say on those little printed applications in that politically correct box that cordially asks if you've ever been convicted of a felony. It's bullshit that prior convictions will not automatically bar you from employment. You check that you've been convicted of a felony, and watch how long you'll be waiting for an interview, let alone a job offer. But the director at the university was good people and let me do small jobs from time to time. I guess the sister wanted to throw me a bone. To show her my appreciation, I threw her a bone right back, if you know what I'm saying.

Anyway, I was on my hands and knees one day when this beautiful woman walks in with the legs of a dancer. She had on a dress that stopped inches above her knees and stuck to the curves of her body like Super Glue. She was sexy as hell; that was Nadia. She walked by me and gave me a brief but sexy smile.

"Hello," she said, speaking to me.

"Hello," I said, before continuing with my work.

Nadia took a seat at one of the small circular tables near where I was working and pulled out a book she was carrying. It seemed like she was watching every move I made, and she was. She passed me her phone number that day and told me to call her. "I have some work you can do," she said sweetly.

The two of us started talking on the phone after that. That first night, we talked for hours. She told me she was a professional dancer and that she was currently teaching a workshop at the university. She explained that she had just gone through a breakup with an old lover and was trying to get back into the dating scene. "I was here and decided to stop by his office to see what he was doing and to see if the two of us still had a shot," she explained to me.

"What'd he say?"

"He turned me down." Her voice dropped an octave.

I'm a sensitive man when necessary, but the truth is I was not trying to hear about the man who got away. I was trying to hear about how I could slide in the spot he left empty. "If you ask me, it's his lost," I said smoothly. I could feel her smile radiating from the other end of the phone and the rest? Well, not to sound cliché, but the rest is history. When I first met Nadia, I thought I had hit the jackpot. I couldn't believe that sexy, talented, career-oriented woman was interested in me, a former hustler who could barely afford to buy his own drawers. I have always been good looking, and I can fake my way into any crowd or group. I know how to blend in and break bread with the best. Granted, I knew the shit sounded too good to be true, but it was a fantasy, and I was down for playing the role. At first, Nadia acted like our meeting was chance, just a turn of my good luck, but I later discovered that our meeting had been calculated; she needed me just as much as I needed her, if not more. I won't act like I didn't develop feelings for her over time, because that would be a lie. I cared for her and quite possibly could have learned to love her, but for me, loyalty is everything, and Nadia didn't know the meaning of the word. She claimed she loved Damon more than she had ever loved any man on Earth, yet she was willing to sell him out for the right amount of change. No loyalty! In my opinion, if she loved him that much, she would have killed herself before she betrayed him.

"We're not going to argue," I told her. "I've had an eventful day, and I have a lot more on tap."

"Has any part of our plan come together?" she asked, sucking her teeth.

Sucking her teeth all the damn time, I thought. *Damn, that's so unattractive.* "I think we're closer than we were before," I said.

Nadia rolled her eyes at me and walked off. I could hear her in the kitchen pouring herself a drink. "Look," she said, strolling out from behind the wall that separated the kitchen and the living room, with a glass of amber-colored liquid in her hand. "My bank account is getting low. I don't have another gig lined up, and I don't have the body I used to have."

"Okay," I said, wondering what her point was. "So go on a diet or hit the gym. Get back in shape. There's $5,000 equipment sitting in the other room collecting dust."

"I have a better suggestion," Nadia said, glaring at me. "Why don't you call that bitch and ask her for an advance!"

What Nadia was unaware of was that I had all the advance I needed; I just chose not to spend any of my earnings on her. "Why don't you sit down and shut up?" I said calmly. I placed our disagreement on pause when I heard my phone ringing. "Yeah?" I answered. I listened as I was updated on a few changes to my itinerary. "Are you sure?" I looked at Nadia, who was watching my every move and hanging on my every word. "That's cool," I told my caller. "Peace."

"And who was that?" Nadia questioned. "Her?"

"Her who?"

"Octavia?"

I looked at her and shook my head. "No," I said solemnly. I was having a moment of nostalgia. "You know, some of the best moments of my life have been spent with you."

Nadia's expression changed from being pissed off to flattered. She was so simple, so predictable, and so damn easy to manipulate—like a stupid lost puppy.

"Our first date," I said, walking up to her. "The first time we made love." I pulled her into my arms and whispered, "Watching you give birth."

"Giving birth is what landed my body in this condition." She sighed, rolling her eyes. Not only was Nadia simple and predictable, but she was also shallow as hell. The more I looked at her, the more the negatives were starting to stack against her.

"But he's worth it." I smiled, thinking about Donovan.

"I guess."

"I'll tell you what," I said, kissing her nose lightly. "Why don't you go and pick out something sexy to wear, and the two of us will drive to Nashville for dinner?"

The thought of money being spent on her always lightened Nadia's mood. She smiled brightly. "Ooh! Can we stay overnight?"

"Of course we can," I said, staring her in the eyes. "Did you call Bernice to check on Donovan?" I asked, changing the subject.

"No," she answered, pulling away from me, "but I'm sure he's fine."

"How do you know?"

"He's *my* son," she said, placing emphasis on the possessive.

I nodded my head in agreement.

"I'm going to take a shower and get dressed," she said. "I'll be out in a few. Oh, and can you get us a car for tonight?" she asked. "I do not want to ride around in that wretched borrowed Camry."

"Whatever you like," I said.

Nadia smiled triumphantly.

***

A hour later, I strolled outside wearing jeans creased to the max, a dark blue button-down, and gators. I carried my overnight bag in one hand and my cell phone in the other. I walked up to the black Cadillac with smoked-out tint that was waiting by the curb for me. I opened the passenger door and climbed in. "You know I like to drive," I teased.

"Mama is chauffeuring tonight," she said softly. "You look nice."

I looked over at Lena and smiled, letting her know I also approved of the fitted knit dress she was rocking. "So do you."

"Thank you, baby," she said, seductively leaning toward me.

I greeted her properly by giving her a slow, tender kiss on the lips.

"Everything taken care of in there?" she asked, raising her eyebrow at me.

"It's done," I said, looking back at the house.

Chapter 35

Lena

I believe everything happens for a reason but that it's up to us how
we look at it. No one has to tell me it was destiny that brought
Damon and me back together after so many years; this was obvious. It was
meant for him to fall for Octavia so that the two of us could be reunited.
After all, there's something to be said about first love. As I sat in the car with
Kelly, waiting, I thought about how we'd first met.

"I think we both know how you'll benefit," I replied. "Money."

Kelly looked like he was pondering my offer. "And you?" he asked.
"What's in it for you?"

"I told you," I said, staring at Damon's picture. "All I want is Damon."

Kelly laughed lightly. "You and almost every other woman in the world,"
he said.

"Possibly," I said, "but I'm a lot closer to him than all those other
women."

"I want you to tell me how you expect this plan to work."

"Well, you and Damon share a mutual interest," I advised him.

"And what would that be?"

"Nadia," I informed him.

Kelly's eyes lit up. "How do you know Nadia?"

"We've met," I said. I refrained from explaining that Damon had told me during one of our conversations about his relationship with the woman. I also chose not to disclose that my curiosity had me wanting to know more about her, so the first opportunity I had, I sent her a postcard good for $200 of free services in my salon. At the time, Nadia was still a resident of L.A., and after the first spa treatment, she started coming back. One day during her regular visit, I casually dropped a hint about who owned the building my salon was in.

"Damon Whitmore? Really? Damon Sr. or Jr.?" she asked, looking up at me.

"Junior," I said, continuing to trim the ends of her wet hair. "Why?" I asked. "Do you know the Whitmores?"

"I know him," she said flatly. "The two of us used to date."

I acted like I was interested while pretending not to be nosy, and Nadia opened up like a book. One evening when the two of us were alone in VIP, Nadia shared with me how and why she got involved with Kelly. It wasn't love or even lust at first sight. For Nadia, money ruled everything, and Kelly was just another a meal ticket.

"So you want me to be your informant in the Whitmore household?" Kelly questioned. He opened the folder I had given him and scanned the résumé I had made for him. The résumé wasn't the only thing I had presented him with. I set up a bank account for him with a small cushion, a Social Security number, and a completely different background. As fate would have it, there were several Kelly Bakers across the country, but I had to steal the identity of just the right one. Again, as fate would have it, there was one around the same age as Kelly who had passed on. I had the money to cover the changes, but I had yet to build up my contacts, so I had to hire someone for the task.

"A nanny?" Kelly laughed. "Who the hell is going to believe that?"

"I'm counting on the fact that no one will," I said. "That's why we need a trusty back-up plan." I beckoned for the older woman sitting at the bar, watching me and Kelly. I had recruited her in Los Angeles when I found her roaming outside my salon, picking up cans and trash. She was dirty and in serious need of a bath and a good meal. I chose her to be on my team because she had more to lose by betraying me than she did by staying down with our plan. "Kelly, meet your Auntie Contessa." I smiled and introduced my two accomplices to each other. "Auntie, meet your nephew."

Kelly looked from me to Contessa. "Auntie?"

"Well, not blood related, of course, but Octavia will never know." I sighed.

Contessa extended her hand to Kelly and smiled. "Welcome to my family, sweetie," she said.

Kelly looked like he was still weighing his options.

"Contessa, please give us a moment," I said. I waited for the woman to return to her seat at the bar before speaking to Kelly again. "Look, you deserve this," I told him. "Why would you throw this opportunity away?"

"Who said I'm going to?" he asked. "I just want to know how you and Nadia are going to play nice, knowing that you both want the same man."

I wanted to choose the right words to address the delicate situation, but there were none. "You're right. Nadia is a liability. I would say, 'May the best woman win,' but we both know Nadia is not a gracious loser. I mean, the fact that she struck up a relationship with you is proof of that."

Kelly shook his head. There was a pregnant pause between the two of us until he finally said, "I'm in."

***

It seemed like hours, but it was only a few minutes after Kelly exited the house that we began to see flames, followed by a loud *boom*. In less than sixty seconds, the house was engulfed in flames, the inferno lighting up the night sky.

"First stop?" I asked Kelly as we pulled away from the curb.

"Airport," he said, looking out the window.

"Where are we going?"

"New York," he advised me.

I looked at him and smiled. "Then the Big Apple it is."

Chapter 36

Damon

The sounds of laughter and chatter filled the air surrounding my home as my wife and her parents exchanged friendly banter with my parents. It was a beautiful day, and I was enjoying one of my favorite pastimes—standing over my outdoor grill, cooking for my family while listening to jazz on the surround sound. My family was happy and full of joy and laughter. I was basking in it and the expressions of peace on all of their faces. In spite of her cancer and recent surgery, Charlene was looking beautiful and strong. I admired her strength and her faith. My mother and father had come to town, and we were having a true family gathering.

I can't deny that Nadia was also on my mind. I couldn't believe she was actually gone. My grandmother was the one to break the news to me. According to her, Bernice had called her, hysterical, and told her that officers had identified Nadia as the victim of a house fire. I had seen a report on WHNT19 about a deadly fire, but I didn't catch the name of the victim. According to the investigators, it appeared as if Nadia was attempting to light a candle, but a gas leak in the home caused an explosion; she was in a home I was unaware she had in Huntsville. I couldn't believe Nadia had been in the same city the whole time, less than ten miles from the home I shared with Octavia.

It wasn't until I called to offer Bernice my deepest apologies that I was blessed with even more knowledge. I casually asked Bernice over the phone how Donovan was doing, and she told me he was fine and would be returning to Huntsville with his godmother. I didn't want to ask too many questions, so I opted to wait until Bernice had time to deal with Nadia's death. Octavia and I were back on the right road, and I was not trying to hit any speed bumps. If the only thing I had to deal with was a guilty conscious, I'd take that over losing my wife and daughter any day.

The keypad for our gated entrance began to vibrate in my pocket, an indication that someone had pressed the intercom. "Octavia!" I yelled, waving for her to come over and tend to the grill.

She looked up, smiled, and excused herself from our guests. I watched as she walked in my direction, looking like she was glowing from head to toe. She wore a long off-the-shoulder peach satin dress that flowed freely around her ankles. Her hair was swept up in a small bun with curls falling around her face, framing it. "What's up?" she asked, kissing my cheek.

"Someone's at the gate."

"Hmm. I wonder who," she said, looking as puzzled as I was.

"Not sure, babe."

"I'll be back," she said, spinning on her heels and walking off. She intentionally put an extra twist in her hips and turned around to look at me.

"All right. Keep on, and you're going to be in trouble," I teased, licking my lips.

"I hope so," she smiled.

I continued to tend to the rack of ribs and chicken quarters I had cooking on the grill in front of me.

Contessa walked up carrying a plate of shrimp. "Here you go, sweetie." She handed me the plate and smiled.

"Thank you, Ms. Contessa."

"You're welcome." She turned to walk away, then stopped suddenly. "Oh, I almost forgot." I watched as she slipped her hand down inside her shirt and pulled out a white envelope.

I shook my head, wondering if Octavia was going to use her breasts to conceal things when she was Contessa's age.

"This came for you the other week. I forgot all about it," Contessa said.

"I must have gotten busy and accidentally put it with my things. I'm sorry, hon'."

"It's okay," I said reassuringly. "I know how that can happen." I wiped my hands before taking the envelope. I stood alone at the grill and stared at the return address. It was from the DNA Diagnostics Center. I looked around to make sure no one was watching me before I ripped the envelope open. *How did they get my home address?* I asked myself. Then I reminded myself that the technician was buddies with Nadia. There was no telling what else would arrive at my home if the two of them were still living. I pulled the letter out and scanned over it quickly. The letter was from a Dr. Arnadi, at the clinic. I read the letter again before ripping it up and throwing it down in the fire of the pit. I wanted to be 100 percent sure that what I read was not a joke or something Nadia and Gia had sent me before their deaths. I asked Charles to take my place at the grill while I excused myself to make a business call.

Inside the guesthouse, I called the number I had seen on the letter.

"DNA Diagnostics Center. This is Tosha. How may I help you?"

"I need to speak with Dr. Arnadi."

"May I ask who's calling?" Tosha asked.

After giving her the rundown of who I was, verifying my date of birth and the last four of my Social Security number, I was put on hold for the doctor.

Dr. Arnadi sounded as if he was in his early thirties, and he confirmed everything I read in the letter. "I apologize, Mr. Whitmore, but in Gia's suicide note, she confessed to swapping your test results with another man's," Dr. Arnadi told me. "I am sorry for the mistake, but the child in question is not yours."

I told him I understood and thanked him for notifying me. I know I should have been relieved and lighting up stogies, but there was a portion of me that was disappointed and damn near speechless. I knew Gia's explanation of her connection to Nadia was missing some details, but I wasn't ready for that one. I sat down on the edge of the bed, trying to get my thoughts together. I dropped my head into my hands and replayed the last few months of my life. Nadia was a special kind of something to go through all that damn trouble for a child who wasn't even mine. I shook my head and laughed; I had to or I would have driven my fist through a wall.

After a few minutes, I decided to rejoin the party. I was staring down toward the floor when something caught my eye. I reached down to retrieve the diamond stud lying by the bed.

Chapter 37

Octavia

Contessa informed me that it was probably Kelly at the gate. "He is supposed to be bringing me some more insulin," she said.

"Well, tell me next time, and I'll pick it up for you," I said, smiling politely. I loved Contessa and wanted to help her, but I also wanted to keep Kelly as far away from me as possible. I opened the front door to find him smiling from cheek to cheek.

He was wearing a mint-green Ralph Lauren polo shirt and jeans, and he looked completely relaxed and refreshed. I noticed he wasn't driving Contessa's car; he'd pulled up in a midnight-blue Nissan Armando with tinted windows. "How are you?" he asked.

"I'm fine. And yourself?"

"I'm good," he said. "Real good."

I waited for him to say something slick or inappropriate, but he didn't.

"I'm actually glad you answered the door," he said.

"And why is that?"

"Because I have someone I want you to meet," he said, backing away from the door.

I wondered if he had finally found a woman who could put up with him. My question was answered quickly when I saw him open the back passenger side door and assist a beautiful little boy out of the car. The child was dressed exactly like Kelly, from his shirt down to his classic white Nikes. Kelly walked hand and hand with the child back up to my doorstep. The boy smiled up at me, batting his big brown eyes.

"Hello, cutie," I said, bending down so to meet his eye level.

"Hi," he said, giving me a shy smile.

"I'm Octavia," I said, extending my hand to him. "And you are?"

"Donovan," he said slowly, giving my hand a gentle squeeze.

"He is adorable." I smiled, looking at Kelly. As I looked at the child, I realized he favored Jasmine. "Whose son is he?" I asked, curious.

Kelly stroked the bundle of tiny curls on top of the child's head. "Mine," he said proudly.

Chapter 38

Damon

I had an abundance of thoughts running through my head as I walked up the lawn back to where my family was waiting. My mother and Charlene were huddled around Octavia, talking and laughing with their backs to me, while my father and Charles stood by the grill, talking with Kelly, of all people. He was the last person I expected or wanted to see.

"How's it going?" Kelly asked, extending his hand to me.

I gave his hand a firm shake. "Good," I said. "And yourself?"

"I'm much—"

"Damon!" Octavia interrupted, cutting Kelly off. "Come over here," she said excitedly while walking toward me.

"What is it, love?" I asked, stepping away from the other men.

"Well, I don't know if Kelly told you or not," she said quickly, "but he has a son!"

"Oh, really?" I asked, looking back at Kelly, who gave me a cocky smile.

"Yep, and he is too handsome," she exclaimed. "Mama Ilene, turn around."

My mother turned in her chair, and I felt like my knees were going to drop out from under me and send me to the ground. Sitting on one leg was Jasmine, and on her other knee was Donovan. I looked from Donovan back to Kelly to my wife then back to Kelly again. Slipping my hand in my pants pocket, I touched the earring I had picked up in the guesthouse. I didn't know if I was losing my mind or if my life was truly capable of spinning that far out of control that fast.

"Damon, darling," Mama said, staring at me, "doesn't this child look like Jasmine?"

I didn't answer.

"I said the exact same thing," Octavia said, watching me.

Kelly and I locked eyes with each other. I had no idea who he really was, and I didn't give a damn. The only concern I had for the time being was figuring out what his connection was to my wife and ensuring he was not any kind of threat to my family. The smile on his face told me he knew exactly what he was doing when he showed up at my home with Donovan. He had made his move, and it was time for me to make mine.

Epilogue

Ilene

I felt no sadness when Damon advised me of Nadia's passing, but I did feel empathy for her child. It's hard growing up without a parent, even if that parent is a snake in the grass. I hate to speak ill of the dead, but Nadia had been on my hit list for years. It all started when she was interning at Nomad, working for my husband. For reasons beyond my understanding, that bitch decided to do some snooping while she was in my home. I found her in my bedroom wearing nothing but her bra and panties and some of *my* minks, with her feet stuffed in *my* Jimmy Choos! I can understand the need to play dress-up and fantasize about what you wish could be, so it wasn't the fact that she was trying on my clothes that turned me against her. It was what she said when I caught her. "Next time come to me," I said, watching her as she put her own things back on. "I have no problem with you trying on my wardrobe, as long as you consult with me first."

"I'll keep that in mind," she said. "I do have a question though."

"And I hope I have an answer," I said politely.

"When are you going to tell Damon and Damon Jr.?" she asked.

It was then that I noticed she was holding the confidential paperwork I had strategically placed in a lockbox in the bottom of my closet behind some of my shoes. I looked past her on the floor and saw that the box had been pried open. "Why would you do that?" I inquired.

"I figured if you went through that much trouble, to lock something up," she admitted, "whatever that box contained must have been big."

The two of us put the incident behind us, and things went on as usual, until a few years later, when she visited my family unannounced, and I came home and caught her in a compromising position with her head between my husband's legs and his Johnson in her mouth. I forgave my husband for that little indiscretion and promptly threw the hoe out on her trifling ass. I had allowed Nadia to stay with us as if she was a part of my family, and I'd treated her like a daughter. It wasn't enough for her to have my son. Why? Because at the time, Damon Sr. was the breadwinner, and DJ was working on an allowance—a substantial allowance, but an allowance nonetheless. Nadia never mentioned the documents she found in my closet thereafter, but each and every time she got the opportunity, she made it evident that she would sell me out if the right opportunity presented itself and she had anything to gain from it.

I checked my appearance in the mirror before exiting the bathroom. I walked out and practically ran straight into Octavia and Damon's visitor.

"Pardon me," he said, eyeing me.

"Excuse me," I said, giving him an innocent smile.

"You know, you are truly gorgeous," he said, shaking his head.

"Thank you." I smiled. "It's called good living," I joked. I looked at him and admired how stunning his gray eyes were. "Well, I'd better get back," I said, turning on my heels. I was halfway back down the hall when I heard him call me.

"Ilene!"

"Yes?" I answered, turning to face him.

"Don't you recognize me?"

"Have we met before?" I asked, walking back toward him.

He looked down at the floor and then back up at me. "You're Ilene Lawson," he said.

"I used to be," I said with a nod, "before I married Damon Sr." It had been many years since anyone had referred to me as Ilene Lawson, and I was curious to know how he knew me by that name. "I'm sorry," I said, "but what is your name again?"

"Kelly," he answered. "Kelly Baker."

"And the little boy out there is your son?" I confirmed.

"Yes, Donovan," he said, stuffing his hands in his pockets. "You remember his mother, don't you?"

I frowned. I had never seen the child before, to the best of my knowledge. "I can't say I do," I said.

"Nadia," he said. "Nadia Jones."

The mere mention of Nadia made my blood boil.

"Donovan is your grandchild," he said, looking at me.

I shook my head and frowned. "You are not telling me Damon is that child's biological father," I whispered through clenched teeth.

Kelly raised his hand. "No," he said quickly. "I know without a doubt that Donovan is mine—the same way I know without a doubt that *I'm* your son."

I took a few steps back to put more distance between us. I studied his face as images of the baby boy I'd birthed thirty-six years ago came to me:—the knitted receiving blanket I held him in, his gray eyes that matched mine, looking up at me, the tiny birthmark on his shoulder, and the way I'd cried when I had to give him away. "Kelly…?" I watched as he unbuttoned his shirt and turned around so I could see his right shoulder, and I backed up against the wall for balance at the sight of the small birthmark there, in the shape of a crescent moon.

Prepare for everything to unfold in
Part 4
Love, Lies and Lust

Coming soon . . .

Coming soon from Mz. Robinson

Havoc On A Homewrecker

Finding a man has never been a problem for Toi Underwood. Finding a man who understands and respects her devotion to her career, lack of availability, and need for her *me time* is another story. Toi is so career driven that when she meets a man she either intimidates him or she pisses him off.

When Toi meets Carlton Thomas she begins to think that her prayers have been answered. Not only is Carlton attractive, he's hardworking and understands her busy lifestyle. He's patient and respects that Toi can't be readily available to him due to other commitments. After all, he has his own *extracurricular activities*. Toi thinks she has met her match until she discovers that one of Carlton's *extracurricular activities*, just so happens to be another woman—his wife, Lisa.

Toi knows in her heart that walking away is the best option, but sometimes the right thing to do is also the hardest, especially when emotions and feelings have gotten involved. Toi's mantra becomes, *It is…what it is.* Toi's not looking for a ring and currently she could care less about being anyone's wifey. To be honest she could care less about Lisa. It's obvious that she's doing something wrong that would make her man have to look elsewhere. Right? And what Lisa doesn't know can't hurt her. As long as everyone is happy, what could possibly go wrong?

For six years Lisa waited anxiously for Carlton to propose. Now, two years later, she has the ring and the papers. Granted, marriage hasn't been what she expected, but she's determined to make the best out of it. When she discovers Carlton has not only been playing the field but that he and Toi refuse to end their affair, Lisa becomes a woman on a mission. Lisa throws all logic and reasoning out the window and decides it's time to teach some unforgettable lessons.

Toi quickly learns that ending her affair with Carlton is not only the right thing to do but could possibly save her life. However, some awakenings come a little too late. Toi will see that when the right woman gets fed up she can truly be *Havoc on a Home Wrecker*.

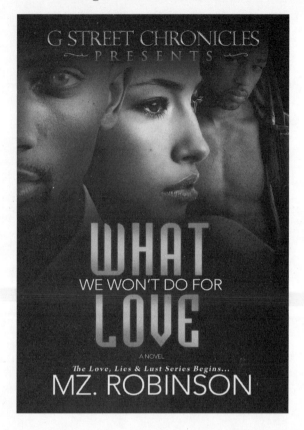

Octavia Ellis is a sexy and independent woman who plays it safe when it comes down to relationships. She lives by one rule: keep it strictly sexual. Octavia is living her life just the way she wants. No man. No issues. No drama. When she meets the handsome Damon Whitmore, everything changes. Octavia soon finds that Damon has become a part of her world and her heart. However, when temptation comes in the form of a sexy-hardcore thug named, Beau, Octavia finds herself caught in a deadly love triangle. She soon learns in life and love, there are no rules and she's surprised at what she herself, will not do for love.

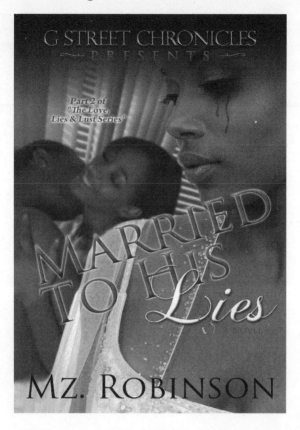

Shontay Holloway is as faithful as they come when it comes to her husband, Kenny. For eight years she's been his support system physically and financially. She's managed to overlook the fact that he's a woman chaser and even turned the other cheek when he got another woman pregnant. Shontay would rather work it out with Kenny than start fresh with someone new. She's not satisfied but she is content. Is there really a difference? Shontay doesn't think so, but that soon changes when she meets Savoy Breedwell.

Shontay finds herself torn between her vows and the man she's falling for. When tragedy strikes, Shontay learns that the love she thought her husband had for her is nothing more than a cover up for his true intentions. She becomes a woman on a mission. When she's finished, Till death do us part, may have a whole new meaning.

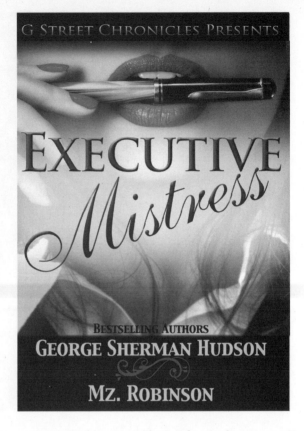

G STREET CHRONICLES PRESENTS

EXECUTIVE *Mistress*

BESTSELLING AUTHORS
GEORGE SHERMAN HUDSON
MZ. ROBINSON

G&L Enterprises is the biggest marketing firm in the country. Each year thousands of intern applicants apply with the hope of securing a position with the illustrious firm. Out of a sea of applicants, Asia is bestowed the honor of receiving an internship with G&L. Asia is beautiful, ambitious, and determined to climb her way up the corporate ladder by any means necessary. From crossing out all in her path, to seducing Parker Bryant the CEO of G&L, Asia secures a permanent position with the marketing giant. However, her passion for success will not allow her to settle for second best. Asia wants the number one spot, and she'll stop at nothing, including betraying the man responsible for her success to get it. Asia, is taking corporate takeover to a whole new level!

Essence Monroe went through great lengths to escape her sordid past and the lovers in it. Using extreme and deadly tactics she re-invented herself and now she's well on her way to a promising future. Not only is she engaged to Andrew Carlton, one of Atlanta s most sought after athletes, but she's slowly creating a name for herself in the fashion industry. Essence is a former bad girl - gone good and she's living a life that others can only dream of. That is until Essence's life is shaken, when she discovers that someone knows her secrets. Essence must revert to her bad girl ways, in order to protect herself and the man she loves. While she's focused on keeping her skeletons buried, there's another woman focused on taking her place by Andrew's side. Not only does the mysterious woman want to take Essences man but she wants Essence life for her very own. In the end there can be only one winner and no one is prepared for the outcome.

G STREET CHRONICLES
~ PRESENTS ~

CHASING
Bliss
A Novel

Sabrina A. Eubanks

Chase Brown has it all…he's wealthy, owns three of the hottest night clubs in New York City and he's boyishly handsome. Chase's rise to the top hasn't been easy and memories of his mother's murder, as she died in his arms when he was only twelve years old, still haunt him. These memories birth Smoke, his monstrous alter ego, who is psychotic and very dangerous.

Chase and his younger brother Corey are close—so close that his older brother, Cyrus, uses emotional blackmail to make Chase carry out his deceitful and murderous deeds. While attempting to bury Smoke and break free from his brother's spell, Chase meets the beautiful Bliss Riley. They fall madly in love but there is only one problem…Bliss isn't aware of Chase's murderous appetite and the demon that lives inside of the man she loves.

Will Chase be able to bury his demons for good and live happily ever after with the woman of his dreams or will Smoke take Chase and Bliss on a journey that will leave dead bodies throughout the city of New York? Only time will tell!

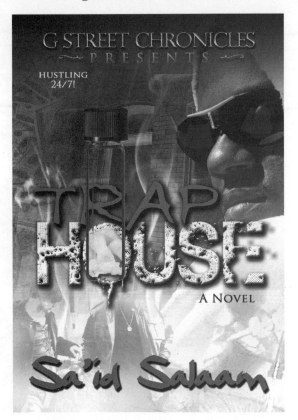

Trap House is an unflinching account of the goings on of an Atlanta drug den and the lives of those who frequent it. Its cast of characters include the Notorious P.I.G., the proprietor of the house, who uses his power to satisfy his licentious fetishes. Of his customers, there's Wanda, an exotic dancer who loathes P.I.G., but only tolerates him because he has the best dope in town. Wanda's boyfriend Mike is the owner of an upscale strip club, as well as a full time pimp.

Tiffany and Marcus are the teenage couple who began frequenting the Trap House after snorting a few lines at a party. Can their love for each other withstand the demands of their fledging addiction, or will it tear them apart?

P.I.G.'s wife Blast, doorman Earl and a host of other colorful characters round out the inhabitants of the Trap House.

Trap House is the bastard child of real life and the author's vivid imagination. Its author, Sa'id Salaam, paints a graphic portrait of the inner-workings of an under-world. He takes you so close you can almost hear the sizzle of the cocaine as it's smoked—almost smell the putrid aroma of crack as it's exhaled. Yet for all the grit and grime, Trap House has the audacity to be a love story. Through the sordid sex and brutality is an underlying tale of redemption and self empowerment. Trap House drives home the reality that everyone is a slave to something.

Who's your master?

Lies, deceit and murder ran rampant throughout the city of Atlanta. Real and his lady, Constance, were living in the lap of luxury, with fancy cars, expensive clothes and a million dollar home until someone close to them alerted the feds to their illegal activity.

At the blink of an eye their perfect life was turned upside down. Just as Real was sorting things out on the home front, the head of Miami's most powerful Cartel gave him an ultimatum that would eventually force him back into the life he had swore off forever. Knowing this lifestyle would surely put Constance in danger, he made plans to send her away until the score was settled but things spiraled out of control. Now Real and Constance are in a fight for survival where friends become enemies and murder is essential. Atlanta's underworld to Miami's most affluent community—no stone was left unturned as Real fought to keep Constance safe while attempting to regain control of the lifestyle he once would kill for.

From the city of Atlanta to the cell block of Georgia's most dangerous prison, life under the City Lights would never be the same.

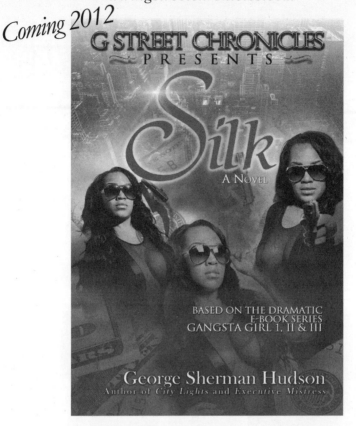

Relocating to Miami, Silk looked to retire and stay far away from the street life she'd grown accustomed to. After living the high-life and carelessly spending the money from her past licks, she had to resort back to the only thing she knew…murder and robbery.

This time she'll play the game differently. Silk built a team of females to pull off her deadly plots. Tiah, Lexi and Kya—they possess all the qualities she needed. Tiah is sexy and knows exactly how to use her charisma to lure in the next vic; Lexi is street smart and real clever when it comes to the game; and Kya is a real killer who doesn't hesitate when it comes to pulling the trigger.

Silk and her team began their missions to get paid. Everything is going smooth until their paths cross Sherm. Out of prison for over a year now, Sherm is the go-to man in many cities but when his connect is killed, his right-hand man set up a meeting with a new connect. After this meeting, Sherm will never be the same. Not one to accept a loss, Sherm set out to get his money and find the person responsible.

Now it's robbery, murder, deceit and revenge coming full steam. Will Silk, the real Gangsta Girl, survive this mayhem or will Sherm, the man who taught her the game, be the one to take her down?

G STREET CHRONICLES
~ SHORT STORY EBOOK SERIES ~

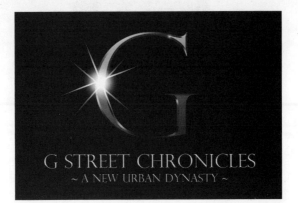

We'd like to thank you for supporting G Street Chronicles and invite you to join our social networks. Please be sure to post a review when you're finished reading.

Facebook
G Street Chronicles Fan Page

Twitter
@gstrtchroni

My Space
G Street Chronicles

Email us and we'll add you to our mailing list
fans@gstreetchronicles.com

George Sherman Hudson, CEO
Shawna A. Grundy, VP

Name: _____

Address: _____

City/State: _____

Zip: _____

ALL BOOKS ARE $10 EACH

QTY	TITLE	PRICE
	The Lies We Tell for Love	
	What We Won't Do for Love	
	Married to His Lies	
	Chasing Bliss	
	Still Deceiving	
	Trap House	
	City Lights	
	A-Town Veteran	
	Beastmode	
	Executive Mistress	
	Essence of a Bad Girl	
	Dope, Death and Deception	
	Dealt the Wrong Hand	
	Two Face	
	Family Ties	
	Blocked In	
	Drama	
	Shipping & Handling ($4 per book)	

TOTAL $ _____

To order online visit

www.gstreetchronicles.com
Send cashiers check or money order to:
G Street Chronicles
P.O. Box 490082 College Park, GA 30349